THE LAST

A NOVEL BY

COWBOY

LEE GOWAN

ALFRED A. KNOPF CANADA

PUBLISHED BY ALFRED A. KNOPF CANADA

Copyright © 2004 Lee Gowan

All rights reserved under International and Pan-American Copyright
Conventions. Published in 2004 by Alfred A. Knopf Canada, a division of
Random House of Canada Limited, Toronto. Distributed by
Random House of Canada Limited, Toronto.

Knopf Canada and colophon are trademarks.

National Library of Canada Cataloguing in Publication

Gowan, Lee, 1961–
The last cowboy / Lee Gowan.

ISBN 0-676-97582-8

I. Title.

PS8563.O882L38 2004   C813'.54   C2003-901781-8
                PR9199.4.G68L38 2004

First Edition

www.randomhouse.ca

Text design: CS Richardson

Printed and bound in the United States of America

2 4 6 8 9 7 5 3 1

To Mom and Dad, and to Alison,
for loving a boy and a man who gives
such unfortunate gifts.

What sense am I trusting? Sight?
There is nothing to see. Feeling?
There is nothing but cold. Direction?
There is no such sense.
There'd better be, and a good one.
There are 359 wrong directions to be going
and no angel out here.
Can this be death?
Senses without value and value without sense?
Death can't be so completely boring—
like hell it can't.

HOWARD GOWAN
"WINTER RIDE"

THE LAST COWBOY

SAM MCMAHON FROZE, the steaming kettle in his hand poised over his stainless steel designer teapot. He didn't pour. He was listening for something. Probably only the wind. Yes, the moaning of the wind sweeping across the valley and thrumming his corrugated metal roof. But there was no wind. The air was still and dry, the sun bleaching the whole world with angry light. Even the sparrows were too hot to sing. In the silence of the room he could hear his ears humming, his heart beating, a fly buzzing between the Venetian blinds and one of the sheets of glass that ran the length of the house on the southern exposure. And then there it was, the faint whispering of a faraway voice.

"Hello?" he said, standing up straighter, focussing on that one sound.

He'd noticed it as he lifted the kettle from the stove, interrupting the shrill whistle. On the stereo the last strains of Mozart's *Don Giovanni* were fading away. For a moment, in the revealed silence, he heard the voice murmuring fitfully, mournfully, and he couldn't stop himself from answering: "Hello?" Now he concentrated, and the faint whispering was still there, but he knew by the way it droned on that it was not a reply. He strained to decipher its source and meaning, until it was interrupted by the beat of some insipid pop song.

He was talking to a voice on the radio. Michael had left the radio on in his room.

He was alone. He might be alone for the rest of his life. All of the rooms of his beautiful home were empty. Except this

I

one, the kitchen, where he still stood holding the kettle in mid-air—had held it for so long that the water had stopped boiling and the tea would be spoiled if he poured. He set the kettle back on the burner and turned on the gas.

Yesterday was Saturday, and he'd spent it at the bank, catching up on the paperwork that had piled up all week. He loved the bank when it was empty—only the tubular chrome chairs with the gaudy green-striped upholstery in the waiting area, the reams of paper neatly in their files, the stacks of money in the sealed vault, and him. He'd planned to spend Sunday with the boys, but when he'd arrived home last night Gwen had ambushed him, pronouncing him the worst father in the history of the family. It seemed like something of an over-statement, and so he had fought back and ended up sleeping in the guest room. It had got so that the boys called the guest room "Daddy's room." He'd rolled around for most of the night, imagining accusations and apologies, and in the end slept for only two hours, awaking to see the light funnelling through the narrow window knocked in the concrete, Gwen's framed needlepoint surrounding him. The master bedroom had a whole wall of glass looking out over the valley.

When he walked into the kitchen and sat down for break-fast, Gwen announced that she was taking the boys to see their grandparents. Her parents. There was no question of Sam coming. Her father had not spoken to him in the eight years since the bank had foreclosed on his farm implements dealership.

"I was going to spend the day with the boys."

"Well, I'm taking them to see their grandparents."

She pushed a lock of blonde hair behind her ear, a motion he knew so well it was almost part of him. Sam poured some corn flakes into his bowl.

"Why don't you go and see your parents and leave them with me?"

He meant it as a concession, an apology, but somehow his voice emerged sounding not the least bit remorseful. Her eyes might have swallowed him whole.

"I'm taking the boys with me."

And with that, she rose from her chair and strode out of the room.

Last night, moments before she'd locked him out of the master bedroom, she'd told him she was leaving, and he'd better call a lawyer and start thinking about how they would organize living apart; start thinking about all of those terrible intricacies. It was a threat she'd made a hundred times in the last five years, and for that reason Sam tried not to take it seriously, though it still unnerved him by pointing out the essential fragility of his seemingly unshakeable position in the world. Bank manager. Excellent health. Married fourteen years. Two children, nine and three, both healthy boys.

As his family left, Sam ruffled Michael's hair, received a sloppy kiss from Ben, and sent his regards to Gwen's parents. She did not respond. He stood in the living room and waved through the wall of glass as her new Buick pulled away. He hated the ugly thing, which only made her love it all the more.

Now he poured the boiling water over his tea bags, set down the kettle and walked out of the kitchen, across the living room and down the hallway towards Michael's room. Clothes were strewn across the floor. He picked them up, threw them in the hamper and turned off the radio on the bedside table. Quiet. He sat down on the bed and ran his fingers through his thinning hair. Perhaps he should just shave it all off. That was the style now. The clients likely wouldn't say much. Some of them kidded him about his fancy suits, but to most of them a suit was a suit. It was the guys back east who would never let him live down a haircut with too much attitude.

A group of tough-looking young men sneered at him from a poster. Were these Michael's heroes? Obviously. They were on his wall. He thought of the time Old Sam—his grandfather—had torn down a poster of the Rolling Stones from his older brother Vern's bedroom wall. Vern was furious, and Old Sam's only explanation was that he didn't like the look in their eyes. Sam would not tear down Michael's poster, even if he didn't like the look in the men's eyes. He was not given to the dramatic actions of his grandfather.

What was that smell? Dirty laundry or some forgotten snack? His mother would never have allowed his room to get this messy. He felt tears in his eyes, took a deep breath, and rushed out of the room.

In the living room, where he'd stood watching his family drive away that morning, the blinds were closed against the sun, the room in shadow, the floor cut by slivers of light. The kettle clicked as it cooled on the stove. His tea would be steeped. He was about to put on another CD, *The Goldberg Variations*, but he paused and walked to the glass wall, wound open one of the blinds and peered out across Gwen's green yard and blooming delphiniums to the expanse of the yellow valley. Not a soul. He'd been careful to pick a spot where they couldn't see anyone and no one could see them. His parents' house was only a mile away, and his older brother Vern's trailer only half a mile, but both were safely obscured by a small hill of aggregate deposited during the last ice age. A beautiful hill. One side of it had been cut away by the creek, but the rest had been dense enough to resist thousands of years of wind and water.

He should close the blind and go back to his office with his tea and get some work done, but he knew it was pointless. His muscles ached. He couldn't focus. He couldn't escape the thought that his family might not be coming home. Though he tried to ignore it, the silence kept telling him. He loved Gwen and he loved his boys and he did not want to think of what would be left of his life if he lost them.

He could no longer please her. He'd tried desperately, but nothing worked. Her resentment always showed, even when he caught a smile on her face like the smiles he thought he remembered. He really had no idea why she resented him so much. She told him it was because he left cereal in the bottom of his bowl every morning and it stuck there. He started rinsing out the bowl. She told him it was because he was always shedding his hair in the bath and the sink. He did his best to clean away the evidence. She told him it was because he always wore black suits. He bought a blue one. She told him it was because he did not do his share of the housework. He hired a cleaning service and offered her a day on the weekend without the boys and an evening or two a week. It didn't make the slightest difference. She told him it was because he was too lazy and unmotivated to change his career, and so he arranged a transfer to Head Office in Toronto, and she told him she wouldn't go to Toronto if she were in a pine box. She told him she couldn't understand why he was satisfied with being a banker when everyone hated bankers. She wondered how he could help but hate himself if everyone hated him. And how could she possibly be expected to love him if he hated himself?

Once she'd loved him. Maybe she still did. Sometimes, in remorse, after she'd said something particularly ugly—that she was living with a zombie or that his boys would grow up to hate him—and she had had time to begin to feel guilty, she would tell him she still loved him. But he wasn't sure he believed her anymore. He suspected she was merely afraid to walk away from this home she hated so much. *His* home, she called it. Built by *his* architect. His parents a mile down the road. His whole life mapped out by the section lines.

But once she'd loved him. Here, in this house, a mile down the road from his parents. Once she had loved her garden, and only made silly jokes about how much she hated the institutional modernist box his architect had forced her to raise her children in. "We're living in a work of art," he'd told her, "and that makes us art. Or pests. We're a patina." Once he had known how to make her laugh. Now she told him she didn't like his sense of humour. No matter how hard he tried he could no longer reach her. Touch her. Breasts. The freckle beside her navel. Her thighs.

Across the creek, high over the world, a hawk circled, waiting for a gopher or a mouse to show itself.

He knew what Gwen wanted. It was simple enough: she wanted him to give up his career and sell this house and take her and the boys away to some new life. And he would do it if he thought there was a chance it would satisfy her. But the only alternative future he could see for them was in the city. He'd arranged that transfer to Toronto four years ago, before Ben was born, but she would not go. She hated cities. Even Broken Head was too big for her. So what did she expect him to do? Move back to the tiny town of Meridian, where she'd grown up, and live up the street from her father, who would never forgive him no matter what he did?

The problem, he'd begun to admit to himself, was that Gwen would never forgive him either, because no matter how hard he tried to please her he would still be Sam McMahon. That he could not change.

He wound the blind closed and put on Bach.

But when he tried to work, the numbers made no sense. Glenn Gould was no help either. Sam turned it up enough that he could hear Gould humming along with his playing; the house only seemed emptier. He needed to talk to somebody. He had to tell someone that his life was falling apart.

He walked to the phone and called his mother.

"Hellllo?"

For a moment Sam considered hanging up, but he was not that much of a coward.

"Hi, Dad."

"Who's this? The banker? No, we don't need any money, thank you very much. We've got enough hands in our pockets at the moment as it is, and you bankers've got the stickiest hands of them all, don't you?"

"Oh, I'm not so sure. There's the government."

"That's true. But it's you guys who run the government, isn't it?"

"That's right, Dad. I was just talking to the prime minister before I called you."

"You were? Funny thing. What would you need to talk to me for then?"

"I don't know. Talking to him left me feeling starved for intelligent conversation."

"Uh-huh. I guess it would do that. Did you want to talk to your mother?"

"Sure."

"You could come and visit her every now and then. You only live a mile away."

"Thanks for the invitation."

"Here she is."

He heard the phone fumbled from one parent's hand to the other's.

"Saaam?"

"Hi, Mom."

"How are you?"

"I'm okay. Just hadn't talked to you for a while."

"No. I'm sorry, dear. I never seem to get you at home."

"No. Pretty busy, as usual."

"How's Gwen?"

"She's fine. She took the boys down to her parents for the day."

"Oh? So you're home alone? Did you want to come over for supper?"

"Oh, no. That's okay. They'll likely be home for supper."

"Well, you could all come over."

"Thanks, Mom. That's all right. School tomorrow and everything."

"Yes. Michael's got a field trip, doesn't he? They're going to the Creamery."

"Is that so? I guess it's that time of year. They'll get a free ice cream."

He listened to her breathing, trying to think of something to say. She began to talk about the weather, how the heat would be hard on the crops. He agreed. She mentioned a relative who was ill, and Sam voiced his concern. At last they ran out of things to say. He heard her swallow.

"I walked over to Vern's yesterday and the boys were there helping him work on the tractor. Having a great time. I was thinking what a treat it would be if you took them into the bank with you one day. Do you ever do that?"

"I'm not so sure the bank's ready for them."

"Oh, there must be a way you could figure out to make it work, even for an hour or so. I think it would mean so much to Michael especially. Maybe Ben is too young."

"That's probably a good idea. I'll think about that."

"It would be nice."

"Yes. Well, I'd better go. I should get some work done."

"All right. Nice to hear from you, dear. Are you sure you don't want to come over for supper?"

"Not tonight. Maybe next weekend. I'll mention it to Gwen."

"That'd be nice. Okay, we'll talk to you soon."

"Bye, Mom."

He placed the receiver in the cradle and put his hand on the wall to steady himself.

The phone rang. He stared at it. He'd been so deeply lost that for an instant he wondered if he'd actually heard anything or only imagined it. It rang again. His mother. She was calling to ask if there was anything wrong.

"Someone still loves me."

He'd spoken aloud before he knew it was out of his mouth. The phone kept ringing. Tears came to his eyes, and he struggled to get control so she would not be able to hear them in his voice. He would go over for supper. Or maybe it wasn't her—maybe it was Gwen and her mood had broken and she was calling to tell him that she and the boys were on their way home and he should thaw something for the barbecue. He would tell her he was sorry. He would tell her he loved her.

He picked up the receiver and said "Hello" in his practised banker's professional tone.

"Hi, is that Vern?"

A woman's voice.

"No. You've got the wrong number."

"Really?" She giggled. "That is you, Vern."

It wasn't a voice he recognized.

"I can assure you I am not Vern. This is 3568. You want 3569."

"Oh?" He could hear her cheeks turning red. "I'm sorry."

"No trouble."

After listening to her lower the receiver into the cradle, he did the same.

He walked to the window, cranked open the blind, and stood looking out across his valley, listening to the silence.

I AM SAM MCMAHON.

That's clear enough, or nearly as clear as enough needs to be. I was once a cattleman. I'm not anymore. I was foolish enough to figure I was done with what I was and could become what I'm not: a man of leisure. I signed all of my land over to my son, John McMahon, a mistake I'll spend the rest of my life regretting.

I do not miss the cattle—they are still here, wandering the rolling hills of the creek valley, searching for nothing more than a mouthful of grass and a drink of cool water—but I miss them being mine. I miss the land being mine. I don't miss the owning, I miss the meaning the owning gave me. It made it clear what I meant when I said any stupid thing such as, "Pick up your feet, ya lazy bastard," or when, as was apt to happen, some spirit would appear to me from a blizzard or a fire and ask me to introduce myself and I would answer, "I am Sam McMahon."

No longer a cattleman, no longer anything. I have not been a husband for longer than I care to remember. My wife, Mary, died of a cancer of the breast in '31, at the beginning of the dust bowl years. The boy John was only nine months old at the time. I hired a housekeeper, Molly, to look after him for the twenty-five years until he married. To avoid false sentimentalities I will frankly admit that I never missed my dearly departed very much. I do not blame this on Mary, who was ever the gentle and attentive wife. (I wouldn't call her affectionate—not because she wasn't, but because even if she was that wouldn't be anyone's business). I suppose I should think of her more often, but she was never much to think on. I was no good at husbanding. There was something in me that wouldn't allow me to love her as much as she expected I should. I loved my freedom. I loved women. I loved my horse. I never in my life lost an hour's sleep over Mary or any other woman. I don't see that there's much point blackening your soul over not being what you can't be. After all, who would I be if I weren't Sam McMahon?

Which is exactly the kind of moronic question I find myself asking myself these long empty days, now that I am a man of too much leisure, sitting in my battered old La-Z-Boy in the living room I framed and plastered with these scarred old hands, looking out the picture window at a magpie eating the gruel from the dog dish. I suppose this "Who would I be . . . ?" must be a modern sort of question, a 1970 sort of question. It's in a different category of nonsense than I was given to asking myself in days gone by—back when the world was real, which is where I generally spend most of my time trying to get to these days. Back in those days I wouldn't have got so far as, "Why am I not dead, instead of her?" And even if I got there I'd never have dug too deep into the question, thinking the answer was clear enough: I was stronger than Mary.

But now I am old and no longer strong, and I have little time left to waste but apparently nothing else to do but waste what little time I have left. I spend most of my hours looking through this flyspecked window, watching John and his wife and their two boys crossing back and forth and getting on with the business of using up their lives. I watch a world I used to be part of, cut off from the land that was mine until I was stupid enough to give it away—my own stretch of earth that

I sweated over for decade on decade on decade, and never a man to take my place in the saddle no matter how many nights of sleep I'd gone without.

What good is the world once it's been sealed up behind a plate of glass?

The thing that hurts the most is that I did it to myself. Willingly. I cast my pearls before swine. I gave it all away to the son, believing, as I'd been told, that that was the way it was meant to be. Believing that it would provide me the time and the space to do exactly what I wanted to do: ride old Nitro, check the cattle, think about those better days. It's a mistake you'll find repeated throughout history. To give you one related for instance, the Indians gave away this land, which is the only reason I am here to begin with. They were as much fools as I am. Sure, you could say they had it taken from them, but in the end they signed it away, just like me. There's little point in blaming your enemies for your weaknesses, even if your enemy is your own son. It's a silly and sentimental idea to think of a son as anything but an enemy, so what use is there in blaming him when you discover his boot on your throat?

What I never would have believed if I'd found it written on the outhouse wall, I must confess, was the betrayal by my greatest friend and most loyal servant, old Nitro. He who had pulled me through a multitude of scrapes where I would have been pulverized under stampeding hooves or found frozen in the spring, clinging like a tumbleweed to a snow fence, was suddenly taken by some devilish spirit and galloped under a branch low enough to catch me square across the neck and wipe me clean off his back. The son found me lying under that tree twelve hours later, after Vern, the older grandson, came across Nitro in the barn, still in his bridle and saddle, waiting in his stall for some oats.

John says I'm lucky. It was a new moon and already deathly dark, and they wouldn't have found me at all if I hadn't managed to signal them by tying my bandanna to a branch and waving it around like I was surrendering to all the cruelties of the universe. My hip—according to the doctors, if you care to trust the words of men who make a habit of dressing in hairnets—was fractured like the dry old limb of the willow that caught me across the neck.

This gradual wasting away is what my son John calls luck. Well, if it's luck, then I don't deserve it. It's not a prize I desire. And desiring is all I have left.

Any stranger might have already detected that my blaming of Nitro is but the weary rationalization of a sick old man, and that it was my own decrepitude that landed me here, in this La-Z-Boy that's jammed in a slight recline, so that I find myself staring up into the sky and have to kink my neck to see the earth. I know all too well that the demon that urged Nitro under that branch has dwelt within his horseflesh all of his twenty-two circuits of the sun, and that it was only my mushy old brain that made me unwary enough to allow him to get the better of me, and only bitter and brittle age that allowed the result of his little practical joke to splinter my bones like kindling. I'll wager Nitro was more surprised than I was when he looked back and saw me there on the ground, and I'll bet my boots it was his fright at seeing his old friend laid so low that sent him galloping back to the barn.

That beast and I are of one blood.

Which is my chief worry at the moment, as I most certainly am my brother's keeper, and I fear my brother has been ill-kept in my absence.

The small one let this possibility slip. My namesake, Sam the Younger, who, I must caution, has as much in common with Sam the Elder as an earthworm has with a rattlesnake. He is only nine, but already has a pair of plastic frames perched on his nose, the product of too many hours spent staring into that infernal picture box his father installed in the corner of the living room where the Victrola should properly stand. If the small one is not in front of the idiot box, you'll find his nose in a book, or his ear tuned to the tinny blaring of a transistor radio some sadistically inclined jester bought him for Christmas. And, of course, he dresses like they all dress now: there's enough denim in his trousers for three pairs, and when he walks across the corral his jeans flap like a matador's cape—and then he wails like a baby when a tiny calf naturally becomes alarmed at all that flapping and kicks him a swift one in the shin.

The older boy, the one called Vern, dresses the same and has some of the same weaknesses—in fact, might even be blamed for instilling them in his younger brother—but at least he seems to have a bit of spunk in him. When I watch him cross the yard, I can see something of myself out there. But they call him Vern. Her father's name. A man who I remember selling rotten bananas in that claptrap grocery store up by the highway back in the thirties. Who in hell names the oldest boy after the woman's father? It ain't right and it ain't done; or it wasn't until the world began to come apart and the women started dressing like men and the men started wearing women's hairdos.

I suppose they named the next one Sam to try and sweeten me up. It didn't work. When I face the child who is to carry my name on into the future, I am looking at a longhaired, four-eyed, weak-kneed, bed-wetting boy who is already old—who prefers to spend his days looking through glass rather than be out taking part in the world.

One might think by the way I'm carrying on that I have given up on the child. Don't you believe it. Despite myself, I have a special fondness for him. I realize this soft spot is probably another sign of the rotting of my soul, and I'm only grateful to the useless excuse for a boy because he spends more time with me than the rest of them do, though I am well aware that his attention to me is nothing more than a consequence of the fact that my reclining throne is stationed in the living room, just opposite the television, making it impossible for him to partake of his narcotizing elixir without my resignation to his horrible need. It's a pitiful bargain we've struck: I do my best to warn him away from the box's evils by pointing out as many of its improbabilities as I can stomach myself to witness, urging him out the door every ten minutes, while all along trusting he won't go away and leave his poor grandfather at the mercy of his mother's whims. In return, the boy fetches what I need from my bedroom or the kitchen—be it whiskey or bread—and promises me he'll go and help his father "just as soon as *Bugs Bunny*'s over."

I must confess I have an affection for old Bugs. They can keep their Ki-yo-tee. They don't even know how to properly pronounce the varmint's name: it's Ki-yoot, as anyone with half a mind should know.

According to his teachers, the small one has something more than half a mind, though their methods of measurement are suspect. So far as I've been able to decipher, the boy has nothing in the way of useful skills, and so I've taken it upon myself to teach him some. He's my one remaining project: if I can save such a sorry soul, if I can temper his bookish and girlish mind with the hard lessons I was forced to learn, maybe I can still leave something significant in this world, something I failed to pass on to my own son. There's the older boy too, it's true, and he seems the more likely candidate, but he's not so easily within reach. A bird in the hand, as they say. Yes, I've taken it upon myself to teach the sparrow a song or two. When his mother's out of sight, I let him practise with my rolling papers and fixings. It's little enough, but it's a trick he might actually find use for some day, unlike algebra or reading about people on the other side of the earth he's never likely to meet. So far, the lessons have amounted to a sad waste of paper and tobacco, but in time he'll get the rope to hang down instead of up.

This afternoon we were in the middle of one of these educational sessions when the Chinaman who bought the McAllister place drove into the yard and started talking with the son out by the barn. When I asked the small one what the hell that fool was doing here, he got all nervous and mumbled something about him buying eggs from us on a regular basis. I've only seen the Chinaman in my yard once before. A couple years back he showed up with a horse trailer, and it turned out the son had sold one of the mares to him, a gentle little thing called Willow that any fool should have been able to ride and keep happy. Well, I wasn't too pleased about the transaction, but she was the son's horse even before I'd signed the whole shitamaroo away, and so what could I do but tell him what I thought and leave it there. It wasn't two weeks later that the phone rang, and since I was the only one in the house I answered, and who was it but the Chinaman telling me that Willow had tried to jump the fence and caught a hoof on the top wire and fallen, and as a consequence was in some difficulties. He calls himself an agricultural scientist, but he had no idea how to deal with the matter in a prompt and merciful manner. I scooted up and found her lying there, panting her lungs out with the pain but still trying to get to her feet, and the Chinaman standing by, shuffling from foot to foot, watching her suffer. He told me it was okay 'cause he'd called the vet and help was on its way.

"The vet? You might just as well throw your wallet in the crick," I told him.

I walked back to the truck and got my rifle and fed in a shell and walked up to Willow and put the barrel against her forehead and pulled the trigger.

As I was walking back to my truck, the smoke from the spent shell still hanging in the air, Shanghai Sammy came up and started squealing at me about how she might have been okay and how I should have waited for the "pro-fessionals" and who the hell did I think I was, shooting his horse. So I told him that no "pro-fessional" was gonna save his horse and that he must have been torturing her something awful to make her jump over that fence and kill herself and that he was lucky I didn't put him out of his misery too. Then I drove home and got the tractor and drove back up the hill to the Chinaman's again and hooked a chain around Willow's neck and dragged her sorry carcass to the burnhole, where I set her free from all China with a splash of diesel fuel and a match.

Well, you better believe the shit hit the fan. He was mad as hell that I'd burned his horse. Said she didn't need to be shot in the first place and even if she did he could at least have used her for dog food. He threatened to take me in front of a judge for saving Willow another minute's misery. Threatened to have me arrested for threatening his life.

Now, I know as well as anybody that Chinamen eat horses. It ain't that I hold it against them: I suppose that poverty is generally responsible. But in the case of a man with a government job it could only be poverty of spirit we were dealing with. In the end, in order to get the fool to shut up, the son offered to pay him back his money. Well, damned if he don't tell the son he'd just as soon have another horse as a replacement. I told the son that if he gave another horse to that slanty-eyed bastard to try and eat I'd sell *him* to the white slavers first chance I got. To which the son says that I can't tell him what to do with his horses and blames me for "souring the relations with the neighbours."

Anyway, that was two years ago, and I hadn't in the meantime noticed any horses missing, so I figured the son and the good neighbour had settled the matter with money. Whatever they done, they must have since managed to re-sweeten relations, 'cause this afternoon I see the Chinaman out in the yard, and I ask the boy about him, and the kid spins me this yarn about him buying eggs, but meanwhile I can't help thinking about the boys over there on the other side of the world being shot at by Chinamen everyday, while me and Young Sam watch them bloodied and dying on the black-and-white box, and here's my own son in full living colour standing talking to the genuine article out in my yard. I'm thinking about that, but I know if I was to mention what I was thinking likely nobody would even see the connection. People have a way of refusing to see connections. Certainly Young Sam wouldn't, and so I didn't bother mentioning it. But I'm also thinking about the day Willow's hoof caught the barbed wire, so instead of mentioning those men dying in the jungle I ask the boy to take an apple out to Nitro when he goes to help his dad, and the boy jerks his eyes up from the tobacco and rolling paper he's managed to crumple into some kind of sorry paper doll, and he meets my eyes with his scared little puppy dog eyes and tells me he thinks maybe Nitro is gone.

"Gone? Gone where?" I say, and the boy drops the tobacco and the paper in the pouch and sets it on the arm of my

La-Z-Boy, his hands shaking like a leaf in messy weather. He shuts off the television, sucking Bugs into that tiny white dot, and heads out the door, saying he'd better go and help his dad. He leaves me yelling for him to come back, yelling so hard I start to cough and cough and cough until I think my lungs are gonna come up into my lap, and by the time I get the best of that coughing spell all I can do is watch the young dodger crossing the yard the way I've crossed it a million times myself, except the small one never lifts his feet when he walks, so that if you look close you'll probably be able to see his path as two parallel lines in the gravel.

He left me to sit here asking myself silly questions about who I'd be if I weren't me, when I should be going out to that barn, crawling if I have to, and checking on Old Nitro.

The awful truth is that I am reluctant to go. It is easier to stay in this chair, staring out this window, and live up to my grandson's name. Yes, I am tired. I am reluctant. If the truth be known—and I might as well state it, as the truth will always be known sooner or later, no matter how hard you try to hide it—I would prefer to sit right where I am until I die, and I would prefer that occasion to come sooner than later.

But this is 1970, and old men seldom get what they prefer.

And so I stretch back in permanent recline and do my best to travel off to a better day, a summer day fifty years past, a few days after a big rain, when everything was green except for the cuts in the draws where the runoff had chewed right through the grass. There was a glow to the world back then. I sit here stubbornly trying to restore the shine of it, but it's painfully elusive. I begin with a sky that was as blue as the better skies now, and work my way down to the green, with only a breath of white dividing the earth from the heavens. I should point out that there was nothing all that special about the particular day I am trying to recreate—nothing special for those times. It was what anyone might have called an average day.

I was building fence. Had a load of split cedar posts piled on back of the Model T pickup, and I was hammering them in one at a time with a forty-pound maul. A mile of pasture, four square miles of fence, and this year's chore was one whole side that Janson warned me needed to be done when he sold me the place—advising me that it was best to keep up with it a chunk at a time. But if Old Janson had been there to ask me that day, I would gladly have told the lazy old Scandahoovian that a mile was maybe more than should ever have been let go to rat-shit. A mile is a mean chunk of posts and wires.

So there I was for the sixth day in a row, hammering away at a post, then moving on to the next one, muttering curses at Old Janson under my breath, not really believing I'd ever see the spot where the corner post went, when what should come over the hill but my horse Dynamite, the grandfather of Nitro. The old stallion had heard me hammering away and decided to come and see if there were any oats on the truck. He flapped his lips at me the way a horse will when he wants to tell a man what a fool he is for wasting away a day by hammering bits of dead tree into the ground.

Well, it was too much for me. I dropped the hammer, went through the old leaning fence I'd left standing—I was building a few feet outside it, figuring it only made sense to expand your borders if you had to build fences—and swung myself up onto old Dynamite's back, and he took off like a shot.

Oh, what a ride. It was the horse who was driving, not me. I hoped he was watching for holes. At first I figured he wanted us dead, and I considered jumping, but I decided if that's where he was going I'd let him take me. We were charging through some rosebushes, and a bunch of pheasants or grouse exploded up underneath us, and Dynamite reared, and I had to ride him back down to earth, smacking him on the neck with my right hand and only a hank of mane in my left and my knees gripping his sides, and all in a flash we were off again towards the crick.

There has never been a more glorious pursuit of happiness. I caught up to it that day. I felt the wind in my hair and realized I'd lost my hat.

In the end, of course, I had to ride back and collect my hat and continue with the hammering. When I picked up the hammer, I was still thinking about that wondrous ride and that bloody fence I couldn't quite believe would ever be built, and all of a sudden I imagined myself in fifty years, sitting in a crippled La-Z-Boy, my hair white, my teeth gone, my backbone collapsed by all the years of hammering and riding, so that I'd be two inches shorter than I was that bright day. I actually saw myself sitting here, staring out this window, and I thought, "That old man will not recall a single moment of this day. Not one single solitary second. It's too small. It don't mean nothing. It's just your average day."

And, of course, I have always remembered that day, if only because that particular thought scratched my mind and stuck the image of it there, to repeat and repeat until I give up my average life.

The fence is still there.

JANUARY 2nd, 1971: NEAR BROKEN HEAD

"I SING OF IRENE," sang the man on the radio, his voice dark and rumbling and plaintive with a terrible wanting. Irene turned it up. She had never heard the song before, and she would never hear it again. Perhaps there never was such a song. Luke took his right hand off the steering wheel, turned off the music, then replaced the hand at two o'clock. "Driver rules the airwaves," he'd said before they left the reserve, though at the time he'd been joking about a Beatles song that Irene liked and he couldn't stand. He said nothing now. He'd said nothing all morning, and nothing all through lunch while he'd picked at his French fries, and nothing all afternoon.

The cold was on the verge of cracking the pale blue and grey sky. Forty below. The sundogs had their prey surrounded and were closing in for the kill. On either side of the highway, the bleached stubble poked up through the sparse snow. Ahead of them, to the west, the sky was boiling, and they could see they were driving into something nasty. She could peer out to the north through the oval portal of plastic stuck to her side window. Around the opening, the window was opaque with frost.

Every bump and ridge the Studebaker passed over gave her a small jolt.

One day ago they had been so happy. It was the first day of 1971, and they were purposely beginning the year by heading out two days earlier than they'd planned, having decided it would be appropriate to start their new life on the first day of

January. Unfortunately, they didn't get started until after noon because Luke had stayed at the New Year's Eve party and drank more than he should have, but even that didn't matter. Even hungover, Luke was still happy, and she was happy, and the road pointed out in front of them in a way that made her certain anything was possible. They were driving into a future that was theirs, together, and nothing could stop them.

But then they'd made their first mistake. To save money, they decided to stay at her aunt and uncle's place in Winnipeg. Her uncle was hungover too, and he gave Luke a hard time about the Studebaker. Where did his cousin get it? Where was the registration? What would they tell the Mounties if they were stopped?

Luke's cousin had bought it off a bald man named Curly in the parking lot of a convenience store. Told Curly he liked his car, and the man said he'd sell it to him for thirty-five dollars. The registration was lost somehow, but there were papers at the cousin's in Calgary proving it was his cousin's and properly insured, and that's what Luke would tell the police.

Irene's uncle was not satisfied and kept repeating variations on the questions over and over, and he told Irene there was no way he'd let her go any farther with a Blackfoot who papered himself in so thin a story. Her father would never forgive him, he said, though it was he who would never forgive her father for being a lazy Indian and staying on the reserve. Luke said her uncle was no better than a white man, and it was true that her uncle hated Indians as much as any white man she'd yet met despite the fact that he was one himself.

"My grandfather warned me that you Cree are all a bunch of bad apples." These were the last words Luke had spoken last night as they lay in the dark on the pullout couch in the basement. Even after he was snoring, Irene lay awake a long time, listening to the whistle in his nose until it was drowned out by the roar of the furnace. She prayed to Jesus to let Luke see that she loved him with a love as pure and strong as the Lord's love for all mankind. There was only one tribe in the Lord's eyes. She prayed to Jesus to show her the way to make Luke's heart as strong as hers.

On this second day of 1971, they got up before sunrise and left. Her aunt got up too, and insisted on making them breakfast even though Irene told her not to worry, that they'd get something on the road. Her aunt mentioned that the radio said it was already blizzarding in Calgary, where they were heading, and they'd probably hit it in Saskatchewan. Luke didn't say a word, just ate his eggs and toast and went out and started the Studebaker to warm it up. Her uncle did not even get up to try and stop her. She'd thought the leaving would satisfy Luke that she was on his side but it had not done so. Maybe it was only that he had the need to feel wronged and, as she was the only one present she'd have to skin the goat.

Love was such a terrible puzzle. What if she were to reach across and touch the hand that had turned off the radio? Would that erase the wrong? Or would he tell her not to touch him and make the whole thing worse? Or would he pretend not even to notice that she was touching him and make things worse in a different way? Did he just need more time to burn out the anger her uncle had stoked in him? A man's anger was a fire too hot for cooking, her mother had once told her. Or had that just been something she'd heard in another song on the radio? Another song she had perhaps never heard at all.

The '52 Studebaker was the same age she was, Irene had pointed out to her uncle, trying to lighten the mood of their talk, and how could that not be a good sign?

Because there's nothing the same in a car and a girl, her uncle had replied. At eighteen years a girl's still a girl, but a car

that's eighteen years has already covered too many miles and
seen too much road and run down too many gophers, and this
one has too much mystery in its cracked lamps and dented
body. Don't ride in a mystery unless you're wanting to arrive
in a mysterious place.

Which meant nothing to Irene, for wasn't every place but
the reserve a mystery to her? Life was one long beautiful question to which the Lord's love was the only answer, even on a
forty below afternoon with a lover who would not allow her
song to be sung. But she should not even think that. That was
not fair to Luke. Even in his silence he was singing her song
with a deep plaintive wanting, singing his need and his love
and his terrible possession. Her mother had told her that Luke
was so in love he was afraid of her. Her mother could see these
things.

Her mother was generally right. Knowing this, she could
not help reaching across and touching him, but on the leg
instead of the hand. He looked down at her fingers there on
his leg, before he looked into her eyes.

"What do you want?" he finally said.

"I want to hear you still have a voice," she told him, and
gave his leg a squeeze.

"Well, now you've heard," he said.

"Not good enough," she said. "You won't let the man on
the radio sing to me, so I want you to sing me a song."

"I'm driving," he said.

"All right. I'll sing to you, then."

And she sang him a Beatles song that maintained that all
that was needed was love.

"The Beatles broke up," Luke said when she was finished
what she knew, which was not all that much. Not that there
was much to begin with, so far as she recalled.

"I heard."

"So, a lot of good love did them."

"Maybe they didn't have enough of it."

She started to sing it again. There were not many words to the song.

"That would explain them singing about needing it."

"It would."

"It would."

Her hand was still on his leg, and he glanced at it again.

"Your uncle don't have much love for me, do he?"

"You want my uncle to love you?"

"No, but I wouldn't mind his respect. I'm bigger on respect than love. That's me. If I was to write a song, that's what it would be about."

"Maybe you haven't had enough respect. That makes you want to sing about needing it."

"Maybe."

She leaned over and kissed his cheek.

"I respect you," she whispered in a breathy voice. "How do I respect you? Let me count the ways. I respect you like a winter morning. Forty below."

He gave her a suspicious look. "I hope not."

"Why not?"

"Because you respect a winter morning because it'll kill you if you don't. That's not why I want you to respect me."

"But I do. It would kill me not to respect you."

"Is that so? I doubt it."

"You don't believe that not enough respect can kill?"

"I do."

"Well, then?"

"You're confusing me," he said, and looked again at her hand on his leg.

"Oh. Sorry. Does my hand confuse you?"

"No. Your mouth. Your hand's not confusing at all."

"Good."

"It's distracting, though. Your hand isn't showing enough respect for the road."

She took her hand away.

He glanced longingly in the direction her hand had gone, and then into her eyes.

"Maybe we should stop and talk about this some more," he said.

"No. It only confuses you," she said. He turned back to the road. "Tell you what," she said, "let's go somewhere and make respect to each other with our hands."

He seemed to like the idea. "Somewhere off the highway?"

"That's probably a good idea. You can't make proper respect worrying about other people watching."

Luke pulled off on the next grid road and drove south a couple of miles until they came to a clump of Scotch pine that had been planted around a farm, now abandoned. There was not much snow on the driveway, so they pulled into the yard. A deer turned and fled through the pine, waving its white tail at them.

Luke left the car running.

His lips were on her breast, her fingers in his hair, cupping his ears, when Irene noticed that the wind was beginning to pick up. The snow had begun to gust across the ground. Even though they'd stopped, the weather was still coming. She considered pointing this out to Luke, but he was so interested in what he was doing that it did not seem fair. A change, she thought. A wind means change, and on such a cold day that could only be good news in the long run. He had already begun to kiss her belly, and she lifted her bum so he could pull off her pants.

JUNE 25th, 2000: NEAR BROKEN HEAD

SAM GAVE UP ON WORK to drink a cold beer and sit out on a patio chair in front of the house, waiting for his family to come back to him. And they did. Gwen and the boys drove into the yard in Vern's pickup truck. The Buick had started making a funny noise near Neville and stopped running altogether just this side of Lac Pelletier, and she'd phoned Vern to come and get them.

"Why didn't you call me?" Sam asked.

"I tried, but it was busy. Anyway, I thought maybe Vern would be able to get it going. No such luck. I guess it's something serious."

Vern had wandered to the edge of the yard and, with his back to them, was pissing under the flowering plum.

"Well, that's . . . a problem," Sam said. "I have to take my car to the airport in the morning."

"You're going to Toronto tomorrow?"

"Yes. You know that. How are your parents?"

"Dad's fine. Mom says hello."

Sam scooped Ben up into his arms. "Did you guys have fun?"

"Sure." Michael shrugged. "We made cookies."

"How much do you love me, Dad?" Ben asked.

"A million billion."

"Do you love me more than you love Michael?"

"No!" Michael said.

"I love you the same," Sam said.

Ben grinned one of his sly little grins. "Is it okay if I love Mommy more than I love you?"

Sam nodded slowly. "Sure, that's fine." He set him down

29

next to his brother. "Go and wash your hands and get ready for supper."

Sam had been on the phone for only a few minutes the entire day, talking to his parents. Oh, yes—and answering a wrong number from some girlfriend of Vern's. What were the odds that Gwen's phone call would have come during those few moments? Perhaps Vern's latest conquest had blocked Gwen's emergency, so that she had had to turn to Vern. Sam imagined a scantily clad young woman calling Vern's number a moment later and finding it busy, the call she had blocked now blocking hers, so that Vern would not get laid that night after all. It made him feel better as he faced Vern's gloating grin, flushed from the effort of playing cavalry.

"No problem, little brother. You'd do the same for me."

But Vern would never have a wife for Sam to rescue. When Vern wasn't eating their mother's or Gwen's cooking, he existed on frozen pizza or drove to town for shrimp and ribs and a beer at the Eye, where he could check out the ladies. Vern's life was too big for just one woman.

"Do you want to stay for supper?" Gwen asked him.

"What are ya havin'?"

She turned to Sam, redirecting the question his way.

"Well, I didn't know when you were coming," he said. "We could barbecue hamburgers."

She turned back to Vern. "Hamburgers?"

"Sure."

"No better offers?"

"Yeah, but I wouldn't wanna deprive you of my company."

"Oh, don't worry about us," Sam said.

Sam's acreage was a postage stamp of prairie stuck on the northeast border of his father's land. When his father refused to take money for a corner of the Big Pasture—Old Sam had called it Janson's, after the man he'd bought it from, but Sam's father had always called it the Big Pasture—insisting that Sam should just build there if he wanted, Sam had bought forty acres from their most despised neighbour.

The house was dug into the side of the valley, facing south towards the creek. The three side walls were concrete and the south wall a plane of glass broken only by narrow vertical stanchions. There wasn't another view like it in the world. The house wasn't too hard on the eye either, especially in the evening, when the bare inner walls (Sam had, after long negotiation, convinced Gwen that her needlepoint should be hung in the spare room) glowed out into the night like polished metal. The lines were clean and straight. The roof was flat, so that after one particularly bad blizzard Sam had had to get Vern to come and help him shovel off the snow before the winter came in on them. Generally this wasn't a problem though, as flat roofs were well suited to the prairie climate of abundant wind and little moisture.

A senior vice president on reconnaissance had come for a barbecue once and was so taken by Sam's place that he'd told a friend of his who published a lifestyle magazine and Sam's postage stamp ended up in a nationally distributed photo spread. Gwen did not share Sam's modernist leanings, preferring a home to look domestic, and for years she'd complained that Sam's star architect had created something to match his cold heart. She felt like she was living in an institution: a hospital, an airport, a bank, maybe a funeral home, she wasn't sure which. So when the photographer showed up that June morning and she proudly escorted him from room to room, Sam couldn't help teasing her about her sudden enthusiasm for their model home.

"What'd you expect me to do? Insult his lack of taste? I'm not that crude."

Despite her protestations, Sam once came home to find Gwen gazing at that magazine. "Our house looks pretty good in these pictures," she admitted, before her face transformed into a wicked grin. "Maybe that's where it really belongs."

The photo spread had happened about five years ago, when their marriage still worked, more or less. Sometimes, when Sam got home, Michael was already in bed, but Gwen didn't complain about his lateness. She didn't eat with Michael so that she could have dinner with Sam, and she'd light candles in the dining room, and they'd sit and talk about his day and Michael's day and his family and her family and what was blooming in the garden, and after dinner they'd go out and sit in the dying light watching the world get dark. He felt that this might be what was known as happiness.

That's all he really wanted, was for everyone to be happy. That was why he worked so hard and traded his portfolio so carefully. He'd done very well indeed, and they would never have to worry about money. Both boys' university educations were already paid for.

Like Gwen, Michael thought the magazine article was cool, and he showed the glossy pictures to all his friends. But the photo spread didn't impress Sam's father or his brother, who still claimed Sam's house was a glorified cardboard box.

"You know why he makes you live in that thing, Gwen?" Vern had joked in the middle of last Thanksgiving dinner. "It's because Dad bought Mom a freezer when we were kids, and they gave Sam the box to make himself a playhouse. I guess he musta spent his happiest moments in there and now he's trying to recreate them. Come to think of it, the inside of your house looks a lot like the inside of that freezer."

Vern house's, the trailer where Sam and Gwen had lived while they were waiting for their house to be built, was considerably more like that freezer box than Sam's beautiful home, but Sam didn't bother to do anything more than think this retort. Instead, he left before the pumpkin pie with the excuse that he needed to catch up on some paperwork.

"What difference does it make?" Sam had asked their mother years before, on the morning he'd announced he would be leaving in the middle of harvest to start working towards a bachelor of commerce. "Dad's got Vern. Why does he need me?" She had no reply except that look in her eye that suggested there might be an entire universe trapped inside her head. Some sappy country-and-western song twanged on the radio. Sam would always associate the steel guitar with that awful moment.

When he returned with his M.B.A., taking the job in Broken Head over a multitude of other possibilities that would have been more favourable for his career, it was to please Gwen, his high school sweetheart, who had followed him to Vancouver to do her undergraduate degree and had accidentally become pregnant just as he was beginning his M.B.A. For a whole week she'd been afraid to tell him, and when she finally did he was so angry he marched out of the apartment without a word and went to an afternoon movie at one of those theatres the size of a living room they built in shopping malls back then. It was a foreign film, and he was the only one in the theatre. Something from South America about a man facing some direction or other. He didn't remember a thing about the film. After the movie he walked back to the apartment. Gwen was at the kitchen sink, weeping into her dishwater. He took her into his arms, kissed the back of her neck, and asked her to marry him.

Two months later, Gwen had a miscarriage. In trying to comfort her, Sam made the mistake of suggesting the child was obviously not meant to be born. Gwen closed her eyes and told him to please be quiet. Sometimes, no matter how hard he tried, it was impossible to say the right thing.

Even if they'd wanted to reconsider, there was no turning back from the marriage by then. Their families had been notified and the arrangements had begun. Gwen's mother had reserved the Legion Hall for the reception and dance. There were over a hundred invitations, and more than 350 people showed up. Vern was Sam's best man. A rumour went around that he'd outstripped his duties by servicing Gwen's maid of honour, Louise Dumais, who was not entirely happy in her marriage. Vern insisted it was all nonsense: Louise had simply been feeling a little light-headed from all those rum and Cokes, and her husband had passed out on the head table so that he was not able to attend to her. Vern had taken her out for a moonlight stroll to clear her head.

When Sam finished his degree, Gwen wanted to go home to show her family and everyone in town what an important man Sam had become. Or maybe it was he who'd wanted that. This was one of their ongoing debates. In any case, Sam had no trouble finding a job in Broken Head.

Gwen had grown up in Meridian, a town fifty miles north of the Montana border where people thought of moving to Broken Head as moving to the big city. Her father's farm implements dealership had made their name prominent in the area. They were The Lowerys. "No wonder old man Lowery's always driving a new Cadillac, what with the price of that new John Deere."

To Meridian, the fall of Lowery John Deere might as well have been the fall of Microsoft. But Sam couldn't explain that to the boys back east, who could read a bottom line as well as anyone. The demographics just didn't work anymore. There was no money in that area anymore. And it was just as impossible explaining the laws of collateral and diminishing returns to people who were begging you for one more year to turn around their personal disaster—that mythical "next year" when it would rain every two weeks like God was turning on a tap, and the price of grain would go up a couple of bucks a bushel. Someone else had done the dirty work, of course, but Gwen's father would never forgive Sam.

Gwen needed to come with Sam to the airport in Saskatoon so that she'd have his car while he was in Toronto, so the next morning, after they put Michael on the school bus, they left Ben with Sam's mother.

"Oh, it's no problem at all." His mother clapped her hands together. "We'll have a great time, won't we, Ben?"

Ben clung to Gwen, insisting that she was not going anywhere.

"You don't want to drive all that way, honey. You'll be much happier with Grandma."

"I will not! I will not! I hate her!"

"Now, Ben, you don't mean that. You love Grandma."

"I hate her. I hate everybody but you, Mommy."

Sam's father and Vern were at the kitchen table, silently nursing cups of coffee.

"You're up early," Sam said to Vern.

"And the early worm gets eaten," Vern said, rubbing a temple and faintly smiling.

"Probably hasn't been to bed yet. Smells like a brewery," their father said. "Are you plannin' on startin' the summer fallow up top?"

"Maybe this afternoon. Thought I'd go get Gwen's car this morning."

"No need," Sam said. "I called my garage to go and get it."

"Your garage? You own one of those now too?"

Sam didn't respond.

"No point throwin' money away. I'll get it."

"The garage'll get it," Sam said. "I think Dad wants you to start on the summer fallow."

Vern shook his head. "If I had half the money he throws away . . ."

"You'd waste it on whiskey and cigarettes and girls with tattoos on their . . ." Their father's voice drifted off, leaving the object of the pronoun to their imagination.

Vern grinned. "That's not waste. That's research and development."

Gwen and Sam's mother finally managed to distract Ben with a colouring book and crayons, and Sam and Gwen made their escape.

"Why don't you come with me?"

The question broke a silence that had lasted for forty miles.

"Because I hate Toronto."

She said this to the wheat field out her side window. They had non-verbally negotiated a cease-fire, but he could still see the muzzles of her guns protruding from a trench that had been so long dug and well furnished it had become as comfortable to Gwen as a summer home. His ditch, he had to admit, was probably just as deep even if it was more tastefully appointed. Perhaps if he invited the enemy over for a drink, she would be surprised how much she liked the way things looked from the other side.

"You'd have a great time. I could get tickets to *The Lion King*."

The strategy was almost as old as their marriage. The strategy was their marriage.

"What about the boys?"

"They can stay with Mom and Dad."

"With no warning? That wouldn't be very fair to your parents, would it?" She actually turned and looked at him. "My, but you're impulsive all of a sudden, aren't you? Feeling guilty?"

They did not speak the rest of the way to the airport. He fell asleep on the flight, not having slept well the night before.

When Sam flew east for these meetings at Head Office, the other guys always called him Cowboy. "How're things back at the ranch, Cowboy," they'd say, clapping him on the back and urging him into his seat at the boardroom table. The endearment made him very uncomfortable. The condescension was inescapable. At times, in certain mouths, he believed the word carried the same sting as "Camel Jockey," or "Nigger," or "Scalp-Hunter." For instance, when one VP, Gregory Kaplan, said the word, there was something in the tone that suggested he believed Sam spent his weekends wearing white sheets, burning crosses on lawns and chanting orations about conspiracies of Jewish bankers.

Still, Sam didn't bother (or, in the case of his superiors, didn't dare) to tell them how much the word insulted him. Once, over martinis, he tried to explain to Gregory Kaplan that, despite what he thought, Sam had not grown up in an atmosphere of anti-Semitism. In fact, his father used to tell them that Jews were the Chosen People, and that they were only hated so much because they had a tendency to be better than everyone else at everything they did. Like Americans, the Jews were the tall poppies of the world. Gregory Kaplan received this information with a blank expression that gradually made Sam run out of steam. After a moment's silence, Kaplan smiled, nodded, lifted his drink as though to toast the great mysteries and said, "Well, isn't that interesting. Cowboys ruminating about anti-Semitism. Who would have thought?" And then he changed the subject to the new quarterly offering of IXP.

It truly mystified Sam, this labelling of him as a cowboy. In any bar back home in Broken Head there were dozens of young men strutting about with pointy-toed boots, tight jeans and pearl-buttoned shirts with satin yokes. Most of them were no more cowboys than Sam, but they at least had romantic inclinations in that direction. Vern sometimes wore the costume when he went to town for parts—though he preferred plain white cotton undershirts to any finer weave—but when Sam drove his BMW out of his manicured yard each morning he was always wearing a suit of impeccable quality.

Not that the cut of Sam's jacket meant anything to his father. Or his brother. Or his wife.

In a drugstore on Queen Street, Sam stood at the condom rack, eyeing the different choices, and decided on the twelve pack over the three. That way they'd think he was just another happily married businessman buying them to take home and put in his bedside table drawer.

They?

The clerk. The clerk would never suspect a thing. Sam had only come in here for a small bottle of Tylenol, and he'd seen the condoms and decided he needed them. That's what he told himself, though he could easily have bought Tylenol in the lobby of the hotel. Condoms too. But who knew when somebody from the conference might wander into that little shop?

He had no definite plan in mind for using a condom. Well, there was that branch manager from the Maritimes, but he really didn't think she was interested in anything but a little harmless flirting. On the other hand, she might be. What did Gwen expect from him? He had a right to want sex. There was nothing abnormal about a man needing sex every once in a while. The last time he'd had sex was on his birthday, ten months ago. He'd attempted to roll Gwen on top of him, the way he used to (he liked the bottom best), but she held him tightly in the missionary position until he was finished.

He grabbed the package and marched to the front of the store, studying the clerk as he approached her. A young woman with a silver stud through one nostril. That must have hurt. He hoped the boys would never be tempted to such foolishness.

As he neared the counter, a dissolute man lurched in front of him. The man wore a torn and filthy fireman's jacket, the kind that had been fashionable among young urbanites a few years ago but had long since been discarded. The smell of him made Sam take a step back.

"Can I help you?" the clerk asked, eyeing the man doubtfully.

"Do you mind if I call you Marie?" the man asked.

The clerk studied the man, her withdrawn expression quickly changing to full fledged revulsion. On her left breast she wore a name tag that said BRIANNA.

"Yes, I do mind."

She looked at Sam as she spoke, and he smiled his sympathy for her plight.

"I can't call you Marie?"

"No."

"Why not?"

"Because Marie's not my name."

"No?" He swayed, but was obviously lucid enough to read the tag on her breast. "Your name is Brianna. See, I know your name. I'll call you Brianna."

"Very impressive. Can I help you?"

"Yes, Brianna. Can I get some razor blades?"

Brianna considered this request. Perhaps she, like Sam, had been expecting the man to ask for cigarettes. Still, there was no doubt that the man could use some razor blades. One had to remember, though, they were kept behind the counter for good reason. But Brianna was not a psychologist, and even if she were the man's suicidal tendencies were likely passive. He had his next drink to live for. One might argue that his willingness to waste the money on razor blades—money he might have spent on that drink—was a dangerous sign, but he might mean to use the blades to shave his face and reclaim himself for the work force or for a visit to his family or his church. Or even to the bar. Razor blades were ambiguous. If the man wanted razor blades, she would give him razor blades.

She swept the package over the register's eye, and told him the price. He began to measure out coins from a cache he had been clutching in his fist. His motor skills were not what they should have been, making it a laborious process, but at last he placed the last penny on the counter and she swept the coins into her palm and dropped them into the proper slots in the register. Then she dropped the blades and the receipt into a plastic bag and handed it to the man. Sam clutched the condoms and Tylenol in his folded palms.

"I don't need a bag," the man said, but she ignored him.

"Can I help you?" she asked Sam, smiling widely.

Sam plunked the Tylenol and the condoms down on the counter, and she rang them through. When he opened his wallet, he found, to his surprise, that he was out of cash. Oh, yes. He had paid for that round of martinis. He took out his ABM card, and she swept it through her machine. Sam could not get to the terminal to punch in his personal identification number because the man was still standing in the way, trying to fish the razor blades out of the plastic bag. As he held the bag with his left hand, his right hand kept missing the opening. The clerk looked at Sam and smiled apologetically. Finally, when the man missed again, Sam reached into the bag and pulled out the razor blades.

"Hey! Those are my razor blades! This asshole's trying to steal my razor blades!"

Sam took a step back, worried that the man might take a swing at him. "Here. I'm only trying to help you."

He held the razor blades out to the man, who briefly considered the offering.

"I'm not a baby. I don't need your help. Asshole! Put them back in my bag."

Sam sighed, met the clerk's sympathetic eyes and dropped the razor blades into the bag.

"Asshole! I can do it myself. I'm not a baby!"

"Yes, well, you're standing in the way of the ABM terminal, and I can't pay for my purchase."

"I'm not in the way! I'm not stopping you from paying for your stupid French ticklers. Use it if you like, Asshole!"

Sam stepped dangerously close to the man and, holding his breath, punched the date of Michael's birth into the terminal.

"You think any lady's gonna let you use one of those things on her, Asshole? Not likely. Ask Marie here. You wouldn't fuck this asshole, would you? Or are you one of those queer fellows? Is that what you are? That's what you are, isn't it? Isn't it?!"

Sam nodded politely at the clerk and marched out of the store. He'd gone half a block before he realized he'd forgotten his purchase. He did not go back. What did he need with condoms anyway? He bought Tylenol in the lobby of the hotel. It was time to head back for the afternoon session.

—

Sam was in the city for three days of corporate pep talks enti-
tled "Unleashing the Hunter Within: Attaining Your
Marketing Goals." What that meant was that he was here to
strategize about how to deal with the latest branch closings in
his area. Customers tended to be touchy about branch closings
no matter what the justification, and at the moment the bank
was making record profits, so the left-leaning media were
attempting, fairly successfully, to whip the people in the
affected rural communities into a bit of a lather. Head Office
wasn't overly concerned about feedback—there was little
money or political clout in those rural areas—but they did feel
a slight responsibility to offer Sam, who was on the front lines,
some strategies for dealing with the hate and derision.

During the smoke break he stood at the wall of glass, staring across the street at the TD Centre, an exquisite grid of
black rectangles within larger black rectangles. Black, like one
of those inverse stars, black holes, that lurk at the corners of
the universe. In the evening the structure glowed like polished
obsidian. Wouldn't it be wonderful to look out at such perfection every day at work, instead of at the boarded-up video
store across the parking lot in Broken Head. For five years Sam
had begged and bargained with Gwen, even demanded that
they should pack up their things and move to Toronto, where
they could get on with their lives. He'd promised her riches
she couldn't imagine; unfortunately, Gwen had enough
money already, thank you very much, and had no wish to run
away to some big city where people would make her feel stupid like most of Sam's friends from the city did. Like Sam did.
Besides, it wouldn't be fair to the boys. They had friends. They
had lives. They had this green postage stamp at the corner of
his father's ranch. It wasn't all about Sam and his career.

And so Sam stayed on, though he felt he was walking a road that led nowhere. He'd made as much as he could of his job. Not to say that his position was as unimportant as most people thought. His branch serviced the entire southwest corner of the province, and because Sam was more forward-thinking than his colleagues in Regina and Saskatoon or the other regions, he had soon become the point man for the entire province. If Head Office needed information on the region, they'd fly Sam to Toronto. To the bank, Sam was Saskatchewan. They couldn't have imagined how completely disconnected he felt from it.

Not the place. He loved the landscape. It was the most perfect landscape in existence: an sublimely essential combination of grass and hill and sky and cloud. But the boys here at Head Office could not imagine how alienated he felt from the community he served. After all, he had been raised there. They were his people. But he had no friends. He had no one to share his love of Puccini. His monthly business trips to Toronto were the joy of Sam's life. So it bothered him a great deal that he was forced to play country bumpkin to boorish VPs and investment analysts who'd never even heard of Mies van der Rohe, but who insisted on greeting Sam with a slap on the back and a "Hey, Cowboy. How do you manage to keep those shoes so clean?"

Was it the name? For a time, in university, he'd tried calling himself Samuel McMahon, but not one person had paid him the respect of adding the three letters when they addressed him, and he took so much ribbing from Gwen for the attempt that he finally gave up. Anyway, *Samuel* sounded as much like he was born to ride a horse as *Sam*.

Perhaps his colleagues' endearment was simply a reflection of their condescension towards anything beyond the 401—a condescension he longed to share but couldn't, fearing that something of his background would reveal itself in him: something of his grandfather's or his father's gait in his own stride. After all, his grandfather had made his living as a rancher. His father, on the other hand, had diversified by buying more cultivated land and had given up working his cattle with horses before Sam could even remember, finding that with strategically built fences and corrals the family could manage the herd with a truck and on foot. Chasing them on horses only made the cattle wilder and more difficult, even dangerous, to handle.

He tried to explain this to a woman named Erika over cocktails in a rusty-walled bar on College Street. "Old Sam turned the place over to Dad, and the first thing Dad did was stop using the horses to work the cattle. Made Old Sam furious. He had this beautiful old horse. A black stallion named Nitro . . ."

"Old Sam?"

"No! The horse was called Nitro." He was actually shouting, trying to be heard over the music—if you could call it that. "Old Sam was my grandfather. I'm named after him. He died when I was nine."

"Do you still ride?" Erika shouted back, missing the point entirely. She obviously wasn't hearing him properly. He leaned closer and she turned her head, offering the whorl of her ear and a dangling star-shaped earring.

"No," he spoke directly into her. "Not since I was a kid."

She said something he couldn't catch, and he turned his head, offering his ear to her.

"How big is your ranch?"

"My father's farm? A couple thousand acres."

"A couple of . . . ! How big is that?"

"Ummm . . . Three square miles, give or take . . ."

Her gasp made him sit back and cross his legs.

"I envy you so much!"

Her shout was so loud that he heard every word clearly—so loud that the urban primitives at the next table, sporting enough metal in their faces to warm the heart of a steel company executive, turned to Sam and stared, apparently wondering what there was to covet in this man in the fancy suit.

"What do you mean?"

She read his lips and leaned closer, and he offered himself again, and this time he actually felt her lips brush his ear as she spoke.

"This city is eating me alive. You can't imagine. Eating me . . . from the inside out. It's insidious. I grind my teeth when I sleep. I've had to have three operations because I've worn out the sockets in my jaw."

He nodded and glanced from her eyes to her damaged mouth, and finally down to her exposed cleavage, before he turned his ear to her again. "My dream is to get my own little place in the country some day. Horses, a few chickens, a big dog, maybe a llama. I love llamas. Heaven!"

Erika had been sitting next to him at a production of *Carmen*, had laughed out loud when the toreador stripped off his shirt and flexed his pectorals at them. During the intermission they'd started chatting, she complaining about how her date had stood her up again because he had to do some stupid heart operation, and after the show she'd asked him if he'd like to go for a drink and brought him to this tiny club with walls that looked like the inside of the threshing machine where his father had once caught him smoking. He ordered a glass of red wine and she ordered something called a Stir Trek, which turned out to be a fluorescent blue cocktail. She offered him a taste and he found it much like rubbing alcohol. He told her so: "It tastes like rubbing alcohol." She shrugged and lifted her glass above a candle guttering in a rusted spherical pod that might have housed a hi-fi speaker back in the seventies.

"Looks cool, though, doesn't it?"

When he stopped his rental car in front of her building, intending only to drop her off, she leapt on him, crushing his lips with hers to prevent any attempt at escape. This sort of thing had never happened to him before. He'd often fantasized about having sex with women other than Gwen (or rather, he'd often fantasized about having sex, period) but he had never pursued these daydreams—the condoms this afternoon notwithstanding.

The elevator in her building wasn't working. Holding his hand, she led him up the stairs to the seventh floor. Before she unlocked her door, she kissed him like melting butter and whispered in his ear: "Ooooooooo, Cowboy. You look like you'll be good for a ride."

NIGHT FALLS. Those two words make the passing of the last two hours sound almost perfumey and pleasurable, like a lovely lady in a dim parlour, but as a matter of fact there was nothing the least bit pretty about them. Yeah, I suppose there was the last light glittering the frost on the pines around the vegetable garden, the cornstalks leaning eastward, the blush in the sky where the sun showed its embarrassment for a day of feeble effort, but light and words are separate aliens who have only heard about each other on the radio. The long and the short of it was it was supper as usual. The five of us crowded around the old table, jostling elbows to shovel down what we need to keep us alive for another day's trip to the outhouse.

Except that even the outhouse has been retired.

For some strange reason the son's wife went and paid what had to amount to a half dozen bushels of wheat for a lamb's leg that'd been shipped all the way from New Zealand. The small one sat there looking like the coyote having dinner with the weeping shepherd. Staring into his mashed potatoes and gravy. He was next to me, as usual. Sam by Sam. I've lost my spot at the head of the table. The son's there now. You'd think he'd be embarrassed to sit in my chair—the chair I ordered with the others from the Eaton's catalogue forty years ago, when he was no more than a pooping and screaming and puking little bit of red flesh, clutching at his mother. The chair I ordered to try and make his mother happy. Little good it did in the end.

47

There wasn't much being said, aside from the usual muttered requests to pass the salt or the milk or the devil's sorry
soul—which, in fact, I've never been called on to pass, though
for years now it has always been within arm's reach—and so I
decided to motivate a little discussion by tapping my fork on
the corner of my plate and saying to the son, "The boy tells
me the Chinaman's buyin' eggs."

The son looked at me but, as is his practice, decided to cal-
culate my agenda before responding, leaving it open to his
other half to fill in the blank.

"Mr. Chong?" she asked.

"No. Chiang Kai-Shek."

Once she'd uttered his name, she didn't have much else to
offer, so she looked to her husband and then at her plate.

"Anybody ask him what he figures about what's goin' on
over in Vietnam? Young Sam and I were watchin' it on your
box just now. Watched them carryin' out a few boys riddled
fulla metal."

The son sighed. The young one hunched a little more over
his plate.

"You shouldn't be watching that, Sam," the son's wife said.

"Of course he shouldn't. We should toss the cursed box in
the burnhole tonight. That's the only way you're gonna stop
him from seein' young men bein' shot to pieces. At least he
ain't over there bein' shot at, though. There was a young fellow from Wyoming, couldn't be much older than Vern,
tellin' about how they got ambushed by . . . what do they call
them now? Gooks. Used to be Japs, now they're Gooks. I
spoze that's what they call progress. Anybody ask Mr. Chong
about that?"

The son had figured out the lay of the land by that time,
I guess. "No, Dad," he said, "I don't talk to Mr. Chong about

Vietnam. Why would I? What would he care about Vietnam? He was born in Regina."

I chewed for a moment in order to give the appearance of properly considering his question. "Well, bein' a scientist and all, he must be a pretty smart guy. He might have an innerestin' perspective on things."

"He might," the son nodded in his insolent way. "He thinks we should sell all the cattle and raise buffalo. They're natural to this ecosystem, you know."

That silly grin on his face.

"Yeah? I guess he's never tried to brand a buffalo, then, has he?"

"No, I don't spoze he has."

"Funny how educated people are constantly talkin' about things they know nothin' about, ain't it?"

"It is," the son said, and he tore a bun in half, as if that sealed the matter.

This was generally the son's strategy: work the conversation around to something we couldn't very well help but agree on. He thinks that'll satisfy me, and often enough it does. I am old and tired and reluctant. I am ready for a wooden box without a window.

We ate on in silence for a space, our silver scraping on the plates. Or stainless steel, I guess, as the son's wife has packed away Mary's silver in the china cabinet my brother bought Mary for a wedding present. John. The son's named after my dad, and my brother was too. Buried him three years ago. Wasn't much loss to the world or to himself as the Alzheimer's or something had made him into a baby years before. Last time I visited he peed his pants right in front of me and started bawling like he wanted me to change him.

In the end, tired as I am, I could not hold the peace.

"Well, if the Chinaman wants to turn the prairie back to

the buffalo, then what does he want with my horse?" The son just kept chewing. "Or maybe he wants to make himself into an Injun. Is that it? Is he plannin' on ridin' Nitro while he shoots his bow and arrow at these buffalo of his?"

That got everybody looking at one another, but it was more than a few seconds before the son found his tongue.

"I don't know what you're talking about," he said, glancing at the boys to warn me to the fact that we oughtn't to have this discussion in front of them. As if hearing their grandfather and their father raise their voices at one another is any worse than watching boys die on television. "Mr. Chong doesn't have your horse," he said.

"Where is my horse, then?"

The son looked down at his plate and stabbed a bit of the black sheep. "In a better place," he said, before he put the meat in his mouth and chewed.

A better place. What would he know about a better place? There is no better place than this one, and if he doesn't know that, then he doesn't deserve it, and I'd like it back right now, thank you very much.

But that's not what I said.

"You've got no right to sell my horse!"

Funny how a shock like that can make you so silly as to rely on something as flimsy as your own pitiful moral indignation. The son, bless his heart, just turned around and gave me back a little of his own.

"He wasn't your horse. You gave him to me when he was a colt, when I was fifteen. Remember?"

I hadn't seen that coming. I should have. When you give something to someone and they throw it away and you bend over to pick it up for safekeeping, more likely than not it's about to become their most prized possession.

"But you never rode him."

"I tried to ride him, and he threw me and broke my leg."

"That's right. You couldn't ride him, so you sold him to the Chinaman. You think it's a fine thing to be chasin' the cattle around with a goddamned pickup truck. What kind of an excuse for a cowboy are you?"

He tried to smile, but the smile had long since been wiped right out of him. "He was too dangerous. I should have sold him years ago. He almost killed you."

If I had two good legs, I'd have been jumping up and down. "He did nothin' of the kind. Old age and my own stupidity almost killed me. To give you one for instance, I should've never bin stupid enough to give away this place to a whelp like you. Who'd a thought I'd hear my own son call a twenty-two year old horse 'dangerous.'"

The son looked me up and down as though he was measuring me for that box I was desiring. "Old age doesn't necessarily make you less dangerous."

I had a hard time getting to my feet, which made me all the madder because it spoiled the effect of the exit I was trying to make. "That's a truth you will learn to regret," I told him, as I hobbled out of the dining room and off to my bed, like a whipped child, to sulk and lick my wounds.

At least I still have my old room. The only reason is because the boy built on an addition with a bigger bedroom for him and the wife. But then, maybe there is another reason. Maybe he's afraid to sleep in here with the ghosts. It's the same room I have slept in, mostly alone, for the last forty years. Not that Mary was the only woman who ever slept here. There have been others. Even when Mary was alive, there were others, though not as many as she seemed to think. Not that I give a damn what she did or didn't think. And I told her so too.

I asked her was it natural for a man to unzip his pants for one woman alone? I owned bulls, I told her, that had three heifers in an afternoon. So why should men be expected to be any different, if that was the natural state of things? And she asked me if I was no better than an animal, and I said, No, thank you, I guessed I was not, and that I hadn't seen too many men who could make a claim to being half so good as the average animal.

Oh, yes. I was a cruel one. Cruel enough to speak the truth. If the truth be known. And it will.

I found Mary in this room. Came in from checking the cattle and she didn't answer when I called, and so I called again and the son woke up and started wailing, so I went in to check on him. I picked him up and held him in the crook of my arm, let him suck on my finger to stop the noise, and I walked on down the hall looking for her, calling again, "Mary," already fairly certain what I'd find when I opened the door. I didn't know beforehand—or I knew it, but I didn't know I knew it until that walk down the hallway. I opened the door and there she was, and I didn't even stand and stare but just turned around and took the boy back to his crib and put him down, and he started screaming again.

Then I went and cut her down.

"Cancer of the breast?" the neighbours say. "More like cancer of the heart."

They blame me. Have blamed me all of these many years. As though I had told her where to set the chair and placed the rope around her neck. As though she had no other choice, considering my great evil.

We had talked about that. About choices. I had explained to her that our choice, this marriage thing, had obviously been a mistake, and it was my choice to make amendments. On the other hand, I did not want to take away choices from her, and so I would allow her to stay and live on with me if she could accept the arrangement as I saw it working for me. I would leave the choice to her, but she would need to realize that if she stayed it was by her own choosing.

She called me selfish, and I told her that freedom was a selfish thing. How could it help but be?

And so, in the end, she chose her own sort of freedom. Which was all well and fine with me. The neighbours blamed who they had to, but I guess I can shoulder the weight of an entire world's blame if that's what the world needs to feel all right about itself.

I hired a woman to nurse the son. With a bottle, I mean. Her breasts were empty. Not that I gained that knowledge by hand. I never touched Molly, though once again the neighbours whispered otherwise, which was not fair to Molly. Not that Molly cared any more than me. She, I have come to believe, was the perfect partner for a man. This man, at any rate. Ugly as sin and a bit of a battle axe, but she raised the boy up straight and tall and proud enough to put his father in his place. Five years ago, when her heart gave out, I mourned her more than I have any man or woman since my own mother and father. The son, I think, has not entirely gotten over mourning her yet.

The son does not even remember his real mother, and he has me to thank for hiring the one he did know, but he finds his own needs to blame me for Mary's passing. Always has.

And now he has sold my horse out from under me, leaving me swinging, slowly turning, as Mary was when I walked into the room.

Fortunately, when I point my toes I can still touch the ground.

JANUARY 2nd, 1971: NEAR BROKEN HEAD

"THEY'RE NO DIFFERENT than children, these men are," Irene's mother had once told her. She was rolling some dough into a piecrust when she shared this secret. (It was something her mother had definitely said and the pie had definitely been apple). Irene remembered thinking at the time that "these men" meant her white father, whom she had never seen—not even in a photograph—and who was only ever mentioned in ways that suggested he might have been more than one man, almost any man: there were no real peculiarities about him worth working your tongue over. He was one of "these men," who were this way or that. He was the average man.

It was Luke who taught her what her mother had meant. When he cried or fretted or was unhappy in any of the many peculiar ways he was unhappy, Irene put him to her breast and he was contented again. The only problem was (at present) the door handle against her backbone and (in general) the fact that her nipples were so sensitive the nuzzling gave her little electrical shocks that made her want to push him away, which was why she held onto his ears and tried to direct him. Eventually she would lower him down to her belly and then down even farther. She preferred his tongue down where he could do things to her she would never have imagined possible—things even he didn't seem to be aware were possible. It was not something they talked about, that's for certain, and there was certainly no talking going on when she opened her eyes and saw that outside the Studebaker the whole world had been erased by blowing snow, leaving only a blank white square of windshield.

When she told him, Luke stopped what he was doing to check out the situation, but he said that they might as well go on with what they were doing, and maybe it would let up a little by the time they were finished. So they did, though Irene was distracted by the sound of the wind and the depth of the whiteness outside. And when they'd finished, it had not let up.

They sat awhile, waiting, until Luke admitted it wasn't getting any better and decided they'd better try to get back to the highway. Irene had no idea which direction that was. She was too scared to ask Luke if he did. He must. He was driving.

Once they were out of the farmyard, even the glimpses of objects they'd been allowed—the farmhouse, the wooden grain bins—fell away, and they could no longer see a thing. Luke rolled down his window so he could see the edge of the driveway, and they crawled along towards the grid road, Irene staring ahead of her into the whiteness. And then they stopped, and Irene could hear the wheels spinning, and Luke said, "Shit."

He made her get behind the wheel, though she wondered how she could drive them out when she had no idea where she was going. "Just go straight ahead. Don't turn the wheel, whatever you do. And once you get rolling, stop!"

He got out and pushed from behind, rocking the car, but when she pressed the gas pedal she could hear and feel the tires spinning. Luke opened the door and scolded her for using too much gas, then took the key, and she heard him opening the trunk and getting the shovel. The storm was so wild that most of the time she could not even see him as he worked around the car, but every now and then, when he was only a few inches from the windows, his form would appear, bending, hurling the whiteness into whiteness. When he was satisfied he'd cleared a track, he came back and gave her more instructions, reminding her to keep the wheels straight and to give just a little gas. He went back and rocked the car and she touched the gas and felt the car start to move.

Every time she stopped, worried that they'd roll into the ditch, they'd be stuck again, but after three or four attempts they were finally through the snowbank and Luke took his place behind the wheel. He rolled down the window again, and they crawled the rest of the way out to the grid road. When they'd finally reached it, finally travelled that first hundred yards, he turned to her and said, "Which way is it to the highway?"

She had no idea. Try as she might to visualize the moment they'd turned at the driveway an hour or more ago, she could not do it. After asking her advice, Luke argued it was a right, but that only made Irene think she might remember it being a left. In the end they agreed it would be better to wait until the wind died down a bit before they continued. If they left the engine running they'd run out of gas or die of carbon monoxide poisoning, so they huddled together under the old green wool blanket and after a while dug out the can of Sterno from under Irene's seat and lit it to warm their hands by. At first they talked about what they'd do when they got to Calgary, Luke's short-term plans of the places he would show Irene and her long-term plans of the job she would find. After another hour the wind had not abated in the least, but their talk had dwindled to Luke's periodic curses at the storm. Irene could no longer think of anything to say.

From time to time Luke would start the engine to keep it warm and warm up the car a little, and they would listen to the radio. There were weather warnings and other warnings to stay off the roads. Sometimes Luke would argue that maybe they should try going to the right and feel their way towards the highway, but Irene would shake her head. Luke cursed, but he would not attempt the escape without her blessing.

She was not sure how many hours had passed, but it was growing dark when she picked out a dark shape looming in the ditch and realized it was a boulder she'd noticed there when they first turned in the driveway. The wind, perhaps, was finally receding.

"It *is* to the right," she said.

She had not said anything in a long, long time, so Luke looked at her as if she had risen from the dead.

"You see the rock . . ." but when she turned to point it out it was gone again. "I saw the rock there a second ago, and when I saw it I remembered us turning in the driveway, and you were right. We do have to go right."

"What rock?" Luke said.

"There's a rock at the end of the driveway. Remember? I saw it there a minute ago. The wind must have dropped off."

"Where?" Luke said.

She turned to the window, and a grizzled old face with hoarfrost eyebrows was staring into her eyes.

"Jesus Christ!" Luke said.

Not only the eyebrows were hoarfrost: despite the cold, his head was uncovered and his hair was frosted too. He wore no coat. Only a cowboy shirt that had spots of frost for snaps. His skin was greyish blue, the lips a shade greyer and a shade bluer, and the whites of his eyes were yellow. He stared intently into her, not even seeming to see Luke beside her, and she did not immediately cry out when she saw him there six inches away. She hoped that he would pass on the way he had come. She thought that this unending stare was a look of hateful accusation; she wondered if he wasn't the God the priest sometimes talked about in church—the God of the Old Testament—that other jealous God, who squashed the enemies of his people beneath His icy heels. Except that he was so small.

Of what might He accuse her?

And then he disappeared.

"Jesus!" Luke said again, and he started the engine. Irene had already opened the door, but Luke popped the Studebaker into gear and stomped on the gas pedal, slamming the door closed with their momentum as they started to roll forwards.

"What are you doing?" Irene shouted.

Luke swung the car right and onto the road, fishtailing so badly he almost lost control. She clutched the handle, waiting to feel them hit the man or slide into the ditch, but Luke slowed and rolled down his window and started crawling the car towards the highway.

"Stop right now!"

"Like hell."

Irene grabbed his right forearm. "He'll freeze."

"He's already frozen. Couldn't you see the ice in his eyes?"

She had, but when she saw him turn away from her she knew he must be only a man, and if he was only a man they had to save him, didn't they?

"Stop the car, or I'm getting out." She pulled the door handle, and the full force of the blizzard leaked in like the breath of the dead.

Luke pressed the brakes, turning to her as the car stopped. "Whaddaya want me to do?"

"We'll find him and get him into the car before he freezes." She zipped up her parka all the way and pulled tight the drawstring on her hood.

Luke breathed deeply. "Shut the door, Irene."

"I'll shut it once I'm out."

"We can't get involved. It don't pay to get involved in this kind of thing."

"What kind of thing?"

"This kind of thing."

"This happens to you all the time?"

"Don't be dense. Two-Indians-and-a-dead-white-man kind of thing."

"What? He's not dead yet. We gotta help him."

"They'll blame us. Would you shut the stupid door?"

"For trying to save him?" She pushed the door open and started to step out into the blizzard.

"Irene. What about the car?"

That stopped her. She sat back and let the door close. "What about it?"

"What if they ask about the registration?"

"It's in Calgary. You told my uncle it's in Calgary."

"They're gonna ask a lot of questions."

He was staring into the speedometer, trying to read how fast they weren't moving.

"Is this car stolen?"

"I don't think so. Ricky says not, but who knows with Ricky? Anyway, it's not like it's worth anything to anybody." He stared into the yellowed numbers on his dashboard, refusing to meet her eyes.

"Who knows with *Ricky*? Who knows with Luke? So my uncle was right."

"Your uncle's not right about nothing."

Irene turned away from him and sighed. "I'm going to find him. We'll get him and take him to the hospital and go. They won't be asking questions about the car. We don't need to answer any questions anyway. We'll just say we found him wandering around without a coat in a blizzard, so we brought him in so he wouldn't freeze to death. Okay?"

She opened the door and put her feet on the ground, the wind and snow blasting in her face, biting her wrists between her mitts and her parka. Her boots were good. Her feet were warm even with the frozen road right beneath her. She hunched her shoulders against the storm and walked back towards the driveway. The car hadn't gone far, and in a few seconds she saw the boulder. Then she saw the shape of the man standing at the side of the road, as though he were watching something in the ditch. She rushed up to him and grabbed him by the arm and he turned to her, and when she urged him back in the direction of the car his legs started moving and he followed. A moment later she saw Luke's shape coming towards them out of the white, and he took the man's other arm.

They managed to manoeuvre him into the back seat of the Studebaker, and Irene got in to spread the green blanket over him. Luke walked around and got in the driver's seat. "You riding back there with him?"

"Go," she said.

And they were off, going five miles per hour, back towards the highway, on to the nearest town, which they knew from the radio station was a place called Broken Head. She touched one of the old man's ears and found it frozen like a piece of hard plastic. He blinked his eyelids and looked at her.

"Who are ya?" he slurred, with a thick tongue between blue lips. And his eyes suddenly locked on hers with the same look he'd had as he stared through the window.

"Irene," she said.

To TAKE MY MIND off the fact that the ground is forty-thousand feet below, I keep trying to imagine the moment I will meet the great James Aspen: "I love your films, Mr. Aspen. I'm so honoured to meet you. My name is Ai Lee. I'm your locations manager."

He gives me a peculiar look and responds "I *who?*"

Even my fantasies are awkward disappointments.

When I've finished what I can of the newly hydrated freeze-dried chicken Kiev, I try reading the script for *The Last Cowboy* one more time, but it's not engaging enough to keep my attention another time through. Why would James Aspen want to make this film? The money? Perhaps, but why would he need so much money at his age? He has a legacy to protect. His first western was acceptable, I suppose—he was part of the old Hollywood system, part of the studio's machinery and had to make what they gave him. But he is an old man now and can do as he wants and should have matured beyond shallow romanticism. Why is he reverting? Has his genie escaped the bottle, as his last film suggested? That one, though, was all bluster and pretension: a Kafkaesque allegory of a psychiatrist going mad. Is *The Last Cowboy* simply an old man's bid for lost innocence?

The in-flight movie, a romantic comedy, is ridiculous enough to have been written by the same writer. With nothing to distract me, I am pulled into an imaginary debate with my mother in which I cleverly use the metaphor of my father's journey to justify my own travels. If I could, I would take my father to meet James Aspen. Goodness knows, Dad would love to accompany his daughter to meet the man who made *That Golden Sky*. That first western of Aspen's is one of Dad's favourite movies. But, of course, I can't take him. I must go alone. Just as he, in the end, will have to finish his journey alone. Needless to say, I would like to accompany him as far as the security gate . . .

Oh my god. Death as an airport. What if it's true? What if the hereafter is spent breathing filtered air in a pressurized cabin while bored and uniformed angels serve you processed food and offer a limited selection of glossy magazines to while away eternity? Perhaps there is something to be said for burning in hell.

The man next to me is reading an article in *The Sporting News* about the scientifically proven importance of cheerleaders.

Boy, could I use a cigarette.

It's Wednesday. I should be visiting my father. Wednesday is our day. I do my best to make Wednesdays work because it gives us a routine, and it means I can avoid my siblings, who generally descend on the house with their depressingly busy families on the weekends. I think Dad finds my visits a quiet relief. Mom has moved his bed into the living room, where he can watch the television or the squirrels in the old elm in the front yard. I take my camera and document his progress. He has no objections, but Mom finds it morbid and insists on leaving the room. It is morbid, I know, but it gives my visits form and purpose. It is a way for us to feel comfortable together.

He expects me on Wednesdays. I would go more often, but we have nothing to say to one another. I go as often as I do because I have this idea—I'm not entirely sure from where it arises—that we should have something to say to one another;

that something needs resolving; that one day he will take my hand and turn to face me, his eyes opening into mine so that I know he is seeing me for the first time in my life—so I know he has always seen me, always understood me, but he couldn't show me because he had to be my father.

Then there are my even more embarrassing fantasies of what I will say to him. My list of apologies and complaints and condolences and recriminations and thank yous. I want to tell him I love him. I want to tell him I hate him more than he hates himself, which takes some doing on my part, for he has always wallowed in a fundamental self-loathing. Why else would he have decided to smoke himself to death? I want to forgive him for everything he hates himself for, with the exception of those things he hates himself for that he has no right to hate himself for, and for which I have ended up hating him. I want to blame him for all of my own mistakes, which I'd never have made if it weren't for my own self-loathing, and where did I inherit that if not from him?

I want to beg his forgiveness for all of my vicious thoughts.

Sometimes, when Mom leaves the room to make the tea and his eyes turn from the television and trail over my camera lens, sometimes the first item on the list finds its way to my lips and I hold it there, ripe, bursting, but I can never speak the words. I know they would embarrass him, that he would only awkwardly look away and pretend not to have heard me.

He is my father. We do not say such things to one another.

Instead, when Mom's in the kitchen and I'm snapping his profile and his eyes find me in that slow wanting way, what he asks for is usually much simpler. "Cigarette?"

At first I refused, until he was able to make me understand that he did not mean to smoke; now I always give him one and he presses it to his nose, sniffing the rich tobacco, and kisses the filter with his puckered lips. Small pleasures mean everything to him: the scent of a cigarette, the feel of my mother's skin on his forehead. One day I was shocked to hear him say, "Your hand is so soft," as she was stroking him. It wasn't something he would ever have said before.

He says nothing about the cigarettes, but I've captured the pleasure in his eyes with my lens. They're photos I'll never be able to show to my mother.

The prairie really is a chessboard. With a few imperfections. The rivers and the draws that drain the squares lie like gashes in the game. The grassland is more like skin. I take a few photographs with my digital, but the perspective is too limited to get anything interesting.

Mom was furious when I told her I was going. Her entire life is looking after my father, and she couldn't understand how I could give up my one day a week and take the chance that he might die without me there to watch him go. She called me selfish. For a moment I was a teenager again, shrinking from her accusations, until I braced myself and fought back.

"Mother. James Aspen is one of the greatest directors in history. His films have changed the way we see the world. I can't very well turn this down. If something happens, I have my cell and you can call and let me know and I'll be on the next flight. Nothing's going to happen."

Instead of responding she picked up her spoon and began stirring her tea. I couldn't look at her.

All at once my father raised his head from the pillow, his eyes exuding that strange sheen that I imagine gives some slight hint of the veil of pain and the painkilling cocktail he sees the world through. Mom was on her feet, at his side, and so was I. He was about to impart a message from the other side.

"What is it, dear?"

"Of course she'll go," he said in his hoarse whisper. I couldn't help looking at Mom, but she was staring into his eyes. Dad, smiling peacefully, rested his head on the pillow again.

"Perhaps she'll meet a cowboy," he said.

My father loves cowboys. Though I don't believe he's ever actually met a cowboy. He worked for an insurance company in an office in one of those towers downtown that have genuine flakes of gold in the glass so that when you look out you see the whole world filtered through gold. He'd get up at seven, appear from the bathroom in a cloud of steam and sit at the table reading the paper, a cigarette clenched in the corner of his mouth and a cup of coffee making sporadic passages between the Arborite and his lips, while my siblings and I gulped down our cereal or, if we had been too long rolling out of bed, our Carnation Instant Breakfast, everybody arguing over whose turn it was for the shower, because we only had one bathroom and I had three older sisters and one younger brother and the only person who had a say over the bathroom was Dad. He wanted in, you got out.

He wore a blue suit. Never brown, never beige, never black. Always a blue suit.

So far as I know, my father has not once in his life ridden a horse, but he did ride the subway to work every day. I remember riding with him once, and I looked up and saw this woman glaring down at my Dad because he was sitting, and I suppose she thought he should give up his seat to her. She wasn't an old woman or anything. Just a young woman. Probably off to visit her grandmother in Mississauga. Slight moustache, perhaps evidence of too much testosterone. Enough makeup for two people, but not enough to cover up the moustache. Dad finally noticed her glaring, and he stood up and nodded at her with that silly subordinate smile I'd seen him use on everyone in his office when we visited him there, and he said, "Please, have a seat," with his BBC British accent, clipping the vowels like dried twigs. You might have thought he was urging the Queen herself to take her rightful place upon the throne of England.

The woman sneered and sat down next to me and I heard her say, "Dumb Chink."

I'll never forget that moment. I'm sure the young woman had forgotten it an hour later, but when I'm an old woman with granddaughters who visit me sometimes—probably not often enough—that subway ride will still be repeating endlessly in some dark screening room at the centre of my brain. The train clattered on, shaking its familiar heartbeat rhythm, and squealing on the turns like fingernails down a blackboard. The lovely young Scarborough princess sat there glaring at my father's belt buckle, and I watched an orange roll around under a seat across the car. That orange was alien and beautiful. I wanted to go over and pick it up from the floor and peel it and eat it section by elegant section. Instead, I breathed in the young woman's sickly sweet perfume and felt that chemical smell entering my bloodstream.

There were never any cowboys on the subway.

I got my driver's licence when I was eighteen and bought a Toyota Corolla when I was twenty-four, vowing that I would never again be a prisoner of the Toronto transit system.

My father always hated my Japanese car. He never said why, but I came to suspect this was some kind of throwback to his heritage and my own; some tiny failure to assimilate. I was once obsessed by these glimpses into his past, my past, which had been for the most part so purposefully blocked off. For a time in my twenties I devoured books on China, but most of what I found there was even more romantic and distant and mysterious than my father's westerns. Feeding and worshipping my dead ancestors was a delightfully spooky idea, and there was something appropriate about recognizing my family as my gods, but in the end I could not really take it all seriously, especially since it was the men who were venerated, while the women were soon forgotten. I was left with nothing but these glimpses of what might have shaped me, but with no glimpses of me: a girl who loved red licorice and Paul Newman. My father's ancestral legacy remains almost entirely associated with memories like that young woman on the subway, or the boys in elementary school who called me "Irene, I-*lean*," ignoring the fact that my enunciation was better than theirs.

During the time I was reading all those books on China, I changed my name to Ai, which means "love" in Mandarin and Japanese. I pronounce it the Japanese way, like the personal pronoun or the organ of sight. The Mandarin pronunciation is "Oy." I read somewhere that the original symbol was a figure in shackles. Someone I met in a nightclub who speaks Mandarin told me that my full name, Ai Lee, means "something so disgusting that no one could possibly love it." I don't particularly care. I like the way it sounds.

I suppose I must have abandoned the ghosts of my family on the thirteenth floor of my first home. We lived in one of a cluster of apartment towers that sprout like mushrooms in the ravine beside the Don Valley Parkway. Our apartment was on the thirteenth floor, three doors down from the elevator. But the number you pressed on the elevator was actually fourteen, as was the number mounted on the wall facing the elevators when you stepped off, and the number on our door was 1408. When I first noted this, at age six, I asked my mother about it and she explained to me that the number thirteen was unlucky, so no one wanted to live there. This was why we lived on the fourteenth floor instead of the thirteenth.

I imagined the thirteenth floor existed below us, but that it was a dark unfinished complex of bare concrete and metal and exposed insulation, like the attic of my mother's parents' home in Kingston—completely empty, except for the black spirits who lived there and who had no way of escaping because the elevator wouldn't stop for them. Sometimes at night I could hear them bumping about, searching for a way out into the world. When I told my older sister this, she laughed and informed me that there was no thirteenth floor, or if there was, despite what the numbers said, it was ours.

I told my mother that I thought we'd better move because if the evil spirits were not already living among us, unseen, they would surely arrive as soon as they figured out what floor we were really on. She was ironing one of my father's white shirts, making sure the seams were perfectly straight.

"Evil has no more interest in the number thirteen than any other number," she said, pumping a button to spray a thin jet of steam.

I nodded, not fully convinced.

Every evening Dad got home from the office at exactly six, and Mom would have food on his plate. We girls would take turns helping with supper or doing the dishes and generally keeping the apartment in the state of un-lived-in-ness on which my father insisted. My brother's only responsibility was to take the garbage and dump it down the chute. Anyone would have thought he was off to the salt mines.

I am a fourth daughter. It's been obvious to me since I was a teenager that the only reason I exist at all is that my parents kept trying until they had my brother. Isn't it funny how we can only allow ourselves to imagine our parents engaging in sex in order to satisfy the biblical imperative? What if I could imagine them conceiving me in a moment of unbridled passion? Would I be happier then? Would I be less brittle?

Perhaps my parents were once passionate lovers. In the beginning, when, despite the obvious complications, they obeyed the brave compulsion to fall, they must have seen something exotic in one another: the Chinese man and the woman whose Protestant parents were from Kingston and whose grandparents were from Ireland. I can't even begin to fathom the bravery of their compulsion—or at least of my mother's. My father's choice makes perfect sense, I suppose, considering his overwhelming desire to assimilate; but how could my mother not have seen that marrying my father would only narrow her life into a channel of scorn and ignorance? For years her parents didn't speak to her. She knew this would happen, but she married him anyway. For that alone, she will always be my hero.

I suppose I should tell her.

Or was it just sex? Was my mother only unable to resist my father's touch? Not brave at all? Or can there be bravery in surrendering to one's own body? Yes.

Whatever the case, I still believe they'd have turned exclusively to sex for sex's sake if a boy had arrived earlier. I would have never been born. My father may have turned his back on his past, may have abandoned the ghosts of his family, but his attitudes to sons and daughters aren't much different from those of his ancestors. He sees my brother as his connection to the future, and for that reason my brother is the only accomplishment that gives his life any real meaning.

When I was fourteen, my father bought the Victorian house in Little Portugal where he now lies dying. The house has four bedrooms, which meant that we all had our own space, as my two eldest sisters had already gone off to university and met the men they would marry. It was a bit mind-numbing, all of that space, after our tiny apartment. There is a yard too, where skunks and raccoons sometimes troop through looking for garbage and an extended family of squirrels claim squatters' rights on the proud old elm. There are worms and robins in the spring. The wilderness in our backyard.

I remember once sitting on our floral couch, crying because a boy at school had dumped me for a prettier girl. My father walked into the living room. He asked me what was wrong. What could I say to him? I told him that my heart was broken. He looked me up and down, then opened his paper and said, "Did you take some aspirin?"

You'd never have guessed there was a romantic bone in my father's body, except that his favourite movies were westerns. He had read Zane Grey when he was a boy in England, and once, apparently, he confided to my mother that when he'd left the jolly old motherland it was with a secret expectation that he was coming to a continent populated entirely by cowboys, and that—just maybe—he might become as carefree and easy as those cowboys himself.

I know of only one gift the cowboys gave him. Perhaps that gift is all my father will leave to me: my deep love of tobacco. My earliest memories are of him smoking. I remember being fascinated by the way he could hold the ghost of himself in his mouth, then breathe it out his nostrils in slowly curling tusks. I remember, as a child, thinking of the smoke as his spirit gradually escaping from his body—that my father's soul was made manifest in the shapes he exhaled. He wasn't a sensual man, except when he smoked. I stole my first cigarettes from him when I was fifteen and smoked them in the backyard with that boy who would soon dump me.

Fucking cowboys.

He loved those cowboys so much that when there was a western on, that's what the whole family had to watch. And there had to be complete and utter silence. If you so much as gasped when somebody got shot in the gut, you risked being sent to your room.

Why is violence so aesthetically pleasing?

The pilot announces our descent. I put the camera and the script back into my bag. The locations, at least, might be exciting. It's a brand new landscape. To me. I raise my tray and prepare myself for disaster. I hate landings. They're almost as bad as takeoffs.

We disembark down a stairway to the tarmac. They have a couple of the covered ramps connected directly to the building, but perhaps they want to offer us some fresh air. The sun is brighter than I've ever experienced—must be the lack of smog to properly filter the light—and I find myself reaching for my sunglasses, even though I'd resolved not to put them on at least until after I've met my assistant, Greg Turnball, not wanting to look too "Hollywood." I'm dying for a cigarette, but know I'll have to wait. Apparently there's something dangerous about mixing jet fuel and sparks. Isn't that how I got to Saskatchewan?

Once inside, I stand and wait, looking anxiously at every stranger to see if he or she might be there to meet me. No one is. I watch the other passengers meeting their families, their lovers, their associates—hugging and kissing and shaking hands. Alone among them, I retrieve my bag from the carousel, then watch them file out the door until there is only me and a frustrated couple who have lost their luggage. At last I dig out the business card the associate producer gave me and call the number.

"Chinook Pictures."

"May I speak to Lance Taves?"

"You're talking to him."

"Mr. Taves? It's Ai Lee, your locations manager. I'm at the airport, and I thought Greg Turnball was supposed to meet me. But he's not here."

"Oh? Right. You're at which airport?"

"Here. In Saskatoon."

"Really? What are you doing here?"

"I'm . . . Greg was going to show me the locations he'd tracked down so far."

"Is that so? Well, isn't that a bugger? Greg was really looking forward to meeting you, Ai, but unfortunately I had to fire him."

"Oh!" I wait for further explanation, but the line hums. "What happened?"

"What's that? Oh, with Greg? Eventualities, as they say. No matter. You're here. You're on the job. Which is fortunate, because I just got a call from Herzog, and he and Aspen are flying into town tomorrow, so they'll likely want to see some of the locations."

I can feel myself getting dizzy, and I wonder if I can put my head between my knees without drawing too much attention to myself. "Yes, but . . . it's Mr. Turnball who knows the area."

There is another silence as he considers my statement.

"*Mr.* Turnball is a mean drunk with a wounded and blackened soul and a bad attitude. He hates you. He hated you without even meeting you because your success reminds him of his own lack thereof. He told me it was either you or him. So

I fired him. What else could I do? Not that it was easy for me. He's a friend. I know his family. I've watched his kids grow up. The oldest is thirteen now and needs his teeth fixed. But it had to be done."

"Oh."

"We're hiring a replacement, of course, but it'll take a day or two to get all of that sorted out and them up to speed and all the whatnot and wherewithal sluiced through. Meanwhile, rent yourself a car. Keep the receipt, and we'll cover it, of course. Are you booked in somewhere?"

"Yes. I think."

"So, what makes you so good that Herzog couldn't do without you?"

I consider the question. "I really wanted the job. I really wanted to work with James Aspen. I'm not sure why they chose me."

"No? Neither was Greggy boy. Sure had his shorts in a knot—the fact that they hired somebody from Toronto to oversee him. I told him to look at it as an opportunity. Everything is an opportunity. You obviously know people. Americans."

"I do know a few Americans."

"They're the people to know. Like Jerry Herzog. You known Jerry long?"

"I've worked on a few of his productions. I guess he was happy with my work."

"Good guy to know. How well do you know the area?"

"I've never been here before. I've read over all the material."

"Great. Well, Jerry and Jim are here tomorrow, and they're really looking forward to seeing some of the locations, I'm sure. The old man is really something. I haven't actually met him yet, but I've talked on the phone a couple of times. He's . . . very human. I might have been talking to my own grandfather. He asked me how the fishing was this year. Apparently he's an avid fisherman."

"I didn't know that."

"Very spiritual. He kept talking about his soul—telling me about the danger his soul was in."

"Pardon?"

"Yeah. He said his soul was in grave danger. Two or three times. Couldn't get him off the topic. I'm trying to talk to him about crew and he keeps insisting that he's staring the devil in the face. He was beginning to sound a little off, if you know what I mean. A little lulu."

"Oh."

"Anyway, I guess we'll see you tomorrow."

"Yes."

"Looking forward to it."

And he hangs up.

I rent a Toyota, out of some mistaken sense of familiarity. It's only the name I recognize. What I get is a sleek and silent machine that seems to want to drive itself. At first I can't put it in gear and have to go back into the depressing little cubicle of an office—I have this unfortunate habit of trying to imagine the lives of people who provide me services—to tell them there is something wrong with their car. A young man only half my age comes out, gets behind the wheel, and puts the car in gear. He shrugs at me, puts it back in park, and gets out. The young man wears a muscle shirt and has a tattoo of a high voltage tower on his left shoulder, and the expression pasted on his face tells me I have been worthless since the day I was born. Not that I take it personally. I'm sure it is the same expression he uses on any woman as impossibly old as forty. I get in and try again, but the car refuses to respond to my commands. Helplessly, I turn to him, and he raises his eyes to the ceiling.

"Put your foot on the brake."

I do, and the car slips into gear without any resistance. The young man shakes his head and walks away.

I wonder if venturing out alone into the wilderness in a car that knows more than I do about driving is a good idea.

I've only just pulled out of the airport when my cell rings. It's Mom, of course.

"How soon are you coming home?"

"Is Dad okay?"

"He's getting worse."

"What do you mean?"

"He's failing. It won't be long now."

"That's what the doctor says?"

"What does the doctor know? He says make him comfortable. How could I possibly make him comfortable? I can't even make myself comfortable."

"What makes you think he's failing, Mom?"

"Every day he's just a little less there. Every day he slips away a little further. He's always been such a quiet man, so sometimes I almost forget that this quiet is any different. And then I remember that soon he won't be here. Soon I'll be all alone."

"Mom . . ."

"Have you met James Aspen, yet?"

"No. My plane just landed."

"Well, I won't bother you any longer. I just wanted to hear your voice, to see if this number would actually work."

"It works, Mom."

"Yes, I guess it does. I love you, dear."

"I love you too, Mom."

But she's already hung up. I put the phone back in my bag.

—

*"One must learn to believe in the beauty of compromise without
compromising all that is beautiful." —James Aspen*

EXT. PRAIRIE VISTA. DAY.

The sun rises on an empty world. Then, in the centre
of the long line of horizon, we make out a black dot
that will eventually prove to be the shape of a man
on a horse trotting towards us.

In the beginning there was the word. No location can ever
hope to offer the perfect incarnation of what the word com-
prises. Every location is a compromise. As James Aspen says,
one of the marks of genius is the ability to see the beauty in
the compromise.

In truth, from what I've read, the main element of James
Aspen's artistic credo is control. He'll shoot a scene a hundred
times if he has to, until he gets exactly what he had envisioned.
He is the same with locations, demanding that they conform
to the standard of his imagination. For this reason, he does
much of his work in the studio, constructing the world as he
sees fit. Landscapes, though, can be a problem. That's where I
come in. My specialty is landscapes.

From my briefcase I take out a large-scale map of the district with mileage radii drawn from Saskatoon. All of my
tools are in the bag. My cameras: both digital and 35mm.
Colour and black-and-white film. Tape measure. Compass.
Guidebooks to the district. Propaganda literature from the
government film department. Sketchbook. I also asked Greg
Turnball to send me as many postcards of the district as he
could find, and he sent a half-hearted response before I called
and demanded more. Now I know why. Hates me, Lance

Taves says. Probably he'll always associate me with postcards of harvesting machines in wheat fields. Often I substitute these overly romanticized images with my own versions, shooting them in a more appropriate relation to the director's previous work.

I left the city limits behind a few miles back, and now, after checking the map, I leave the highway, pulling onto a dirt trail. Before long I have left behind any trace of civilization.

It's like diving off a cliff. If not for the vehicle I'm driving, I could easily be in another time, a hundred years ago, a thousand years ago. I might even be on another planet. All that holds me to the earth is a horizon distinguished by a thin white line, bordering the blue from that brown earth. The immensity of space makes me feel more than alone in the world: I feel terribly alone in the universe. But at the same time there's something soothing. Grass growing between the tracks brushes against the chassis. Some small furry animal runs across the road. I stop the car and get out.

The light, again, is alarmingly bright. And the dry wind sweeps across the world and pushes like some greater force demanding you to lean. I take some photos. Earth and sky. Wild rose bushes. Bluff of trees. Earth and sky. I smoke another cigarette, then I get back in and drive on. When I reach the lip of the valley, which is the actual location, I get out and start snapping again.

What distinguishes my work is my talent with a camera. My photographs, however, are meant for a very small and specific audience: producers and directors. A friend likes to tease me about how catering to this audience had made me develop a very specific aesthetic. It seems obvious that the photograph has undermined reality, but my friend says my photographs undermine photography. "Your photographs reveal, to their very particular audience, what needs to be seen, what might otherwise be missed, and they manage to do this while conveying the suggestion that what is there in reality is much more beautiful than what has been contained by the frame. Actual composition is left to those great men and women of vision who are your audience. They are the ones who will undermine reality by making the landscape into a beautiful world on a screen. That is your talent. You convey the potential for exploitation, and you do that by your contrived failure to exploit."

I drive south with another of my fired helper's locations as my destination. When I get there, it is a disappointment: a lovely old barn, but the architecture is clearly twentieth century. Perhaps it could be cheated, but James Aspen doesn't approve of cheating.

I get back into my car and drive towards the city, trying not to think about tomorrow. The car takes me with it. There is nothing for me to do but hold onto the wheel. I am floating to infinity. There is nothing between me and the sky. I can feel the wind rushing across the Plains from the west, pushing the car slightly to the east, to the hard edges the shadows make of the evening. I light each cigarette off the butt of my last one and think of my father and my mother, wondering if they are thinking of me.

As I drive back into the city, I stop to get a few shots of a sign in front of a church: WHEN YOU HEAR THE BELL, THAT'S JESUS AT THE DOOR.

JUNE 28th, 2000: TORONTO

THE LAST TIME Sam had had sex with anyone but Gwen was
a vague and misty memory, recalled only occasionally, usually
during masturbation, but as he unbuttoned his shirt he
remembered details of that afternoon long ago—details that
until now he'd thought were long erased. Cecilia was her
name. She had lived in a basement apartment that smelled of
lemon-scented laundry detergent. Mostly he remembered the
terrible awkwardness of undressing in front of a stranger, an
awkwardness that was all the more acute now that he was
pushing middle age. His belly suddenly seemed much larger
to him, and he wished he had paid more attention to keeping
in shape. He'd meant to have that mole removed.

Erika must have been having the same difficulties. After
they'd kissed for awhile on the couch, she led him to the bedroom and stepped out of her dress and, still standing, they
kissed another while, and he fumbled with her bra, finally giving up, and as she reached back and undid it she suddenly
said, "Sorry, but that's all there is."

He immediately assured her that he liked breasts just the size
of hers. And he meant it. They really were lovely breasts, and he
really was excited, but even as he rolled onto his back and she
rolled on top of him and slipped him inside her, her eyes closing
at the feel of him, he couldn't help thinking about Gwen. Even
as she bobbed on top of him, her breasts bouncing like playful
puppies, he kept thinking, *What if Gwen were to see this? What
if Gwen were ever to find out? How will I explain this to Gwen?
She'll know. She'll know the minute she looks at me.* Even as it

was happening, he could feel it writing itself all over his face.

He didn't even manage to come. Erika definitely did, at least. Unless she was faking, which was not altogether out of the question. It was a particularly showy sort of orgasm; of a kind he'd only seen before on film or television. At any rate, she didn't seem to notice that he hadn't. They were both pretty drunk.

As she rested her head on his shoulder, their sweat beginning to cool in the breeze coming through the balcony screen, he said, "It's funny," approaching the subject with what he hoped was some delicacy, "Everybody calls me Cowboy here."

"Yeah. Why is that funny?"

"I'm a banker. Do I really look like a cowboy?"

"Sorry," she said, "I didn't realize you were sensitive about it. You shouldn't be. It's quite attractive. It's different."

"But what is *it*, exactly?"

She gave him a look that told him to drop the subject, but he would not. "Really. I need to know. What made you call me *Cowboy*?"

Wearily, she raised herself up on an elbow to study his pale, freckled body. "Well, there's something about the way you carry yourself . . . but it's not really looks. There's that bit of a drawl you've got . . . but it's not really that either. I think it's actually more your . . . aura. There's just something old-fashioned about you."

"What do you mean?"

She shrugged. "You just seem so . . . chivalrous or something. It's like you haven't entered the new millennium with the rest of us. Well, for instance, I'll bet you feel so guilty about this tomorrow, you rush home and confess the whole thing to your wife."

She collapsed back onto her pillow. He didn't know how to respond.

"It must be wonderful living in the country," she murmured, as she rolled over and immediately fell asleep, dreaming, he imagined, of horses galloping into sunsets.

He lay there watching her for hours, the hum of traffic and the clanging of streetcars pulling him back each time he was close to surrendering consciousness. There were no curtains on the windows, and the wasted light of the city seeped inside, making it possible for him to clearly see Tolstoy and the Bronte sisters and Jane Austen and even John Bunyan on her shelves and to study the quilt hanging on her bedroom wall. He decided there might be some hint of old-fashionedness in Erika too.

Lying there, he began to see how arbitrary his life was. Why Gwen? Why not Erika? Erika liked opera. Erika liked literature. Erika laughed at his silly jokes. Erika actually seemed to enjoy his company. How different his life would be if he were with this woman. He began to imagine that different imaginary life, and as the night passed his imaginings began to take on shape and weight.

By the time Erika woke, he was sure he'd never been so in love in his entire life. He kissed her, and she eyed him groggily, then rolled out of bed and stumbled to the bathroom, not bothering to close the door when she entered. He lay there listening to her deliciously intimate noises, punctuated by the sounds of the traffic.

"Fuck!"

He sat up straight. That wasn't her voice. It wasn't his Erika in there. Some other woman must have been hiding behind the shower curtain, waiting for the first opportunity to replace her.

"What's wrong?" he called.

"Shit! I forgot to take my tampon out."

It was quite some time before she managed, mumbling indignantly, to extract the offending (and offended) object from herself. At last she shuffled back into the room and fell into bed. He wondered if she'd gone straight to sleep when, once again, that unfamiliar voice came out of the night: "I hope you're aware it's bad manners to still be around when a lady wakes up in the morning."

Half an hour later, after searching for, almost giving up, and finally finding his missing sock tangled in Erika's dress, he slipped silently out the door, down the seven flights of stairs, turning and turning and turning, and eventually entering into the night and the numbing argument of cars and drivers grinding restlessly on towards morning. Five in the morning. Wednesday. A golden halo had appeared in the narrow band of sky revealed between the row of narrow brown Victorian houses to the east. A yellow strip of paper decorated his windshield. As Sam studied the parking ticket for the particulars of his offence, a young woman strolled past, dragged by a drooling German shepherd. The young woman eyed Sam's dishevelled clothing and smiled faintly, perhaps even ironically, to herself.

"Morning," Sam offered, to which the woman looked away nervously and quickened her pace, glancing back once over her shoulder with an expression of terror so profound that one would have thought a caped skeleton with a scythe had just spoken to her.

If it weren't for the dog, perhaps Sam could have killed her. But what would have been the point? There were too many witnesses. All those people at the opera. And the rusty-walled club. He unlocked the door and slid in behind the wheel.

Sam needed air. The boardroom's filtered and conditioned facsimile would not do any longer. He couldn't concentrate on what anyone was saying and had been caught drifting when a question came his way.

"Would you concur with that, Sam?"

Eyes all on him, except Williams from Vancouver, who was fast asleep. Williams was sixty-four, and so this behaviour was tolerated. To the bank, Williams was Vancouver.

"Uh-huh," Sam finally responded, and this seemed to satisfy them, but left him wondering what he had agreed to. Probably nothing. They were only talking in circles, discussing whether Goals 7 and 8 were really different, or were part of the same lofty pursuit. He drifted away again, returning to the reverie about his flight the next day, imagining the jet plane in tailspin, his body pinned to his seat by the force of the fall, the eruption in flames as they met the earth, debris spinning into the air in beautiful bright arcs and the terrible screams silenced.

He was going to die tomorrow. He knew it with certainty.

Everyone including Williams was standing and filing towards the door. Smoke break. He decided to follow them down for a whiff of the smog. There was an alert today, the air heavy with humidity rolling in off the lake. Asthmatics were ending up in hospital. Senior citizens were dying.

"You okay, Cowboy?" Philips, a manager from Winnipeg, asked him in the elevator. To the bank, Philips was Manitoba.

"Yeah, I'm fine."

"You don't look so well."

Sam ran his hand through his hair and pasted on a wider smile. It showed. If Philips from Manitoba could see it, there was no doubt Gwen would.

"I'm just fine. Never felt better."

"You shouldn't let it get to you. I know it's tough where you are, but you have to push it away. You'll never make everybody happy anyway. Would they be happy if we were losing money? Sound management protects their money."

Yes, the pressures of his job were getting to him. It was an interpretation he was willing to encourage. "That doesn't play too well when you're taking away their land."

"I suppose not," Philips nodded gravely. "You should get out of there."

"Maybe," Sam said.

"When are you flying back?"

"Tomorrow."

"I'll introduce you to Tom White. He's the man you should talk to. He'll be coming down for a smoke. Have you finally taken up the habit?"

"No. I just need some air."

"You oughta take it up," Philip chuckled. "With these strict smoking rules, the best place to meet the real movers and shakers you might not normally get a chance to face-to-face with is outside the tower by the ashcans. I saw the big man down there the other day."

"Even he can't smoke in his office?"

"Well, you're right. He's probably got his own smoking room. He was probably just down to mix with the troops."

Outside the building they stood in the cement courtyard like a group of teenagers, baking in the hazy heat, the smoke rising lazily into the leaden air. Sam was introduced to Tom White, who muttered hello and then spent the rest of his cigarette swearing about how he could be at the cottage if it weren't for this stupid meeting. Everyone nodded their commiserations. When they were finished and heading back into the building Sam said he'd be just a minute and wandered over to a bench to watch the traffic roll past.

A man was standing by the newspaper boxes with a sign that read FATHER OF TWO KIDS HAVING HARD TIME. PLEASE HELP. He had a mournful expression that made Sam think of the boys' former dog waiting for his bowl to be filled. The school bus had run over the dog. The man was thirtyish, white, unshaven, his eyes a shade too close together and shallow enough that Sam thought he could see bottom. Certainly an improvement over the man in the drugstore, at any rate. A family man. Sam looked away, up towards the tower. He drifted off and saw the jet falling. He took a deep breath and, meeting the man's eyes, rose and reached for his wallet. He had a fifty, nine twenties, and a ten. He touched the ten, reconsidered, and handed the man the fifty.

"Bless you, sir! God bless you! God bless your family, sir!" The man was actually bowing to him. Sam rushed back into the building.

That evening he packed up his things, put his suitcases by the door, ordered a wake-up call and phoned Gwen to make sure she'd be there to pick him up.

"Yeah. I'll bring your car. Mine's still not fixed. Vern's got the part on order."

"Vern? Isn't it at the garage?"

"Vern said he could fix it."

"Vern said . . . I called a tow truck . . ."

"Vern towed it home with his truck."

"Why? I had handled the situation. I had called my garage." For a few moments he could hear only her breathing.

"He said he'd fix it. He said we were just throwing away money."

"But it's not fixed."

"He's waiting for a part."

"Gwen. I'm going to call my garage and leave a message for them to come and get the car . . ."

"Why? He said he'd get the part tomorrow. What difference does it make who fixes it? Will it help to pay extra money to get it fixed?"

"But it's not fixed."

"He said he'd get the part tomorrow. What difference does it make to you anyway? It's my car. I'll come and get you with your car. See you there."

And she hung up.

He took a tranquilizer to help him sleep.

He'd never before had the slightest fear of flying, but the next morning he found himself clutching his armrests as though his grip might stop the clumsy aluminum bird from diving for Earth. He could barely breathe. The woman across the aisle eyed him with amusement.

"Fear of flying?" the woman asked.

"No," Sam said, brushing away a bead of sweat that was forming on the tip of his nose. The woman smiled and went back to her magazine.

A flight attendant became so concerned that she kept pestering Sam, offering him drinks and pillows and magazines. Apparently her training had taught her that interfacing with the people he'd handed his life over to was supposed to lessen his anxiety. She wanted to prevent the panic from spreading. But Sam wasn't about to make a spectacle of himself. He shook his head grimly and bit harder on the inside of his bottom lip.

"I'm fine," he insisted. "Never felt better."

It was as absurd as it was embarrassing. In reality, what terrified him was a successful landing and the meeting with Gwen that would immediately follow. She would read it in his eyes. Being smashed like a grape inside a mangled piece of metal would actually rescue him from having to look into her eyes. Dying would save him. They'd have a lovely funeral, and his boys would stand over his grave and throw flowers down on his cooling soul.

But, no. He wanted to live. He had bargained with his conscience and had vowed to change. He would be a better husband and father. There would not be another Erika. If Gwen wanted, he would quit his job and do something else. Maybe he could work with his brother and his father. Maybe, at forty, he could become the farmer his father had always wanted him to be.

The possibility of retribution frightened Sam into complete submission. At this moment, just as he was about to save his shattered marriage, claim back the two sons he had so neglected for the sake of financial security at forty-five—at just this moment he was ripe to be smashed by some vengeful god, or by the weight of an irony that had become so close to the only meaning left, it had all but attained godhead. He already had his place in the country, his wonderful wife, his loving family, and what was the sense of risking all of that for vapid sex in the narrow and noisy corridors of an empty city? He was repentant. He would make things right, if he were only given one more chance.

Air Canada was willing to cooperate: they landed fifteen minutes early due to an unusual tailwind. Gwen was waiting, which wasn't surprising, as Gwen always planned for disasters—flat tires, burnt clutches, carjackings—and arrived early when they didn't occur. Sam threw his arms around her, and they clung to each other for so long that Sam began to feel she was actually comforting him; that she had seen everything in his eyes and had already forgiven him. At last she gently extricated herself from his arms and sent him off to get his bags.

"Where're the boys?" he asked, as he lugged his luggage across the parking lot.

"With Vern. Helping fix my car."

"Oh, God. He's probably teaching them to drink whiskey and roll their own smokes."

Sam chuckled aloud, feeling better than he had in years. He'd made it. He was alive. He had made his bargain, and whatever force controlled the universe had granted his wish, and now he would keep his side of the deal. His life would be different from here on. He promised.

As they neared his car, the wind gusted and he caught a mouthful of that clear clean air and pulled it into his lungs. "I feel like a new man," he said.

"What?" Gwen asked.

He blushed and shook his head. "Nothing. Just talking to myself."

She stared at him grimly and nodded.

"I'll drive," she said, when the bags were in the trunk.

"But you must be tired."

"No. I feel like driving."

"Okay."

Sam got in and sat back into the passenger seat of his car. It was a strange new perspective. Another sign that the new world had begun. He felt good. A little ecstatic, in fact. When they were out of the parking lot he couldn't help but tell her. "It was the weirdest thing. I had this kind of . . . vision of the plane coming down and . . . Well, I was sure we were going to crash. I mean I knew for sure we were going to crash, and all I could do was wait for it to happen. Can you believe that? Me? Have I ever been afraid of flying?"

Gwen didn't answer. She stopped at a traffic light and turned onto the highway that led home. When she reached the speed limit, she glanced at him and said, "I hope you can find somewhere else to stay tonight. The last three days without you in the house made it clear to me. I'm not just saying it this time. I really mean it, and I think it would be best for us both to start right now. I want a separation."

```
                 BROKEN HEAD UNION HOSPITAL
              REPORT OF POST-MORTEM EXAMINATION

NAME: Doe, John
AGE:  Early 20s
SEX:  M
DATE AND TIME OF DEATH:  Approx. January 1971
DATE AND TIME OF POST-MORTEM:  13 April 1971


EXTERNAL EXAMINATION:
The body is received dressed in parka, shirt,
jeans and belt, socks and snakeskin cowboy boots.

Deceased is a well-nourished, well-built, young
Native Indian man appearing consistent with the
stated age and measuring 167.0 cm in length. There
is no rigor mortis or post-mortem lividity.

When the clothing is stripped, the skin shows a
reddish black mottling consistent with decomposi-
tion. Most of the exposed parts have been eaten by
animals or birds: coyotes, magpies, crows. Perhaps
other carrion. The affected areas include the
entirety of the face below the hairline, which has
been eaten down to the skull, and also includes
the neck. The eyes as well.

All of the dermis and flesh on the lower two-
thirds of the left forearm and left hand have also
been consumed, leaving nothing but bones and lig-
aments surviving. The dermis and flesh of the
right hand and fingers as well. A number of tat-
toos are present on the extensor aspect of the
right forearm. Due to decomposition, many of these
are indistinct, but one tattoo clearly shows the
name "Irene."

The torso and lower extremities otherwise appear
substantially normal for a man of this approximate
age and in this stage of decomposition.

No fractures or other injuries are noted on exter-
nal examination. Before proceeding with further
examination, photographs and fingerprints are
obtained by the Broken Head City Police
Identification Unit, and complete X-rays of the
body are taken.
```

NOVEMBER 30th, 1970: NEAR BROKEN HEAD

SNOWING ALL DAY, the wind wisping and whirling past my window, dancing one of those fancy ballroom numbers I remember from the old dancehall in Greenview, those gauzy billowing silks, and the winter depositing the stuff a foot deep already over the flowerbed where the withered old blue spruce used to grow that Mary made me plant but that died in the fifties, and so of course the son and his wife decide this is a good evening to be going to town.

"Where'n bloody hell do they think they're off to?" I ask, when I see the car back out of the garage, the headlights sweeping by me as they turn and pull that boat of a Buick out of the yard. They had not mentioned to me they were going out—had not asked my by-your-leave to keep an eye on the yard apes.

"To see a movie," Young Sam tells me, so they've obviously cleared it with the nine-year-old. He is watching the end of *Walt Disney*. Some silly thing with a raccoon as the hero. Being that heroes are hard to come by these days, I suppose.

"What movie'd be worth goin' out into this for?"

"*Doctor Zhivago*," the small one says.

They even told him what movie.

"Doctor who?"

"*Doctor Zhivago*."

"What kind of name is that?"

"Russian, I guess. They said it's about Russians. They wouldn't let me go."

"Well, I should hope not. God knows why the hell they'd

want to go off on a night like this to see a movie about some commie doctor."

Their tail lights have already disappeared by the time they get to the end of the driveway.

"The Chinaman's ancestors walked across the Bering Strait from Russia to get here," I say, because I've been thinking that maybe it makes more sense than I first realized, the Chinaman wanting to bring back the buffalo. The small one does not seem to hear me, tuned in as he is to that raccoon charmer. He is sprawled out on his stomach on the floor, with his chin resting on his folded hands, staring deeply into the winking eye of that evil box.

"Why don't we go for a drive of our own?" I say, and all of a sudden he cranes his head around, hearing in this proposal a threat to finding out whether the raccoon overcomes his adversaries and adversities and advertisements.

"Where? Can't we wait till this is over?"

"Sure. We'll go just as soon as the coon's cooked. I'll fetch Vern."

I limp up the stairs, leaning hard on the banister, resting at the landing and then dragging myself up those last four steps that always feel like forty these days. I find the older boy in his bedroom, enduring some damned racket on his listening phones. Posters of longhaired boys scowling at me. He slips the listening phones off one ear when he sees me in the doorway, and I can hear the tinny buzzing of a demented mosquito in pursuit of some terrible love.

"Let's go for a drive," I say.

"Tonight?"

"Why not tonight? Or are ya doin' somethin' so important ya just can't get away?"

He blows a bubble with the gum he's chewing, and it pops

and sticks to the few wispy hairs growing on his upper lip.

"Where we goin'?"

"On an adventure. Or don't ya like adventures?" He doesn't answer, attempting to clean the gum out of his poor excuse for a moustache. "I should give you some snoose to chew. It's better than that stuff."

"Shouldn't we be takin' the horses if it's an adventure?"

"We should. But I'm gettin' soft. And I doubt if I'd get Young Sam to come at all if we was goin' on horseback."

"He's comin' too?"

"He is. I'll be lookin' to you to keep him in line."

He smiles, gnawing hard on that knob of pink sugar. Just give them power over somebody else, and they'll follow you off the edge of the earth.

"Okay. I'll be there in a minute."

In the end, it takes more like forty, and even longer than that to get the two of them dressed so they won't freeze to death. They'll wear running shoes to their funerals, just in case they need to make a dash for it. Meanwhile, I get the old Colt from where I keep it in the basement, and fill the magazine with shells. No point in taking any extras. Would just be a waste of powder.

When I finally get them out the door, the truck is not plugged in, and so needs to be jumped off one of the batteries charging in the garage. Vern handles it ably enough, while the small one sits next to me complaining that he's already cold.

"You're cold now. Just think if you'd bin wearin' them runnin' shoes."

"It's not my feet that's cold."

"No. 'Cause you're not wearin' runnin' shoes."

The new battery cranks her, and I get her going, but she stalls out when I put her in gear, so Vern has to jump her again, and this time I sit and wait until the heater stops blowing cold, and at last we're off like rotten eggs.

The visibility's not too bad. When you can see.

Doctor Zhivago, for Christ's pitiful sake.

"Yep. The Injuns walked right over the Bering Sea to get here from Russia. Like I say, they woulda bin the Chinaman's ancestors. That's not how *he* got here, though. His grandpa probably came to work on the railroad, and when they tried to send him back, he mighta bin one of them that hid in those tunnels under Moose Jaw. Them tunnels Al Capone's spozed've hid out in."

"Tunnels?" the small one says, and his brother gives him a miserable look, maybe trying to show him he's boss, or maybe trying to tell him not to show too much interest or he might have to listen to the end of the story.

"Yeah. They lived down in tunnels so the police wouldn't find 'em and send 'em home. Had ladies of the evenin' and gamblin' dens down there too. Chinamen are gamblin' fools. You didn't know that?"

The small one shakes his head, his eyes opened wide. Looks like a barn owl. "Did you ever go down in the tunnels, Grandpa?" he asks, and his brother glares at him again.

"No. Not me. I didn't have to go that far east to find trouble."

The way I have it figured, the Chinamen are coming for me. Not that I'm looking for protection. I don't even want to talk about this here Trudeau, who admits he's a communist, but I have to say I wouldn't give you a dime more for those fancy-pants politicians down in Washington who claim they're keen on fighting the spread of communism. Bullshit. They're all communists. I mean, all they want to do is save the world for their own sort of communilizing, don't they? I say, to hell with civilization. In a way, I have more respect for the Chinamen, who come by their communism honestly, than I have for the bastards who tell me they're my friends and then tell me the way I should be wiping my hindquarters. Or, more likely, they tell me that I should be hiring some friend of theirs to wipe my hindquarters for me, 'cause it's only their friends who know the proper way it's got to be done. I mean, at least the Chinamen grew into civilization naturally. There got to be so many of them that they couldn't very well help but live on top of one another. What excuse do we have over here?

So I'm not surprised they're coming over here looking for land when they used all theirs up. I might even likely do the same if I were in their position. They're the civilized ones, and they're gonna civilize us and, who knows, maybe when they're done we'll be better off.

I know I will, 'cause I'll be deader than an honest politician.

"I'm cold. Where're we going, anyway?" the small one asks, just as we're approaching the approach.

"Oh, listen to the baby cryin'," Vern says.

"I'm not a baby. I'm cold."

"You're always cold."

"I just wanna know where we're going."

"Grandpa told you, we're goin' on an adventure."

"But I wanna know what the adventure is."

"We're goin' in here," I tell them, pointing off across the field towards the yard light we can see every now and then winking through the whiteout.

"In here? We'll get stuck," Vern says. "Why do you wanna go through here?" Finally curious enough that he wants to know the end of the story.

"Well, I'm figurin' it would be best to sneak up on him," I says.

"Who?" the small one says.

"The Chinaman. You figure he's got Nitro down in a tunnel?"
The small one looks at Vern.

"There you go," says Vern, and he starts to smile a big smile, "We're goin' to save Nitro."

"But Mr. Chong doesn't have Nitro."

"Whaddayou know about it?" Vern says.

"Dad said so!"

"Well, we'll find old Nitro wherever he is, won't we?" I tell him.

"I'm cold," the small one says.

I pull off the road and through the approach and down the trail along the edge of the field, but damned if John hasn't started a rock pile where there never was one when I was picking the rock in this field, and damned if that hasn't already caught a drift, and damned if we don't get stuck.

I spin the tires until the rubber burns. Smells a bit like hell, I imagine. Guess I'll find out soon enough. Vern and the small one get in the box, bouncing up and down for all they're worth, but there's not enough flesh on them to make a difference. Should have a bag of sand in there for these sort of occasions, but John can't even be trusted to equip his beloved pickup properly. Should have brought the horses. Never yet seen a horse stuck. If it weren't for this bloody leg, you can bet I wouldn't be riding this rusty hunk of metal. And now the leg's gonna have to suffer the consequences anyway. Such are the fruits of compromise.

"Told ya we'd get stuck," Vern says, after I give up and shut off the engine and step out of the truck.

"You want a prize?" I reach into the cab, haul the .22 off the gun rack and hand it to him. "There ya go. First in your class." He looks at the rifle in his hands as though he's never seen one before, and then he looks up at me with the same sort of dizziness in his eyes. "I'll need ya to cover me," I tell him.

I reach inside my jacket, take the Colt out of my belt and bring it out where they can lay their eyes on it. Vern's head makes a slow kind of nod, like his *yes* is about to freeze up, but then he starts to smile again. He's a happy boy, I'll say that for him.

"Cover your what?" the small one says.

"My sorry ass."

I can see the wheels turning, and I think I can smell more rubber burning, but the small one decides to leave the dog lying. "Are we gonna ask Mr. Chong to give us a ride home?" he asks instead.

"I thought you were gonna ride Nitro home."

His brow wrinkles, his glasses foggy from the blowing snow and his nose leaking southward towards his mouth. "Is Nitro really at Mr. Chong's?" he asks Vern, and we both wait for an answer, but Vern only shrugs. "How would I know? Maybe."

"I thought . . ."

"Shut up," Vern says. "Who cares what you think?"

"What did you think?" I ask him.

"I'm cold." The small one decides to change the subject one more time, wiping his nose on his sleeve. "I'll wait in the truck."

"You're such a chicken," Vern says.

"I'm gonna wait in the truck." He starts to get back in the cab.

"You'll likely freeze to death there. I guess you'd better come with us. I need ya to watch Vern. Make sure he don't grow any feathers and fly south."

"Like hell," Vern says, and I give the small one a little cuff for encouragement and head out of the shelter of the truck and into that howling wind, off towards the house, hobbling on my stick through the snowbanks, and by the time we get a hundred yards my leg might as well be lit on fire.

"Either of you bring your jackknife?" I ask, when I'm

stopped to rest it, and the small one reaches into his pocket and brings his out to offer me, the stag-handled one I got him for Christmas last year. His hand's shaking a wee bit, maybe from the cold, but more likely he's fixing to pee his pants.

"You hold on to it for me. I think we might need it to cut off my leg."

And then I laugh to show him there's nothing to be so serious about. Not that it seems to make much difference. I know I shouldn't have brought him, but like I say, there's things he's never gonna learn if he don't learn them from me. Vern seems to be enjoying himself, but you can see he's pretending it's all some kind of stupid game of make-believe. He thinks he's smarter than me. The slow-minded ones always do.

When we get up close to the yard, I tell them to get down, and we crawl over and have a look at the situation from below the bottom strand of barbed wire. Always an interesting perspective. There's a blue glow flickering in the window, like some blue flame might be burning in some Chinese ritual.

"What in hell do ya spoze is makin' that light?" I ask.

"Colour television," says Vern.

I look at him. "Well, I'll be damned. I expect you might be right."

He nods. The small one's eyes are about as big as the opening of a spittoon, and it looks like he might be about ready to start crying, so I figure it's time to get a move on and so I roll under the fence with my walking stick and manage to get up to my feet and hop off across the yard towards the barn, doing somewhere between a snail's and a skunk's pace. Just as I get to the barn and figure I'm in without a hitch, a dog starts barking from inside the house.

The place is so bloody dark I can't see to the business end of my eyeballs. I stumble around a bit, trying to remember the lay of the land, but I haven't been in this barn since McAllister owned it, and I used to meet Lucy, his wife, out here for a little round of hide-the-salami on salty summer evenings when McAllister went to town to pour beer on the fire in his belly. Those were the days. Or, more precisely speaking, the nights, though it never seemed as dark back then. Maybe I was only seeing through my fingertips. But I am beginning to be able to make out the shape of things. Something tells me there's been more than a couple loads of manure cleaned out of here since Lucy packed off and moved to British Columbia, at any rate.

Meanwhile, that dog's still barking in the house, and then I hear the door open and him coming for me. I take the gun out of my belt. It takes that yappy thing no more than five seconds to get here, which surprises me when I see its legs aren't much longer than a snake's. The thing's bouncing around like it's wound a few turns past the legal limit, and I'm waving the gun at the fool thing and warning it to shut up, but doggy doesn't seem to appreciate the jeopardy of its situation. Just my luck to meet an animal who's never been properly introduced to a fire-stick. Not that his owner doesn't have one, 'cause a few seconds later he comes running in the door carrying a .22 rifle, and I figure that he's bound to be as blind as I was when I came in here, and two against one ain't a bit fair, so I fire once in the air and the dog turns and yelps away faster than he appeared.

Dog, meet gun.

"Who's there?" the Chinaman squeals, and starts whirling around like a top losing its bottom.

"Drop the rifle and get on the floor," I yell, and the Chinaman instantly obliges. In fact, he's so good at it you'd almost think he'd done it before.

I stand still, waiting to see what he'll do next, and he raises his head.

"Get your noggin down!"

Once again he obliges. I walk over and grab the .22. "Thank you muchly," I say. "Now, tell me, where've you put my horse?"

He starts to raise his head, but thinks better of it. "Mr. McMahon?" he says.

"Pleased to meet you. I'll have you over to my place next week, and we'll discuss the price of buffalo, but right now I'd like to get my horse back."

He squirms around a bit. "I have no idea what you're talking about," he says. "I don't have your horse. Your horse isn't here. This is all a terrible mistake, Mr. McMahon. You're going to regret this, Mr. McMahon. Your son is not going to be pleased about this."

My backup comes in the door, Vern carrying the rifle high, and the small one following, looking pretty much like the dog did when he left, but he must be relatively braver, or at least more curious, considering he's heading the opposite direction. They stand back in the shadows, apparently waiting for a proper invitation to join the party.

"I don't give a damn for pleasin' my son, and I'm not findin' this little guessin' game the least bit amusin'. I know from past experiences you're not keen on havin' your life threatened, and that's really not what I want either. I'd just as soon be on my way and let you get back to your television program. So why don't you just tell me where my horse is, and we'll get out of your hair."

"I don't know. I don't know what you're talking about."

The boys are standing there staring, and I must admit that I'd just as soon I hadn't brought them, 'cause now they both look about ready to poop their pants, which would not be a bit of help. Anyway, what are they likely to learn from this little circus?

Self-control. So far, I have shown great self-control. Maybe now we could work on their numbers. "What about . . . say, if I were to give you until the count of three? Would that help you remember?"

"Pleeeeease!" the Chinaman starts sobbing like a baby. "I don't know what you mean."

"Three. It's the number after two. Which is the number after one. I'll start with one. Is that clear enough? One . . ."

"Pleeeeeeeeease!"

"Two."

"Grandpa!" Vern yells. I glance over at him, and he shuffles and looks at the floor, shrugging his shoulders. "Dad sold Nitro to the meat packers."

For a minute I actually forget what comes after "two," and by the time I remember I realize it's too late for anything as imprecise as numbers.

"It's true, Grandpa," the small one answers the question my tongue can't get itself around. "The meat packers. Mr. Chong doesn't have him."

There's a high ceiling in this barn, and I hear the boy's words as though they're coming from a long way off and they're meant for someone else. Those kind of words. Like when I was a boy and came walking home from school and into the house and saw the neighbour woman sitting at the table with the minister, and the neighbour woman was looking at the table, and I said, "Are ya vistin' my mom, Mrs. Bell?" and she nodded her head, and the Minister said to me, "Your father's gone, Sam," and I wondered where he could be off to, because he hadn't been planning on going anywhere when I left for school in the morning. Not that I knew of, at least. And the neighbour woman said, "Your father's had a terrible accident," and she started to tell me about how his horse had thrown him and a steer had managed to catch him with a horn right in the throat. "Don't tell me. I don't wanna know," I said, but she told me anyhow.

I haven't thought of that for a long, long time.

The meat packers.

I didn't want to know, but he told me anyhow.

The boys are both looking at me, waiting to hear what I'll have to say next, I suppose, but what can I say? I'm the fool. I'm the one who came here to learn something. They were the ones who had something to teach me. And I am truly ashamed of my ignorance, and they can see it in the look on my stupid face, so I turn and stumble out the door of the barn and into the blowing snow and off towards the road, where I'm hoping I can find an appropriate spot to lay down and die.

The small one had it right. It is damned cold.

JUNE 29th, 2000: SASKATOON

THANK GOODNESS for air conditioning. I remember my former assistant, Greg Turnball, telling me over the phone, with an awkward significance that suggested he might be talking about some relative of mine, that the hotel had been bought and redone by a Japanese company. The appointments look very expensive, very Victorian. Last night, I took a shower, smoked a cigarette while watching a game show, turned it off and lay down diagonally across the king-sized bed, staring across the room at a print of Van Gogh's sunflowers. The air conditioning hummed, the sheets were clean and cool. I turned off the light and must have fallen asleep almost immediately.

I dreamed I was driving down a prairie road in my Toyota. Not the rented Toyota, but my old rusted one. My father was there. He was my passenger, but he told me he wanted to drive because there was something he had to show me. My father doesn't drive. Besides, the wheel felt good in my hands, and I was thinking that the last thing in the world I'd want was for him to be driving. The next thing I knew he was. We were still in my Toyota, but he was driving and I was in the passenger seat. I wanted to tell him to stop, but all I could do was stare out at the prairie. There was something menacing about the endless rolling Plains now that I was a passenger. There was a drum beating somewhere, and it kept getting louder. I was worried my father was driving too fast over that rutted earth. My dear old car needed to be treated more gently. If it broke down, we'd never find our way back to civilization. The sameness of the landscape unnerved me. Just that rolling prairie and the road running straight to the end of it, right into the sky. I wondered what it could mean, what it was trying to say to me, or sing to me, because there was still that drumming coming from all around.

And then an army of horsemen appeared across the entire horizon.

"Never," my father said.

And the road dropped away, and the earth opened up and swallowed us.

The phone was ringing. Reaching out blindly, I picked up the receiver, dragged it to my ear, and was greeted by a voice saying, "Ai, Lance Taves here. Can you have lunch with Jerry and Jim and I and then be ready to show us some locations afterwards?"

I glanced at the clock. It was almost seven. "I . . . guess. Couldn't you give me until after dinner, at least? He'd probably like to see it at magic hour."

"No. Not tonight. Got a big dinner with the government people tonight. What's wrong with after lunch?"

"Well, for one thing, I checked out the barn and it won't work. I'm going to have to find something else. Aspen'll be furious if we take him there."

"What's wrong with it?"

"The century. It's twentieth century."

"Early twentieth century?"

"Early to mid."

"What do you expect? This is Saskatchewan. There wasn't anything here but Indians before that."

"Are *you* gonna tell that to Aspen?"

"You're the locations manager. We'll meet you in the lobby at noon."

And he hung up.

I collapsed back onto my pillow and lay there for awhile, trying to collect myself. The dream would not leave me. The final moment came floating back as though I was still sleeping—the drumming, the horsemen on the horizon, my father opening his mouth to speak that single word, the earth opening—and I had to sit up and stare hard at the Van Gogh to make it go away.

I showered, dressed and took the complimentary newspaper down to the restaurant, where I now sit, trying to distract myself from that dream.

The coffee could be worse. I have a booth by the window, where I can glance from my paper and omelette out at the river valley and watch the joggers trot by. There are a few families down for breakfast, readying for their daily adventure, but mostly solitary men and women march in, their shirts all too crisp, their suits looking too warm for the harsh sunlight already streaming through the windows. Though I should be completely distracted by the fact that I have to display the hidden secrets of Saskatchewan for James Aspen this afternoon, I can't help thinking of my father at the breakfast table, his face buried in the newspaper as he drank his coffee, the cigarette at his lips. Sometimes—not often—he would actually speak to Mom, telling her about some story in the paper he felt she needed to know about, some new horror or medical discovery.

I'll call Mom to see how he's doing before I go blindly off in search of barns. It'll be late morning in Toronto.

My kingdom for a cigarette.

I put my room number on the bill and am about to go outside for that smoke when I see an old man wearing a winecoloured cardigan shuffle in on the heels of a waitress. He actually has a fishing fly in his orange cap, and he scans the room, seemingly delighted by the beige shade of the carpet, the arabesques on the Plexiglas dividers that separate the booths, the tag of the waitress's shirt standing up against the back of her neck. He might be a small-town grandfather on holiday to visit one of his impossibly successful children. He might be, except that I recognize the face. It is James Aspen.

When the waitress passes again, I order a third cup of coffee. Across the floor, the great man studies his menu. The look of concentration on his face suggests that he is trying to extract some secret meaning from what is written there. Benedict. Freshly squeezed. Whole grain. When he looks up, he catches me looking at him, and before I can glance away he is struggling to his feet and crossing to my table.

"You're the woman—the locations scout, aren't you?"

I am so taken aback I can't speak.

"Jerry took me to your show in L.A. That series of self-portraits you did. You look just like your picture. Nice work. You're a very gifted photographer, you know?"

"Ummm . . . thank you."

"Yes. I told Jerry we should get you to shoot the picture, but he thought maybe we should get you to direct it. He said we have a good shooter, and what we really need is a director. That's how deep in the weeds we are: that's what he keeps telling me. The picture's in a shambles. Whose idea was it to shoot exteriors up here in Canada? Yours, Jerry, I always have to remind him. Sixty cents buys a dollar, he kept telling me. He couldn't deny the attraction of paying for trinkets with your cheap little dollar, especially when your government kept throwing in perks."

"Well, we're certainly honoured to have you, sir . . ."

"Sir? Don't call me sir. I don't deserve it. No one deserves it, but especially not an old sinner such as myself. Call me

Jimmy. That's what my friends call me. You're a friend, aren't you? You'd better be, because I tell Jerry you're the most important person on this picture. Did you know that?"

"Pardon?"

"You see things. The whole world's gone stone blind, but you can see things. At least, I see from your show that you can see yourself. And nobody likes to see themselves. That's a curse. Must be a curse for you. I don't blame you for trying to keep it a secret."

"Pardon?"

"That's why I had to have you. This is a western, and the real auteur of the western is the locations scout. I mean that. It's a genre about a dry place where civilization's just sending up a few green shoots. That's why we need someone like you who can actually see the place. Who can actually see. 'But what if it's not even yours in the end?' Jerry asked me. 'If you insist on seeing it all through her eyes, the Asian woman'—that's what Jerry calls you, 'the Asian woman'—'if you insist on seeing it through her eyes, then how will anyone even know it's a James Aspen film?' And I told him, good riddance. James Aspen is just an old sinner anyway, and he hasn't said anything new since he told his father he should have smothered him in his sleep when he was a baby. I told my father that the day before he died. I told him he should have smothered me in my crib. And I feel better for it. I've felt free since I told him that. But I haven't said anything new. Maybe that's all freedom is: coming to terms with your own banality."

"Do you want to sit down?"

"You don't mind, do you? I don't want to interrupt your morning reverie. Some people need a clear, disciplined morning to get them through the day. I used to be that way. Now I don't even try. What's the use pretending? The rats have built nests in all the workings so nothing turns in the proper direction anymore. You know what I mean?"

"I don't mind at all. Jimmy."

"Oh, that's generous of you." He slowly manoeuvres himself into the other side of the booth, and I wonder whether I should help him, but am still wondering when he's finally settled himself. "Ahhhh, so that's how things look from here. Nothing too surprising, which is just as well. At my age surprises are to be avoided. Are you really Asian? You could just as well be Cherokee."

"My mother's roots are Irish. My father's Chinese. I'm pretty much Canadian."

"I guess so," he nods, not particularly interested. "What do you think of the script?"

I nod dumbly, trying to remember what I had decided was the best way of approaching the question if it came. "Well . . . it's . . . I'm not . . ."

"Terrible, isn't it? Carl's usually very dependable. Distracted, I think. His wife just left him for another woman, which was something of a blow, as you can probably imagine. I told him I wanted a western, and he told me he'd write me the western to end all westerns, and I told him I'd already made that one. What I want to make is the western to begin all westerns. At my age you finally lose the morbid fascination with endings. It's beginnings that attract you. I'd crawl right back into the womb if I could. Not yours. I'm not coming on to you, don't worry. I'm too old for all that sweat and disappointment. So, I told him I wanted to make the western to begin all westerns, and he gave me this tired imitation of *The Virginian*. You know what I mean? He didn't understand. I didn't mean that I wanted to make all the same mistakes they made when they invented the thing. What I meant was that I wanted to resurrect the western. And you can't have a resurrection without a crucifixion. Can you? It just can't be done. But Jerry's telling me the script's just fine and the money's ready to spend and we have to go ahead right now. So what do I do? I'm pleading with you. What do I tell Carl that'll save this thing? Do you have a location I could give him that would get us off on the right foot? Something really . . . seminal?"

I nod my head, look at the table and take a deep breath. I think I'm blushing. "I just got here yesterday. They . . . Mr. Taves wasn't expecting you so soon. I've never even been here before."

"Really? So you're saying you don't know the place at all?"

"I . . . ummm . . . had a look around yesterday. It's very beautiful."

"Set eyes. That's what they say in a western: 'Yesterday was the first day I set eyes on the place.'" He sits back in his chair, crosses his arms and shakes his head. I hope there will be no shouting.

"Well, that's good," he finally says. "That's what we need, is somebody who can see right back to the beginnings of this place. Before all the mistakes were made. That's perfect." He slides forwards again, leaning across the table towards me. "What did you see? How did it affect you?"

I am so surprised that I sit staring at him, considering his question, wondering if he is a little mad, or if this bizarre generosity is the real genius that allows him to control large groups of people so that they will help him to create great works of art. "It is . . . striking. The landscape. I had a nightmare about it last night."

"You did? A nightmare. Really? That's likely it. That's likely what we're looking for. Tell me your bad dream."

His tone doesn't sound sarcastic. I don't know what else to do but tell him. He slides even farther forwards to the edge of his seat and sits there oohing and aahing through my halting recitation, the best audience I've ever had for any words I've ever spoken. When I'm finished, he stares up at the ceiling, shaking his head as though he has never been so moved.

"Just opened up and swallowed you. And your dad. Your dad was there with you. '*Never.*' One of those straight-as-an-arrow prairie roads, running across the flat plain, running right up until it meets the pure blue sky, and then, before you can get there, you and your dad, before you can float off into the beautiful and terrible void, a whole tribe of Injuns appears on the horizon, and the earth magically opens up and takes you back inside. That's it! That's our location!"

He takes the slice of toast I never touched and bites into it.

"But doesn't it sound more like an ending than a beginning?" I ask.

"It's a beginning and an ending. It's the whole damn story. Jerry! Over here."

Jerry Herzog swoops up to the table and grabs James Aspen by the arm. "Jimmy! I was just about to call in the Royal Canadian Mounted in their red suits to ride you down. What are you doing here by yourself? You're not supposed to go anywhere without the escorts."

"They're the worst-looking escorts I've ever had in my life. I'm not that old."

"So I see you found yourself someone more to your liking."

"This is the Asian woman. You know? The locations scout."

I am already standing, offering my hand. "Ai Lee."

"For this film? No, no, Jimmy. Locations are typical of the state of this project. We've got no locations. The local yokel told me they just fired the locations scout."

"Fired? Fired! Well, whoever fired her, I fire him, and she's hired again. Who fired you?"

"No one. That was my assistant. Lance fired him. I'm Ai Lee. I'm actually the locations manager. From Toronto?"

Jerry Herzog looks me up and down as if he's trying to find my fin. "Oh, right. Hello, Ai. I took Jimmy to see your show down in L.A. Did he tell you? Ai and I have worked together before, Jimmy. Very happy with your work. Jimmy loved your pictures. Your photographs, I mean. I don't see it myself, but Jimmy says they're brilliant. I told him if they're so brilliant we should get you to direct the film."

"Should get her to write it. That's what we need is a writer, and she's just given me the solution to the hole in the script I keep telling you about. She saw the perfect location in a dream last night."

"In a dream? I hate to tell you, but we can't film dreams, Jimmy. It doesn't matter how many dollars I throw at it, we can't film dreams. That's the problem with this whole picture. You keep asking me for dreams instead of actors or locations or crew. Does it have a dwarf in it?"

"No dwarfs, Jerry. Just the perfect location. I've gotta talk to Carl about it. I think it's a beginning."

Jerry Herzog turns to me. "Is this what you're showing us after lunch."

"I . . . just dreamed about it last night. I haven't found it yet. I . . ."

"Don't worry about that, Jerry," James Aspen waves me to silence. "Ai'll find it. That's your name: Ai? Ai's a locations scout. She finds the locations. That's what Ai does. Right?"

I nod my head less than emphatically.

"And while she's finding it, we get Carl to do the rewrite. You should start looking right away. Are you finished breakfast?"

He is just finishing my toast.

"Yes," I say, "I should probably talk to Lance Taves about . . ."

Jerry Herzog is about to light a cigarette, but at the sound of the name he hurls down his lighter in disgust, and it spins on the table between James Aspen and me. "That fool! Don't even mention his name. If you're relying on him for anything, we're doomed. The blind leading the . . ."

"No," James Aspen cuts him off. "This young woman is not blind, Jerry. She is cursed by a sight that is all too clear. I don't want anyone getting in her way. She can see. That's the cross she has to bear. Do you have a video camera, Ai? Take a video camera too. Get some video when you get there. I'd like to see what you do with video."

I nod and swallow. "Where do I get one?"

"Just go buy it. Jerry'll cover it. Right, Jerry?"

"Yes, fine. Whatever. Get yourself a camera and keep all your receipts. We had a meeting five minutes ago with this Taves bozo, you know, Jimmy?"

"I was hungry," James Aspen shrugs. "An appetite is a blessing. It means there's still a spark of life in this old carcass."

"You're meeting with Mr. Taves? Maybe I should come with you and let him know what I'm doing. He told me I was supposed to meet with you for lunch."

"Forget about what he told you," the great director orders. "Just go. Just go and find that location."

"Are you sure . . . ?"

"Call me as soon as you've found it. Call me and I'll come straight there. Don't stop looking until you've found it. I swear, even if I'm back in L.A. I'll get on a plane and come straight to you. I'll give you my number. What's my number, Jerry?"

Jerry Herzog writes the number on a slip of paper and then drags James Aspen away. Halfway across the floor the great man looks back, and I wave hopefully, but he shows no sign of having seen me.

Dazed, I go up to my room to get my things together. My cellphone rings. I expect it to be Lance Taves, but it is my mother.

"Irene! Get to the airport right now, dear."

"Pardon?"

"You're father's going. Get on a flight right now."

"Mother. What exactly is happening?"

"You're father's dying, Irene. You need to get to the airport."

"The doctor says so?"

She sobs. "I say so."

"But what does the doctor say?"

"What do doctors know? You think I don't know your father better than any doctor? Come now, Irene!"

She begins weeping inconsolably. My head is about to explode.

"All right, Mom," I say. "Take it easy. I've got to go now. I'll see you soon."

And I hang up, pick up my bag, and go down to the parking lot, where my rented Toyota awaits me.

JANUARY 2nd, 1971: NEAR BROKEN HEAD

"IREEENE."

"Ireeeene."

"Ireeeeene."

She managed to get the old man to lie down on the seat and spread the blanket over him to protect him from the blast of wind through Luke's open window.

"Ireeeeeeeeeene."

"Ireeeeeeeeeeeeeeene."

The old cowboy kept singing her name, searching for the tune, until he finally found it floating somewhere deep beneath his frozen brow. "Good night, Ireeene. Good night, Ireeene . . ."

He was drunk from the cold. She had seen it once before, when she was a little girl on the reserve and Erasmus Hard Sky had come back from his trapline after falling through the ice. At first her mother figured he had been drinking and she pushed a table against the door so as not to let him in the house, before she realized it was only that the winter had got inside his brain and froze up all his sense. Then she brought him in and put him into a hot bath and thawed him out so that he was almost as good as new.

"I'll seeee youuu in my dreeeeeeeeeams . . ."

Luke switched on the radio—let the old man have his song, Irene scolded him with a glance into the reflection of his eyes in the rear-view—and the old man looked around, confused, trying to see who was singing. It was Charley Pride, giving his advice about kissing an angel good morning somewhere down in Nashville, but the old man could only see as far as the cracked green upholstery on the back of the Studebaker's front seat.

"Angelllll?" he asked Irene.

Luke's dirty old sweatshirt was lying on the floor, so she rolled it up and put it behind the cowboy's head for a pillow. That way he wouldn't bump against the door handle when they hit a rut. He was human. There was no doubt about that now, which was a considerable relief. When she'd gone back to find him and saw him standing on the side of the road, staring into the ditch, she began to worry that he might be some sort of monster—some sort of abominable snowman who could freeze you with his touch. The tips of his fingers were blue. She pulled the blanket up under his chin to cover the hand, as much to hide it from her sight as to thaw it. Though he could feel nothing, it hurt her to look at those blue fingers. He shifted his head sideways like an owl, studying her from this new perspective.

"You . . . an In-jun . . . I-rene?"

It emerged syllable by syllable, so that she could almost see the words and their connotations forming in his mind as they teetered off his clumsy tongue. She considered the question. The answer was simple enough: it was the question she needed to get to the bottom of.

"Yeah," Luke answered before she could. "You're in a car fulla Injuns. You've been saved by the redskins, Cowboy. A whole tribe of rampaging redskins, out on the warpath, taking back the world for the Blackfoot. Whaddaya thinka that?"

The old cowboy looked at Irene, confused, but apparently not particularly frightened, only wondering where the words were coming from since her lips weren't moving. She couldn't help but smile, and when he saw the smile his mouth made its own slow curl.

"You're . . . an an-gel . . . I-rene."

Luke glanced at her in the mirror, and she warned him to bite down hard on his tongue by showing her tongue and doing it.

"I'm no angel," she told the cowboy. "You're not dead. We're taking you to the hospital, and you'll be all right once they thaw you out."

He looked around him—at all he could see of the Studebaker's green interior. "I've died. Gone to Injun heaven."

Luke laughed harshly. "That's right. You're in the happy hunting ground." He rolled up his window. Irene looked ahead to see why. The wind was dropping. The road had appeared before them, still hazy through drifting snow, but visible for thirty or forty feet at times. Luke grinned at her. "Maybe we'll survive after all."

She nodded and looked down at the old man, who stared up at her in silent wonder.

"The storm's dying," she told him.

"The storm's dyin'," he said.

In a few minutes they reached the highway, and despite the limited visibility Luke accelerated as he turned into their lane. Irene had to hold the old man from rolling off the seat. The mysterious force on his body made him look around for the source.

"Slow down," Irene scolded Luke.

Either in response to her words or to the feel of her hands on his shoulders, the old man grinned a wide peaceful grin that showed his crooked yellow teeth, and closed his eyes.

He must not sleep. She remembered Erasmus Hard Sky saying that he'd felt like going to sleep out in a blanket of snow, but he wouldn't give in, just kept telling himself stories about the warm world of some southern country and yelling out loud about how he'd walk all the way to that land of gentle breezes, and when he got there he'd bow down and worship their gods and eat the fruit that fell from the trees and sleep with the beautiful women and tell all his stories of the cold country he'd come from, even though they'd never believe a word. He shouted out all his most wonderful and terrible desires in order to keep himself awake, and that's what saved him.

Irene lightly slapped the cowboy's cheek, and his eyes blinked open, looking slightly annoyed with her.

"How'd you get lost out in this weather without a jacket?"

She could see him working through her words in his mind, watching her lips even after they were still.

"Lost? Weren't lost. Just went for a walk. Went off in the cold. Way your old Injuns used to do. Once their families were through with 'em. You know?"

She nodded uncertainly. "That was the Eskimos. I think."

Luke laughed and began to sing, "Let's rub noses, just like the Eski-moses . . ."

The old man's face was full of wonder. "You an angel, Irene?"

She shook her head slowly, soothing him with her eyes the way she'd learned to do with her younger brothers and sisters when she was putting them to bed. But why was she doing that? She didn't want to put him to sleep. "Your family loves you. God loves you."

He pondered her words a while. "I have thought much . . . on God lately, Irene . . . and I suspect He does not approve of me." She shook her head, but he was beginning to gain better control of his tongue, and he must have remembered he had much to say to an angel on the subject of God. "I'm not such a bad man. I have my good points. I wanted Him to know I am not afraid of Him, and so I walked out into the cold to meet Him. I didn't wanna be a burden to my son any longer. John thought I was a burden, and I wanted to take that load from his shoulders. Carried enougha them my own day, but that don't mean I wanna be one myself. Are you an angel, Irene?"

He reached out from under the blanket and touched Irene's face with his blue fingertips. She let him, though a chill ran down her spine.

"They'll be worried, your family will. They'll be looking for you."

"Oh, no, my girl. They'll be glad to be done with me."

"You're wrong there. They'll fix you up at the hospital, and your family will be happy to have you home."

"No, no. They'll be happy all right. They'll find my death the greatest gift I ever gave them. And I gave them my land. Truth is, my son hates me. I can't blame him. I killed his son. I killed my own grandson. I killed Young Sam. Led him off in the blizzard like a dumb animal to the slaughter. I killed Young Sam. I killed Young Sam."

The old cowboy's eyes turned inwards, so that you could see him seeing the face of the child in his mind.

"He's out there today? The boy was with you?"

"I killed him, Irene. Didn't do it on purpose. I led him out into a blizzard and lost him. I killed Young Sam."

It was plain from his tone that he was pleading with her to forgive him. She was his angel. Irene placed her warm hand on the frozen skin of his forehead, and he blinked wildly.

"He'll be all right. Everything's all right."

"I only wanted to teach him things. He has my name. There's some things I know I thought he needed to know. His head was mostly empty. I only wanted to make him smarter. And tougher. Don't you figure that's something God would understand?"

"Yes. God understands. Jesus forgives. Jesus loves you. He loves you and me. And Luke. And your grandson. And everyone. Everything's okay. Your grandson's gonna be okay. Did he get lost somewhere around that farm where we found you?"

"He sacrificed His son. That's what the preachers say. You think He'd understand?"

"Your grandson's fine. Everything'll be fine. There's nothing to worry about. He's probably already with your family. Everything's gonna be fine."

Which is when the lights started flashing, and the siren wailed.

"Oh, shit," said Luke. "Now we're fucked."

He slowed down and stopped, and Irene watched through the drifting snow as the cruiser stopped behind them, both officers studying her face through the rear window. While the one sitting in the passenger seat talked on the radio, the driver got out and started walking towards them. The old cowboy reached his hand up so that the light touched his skin— watched the blue and then the red flash and disappear on his greyish blue hand.

Irene rolled down the window and stuck her head out. The officer stopped and touched his holster.

"We found a man out wandering around without a jacket. He's in bad shape. We need to get him to a hospital. There's a boy lost out there too."

The officer slowly approached her window and looked inside at the old cowboy, then at Luke, and finally at her.

"We found him in the blizzard this way," she said again, not sure if he'd heard her over the wind. "We gotta get him to a hospital. There's a boy out there too."

The officer was not that much older than Luke. He studied her with his pale blue eyes. "You saw a boy with him?"

"No. But he mentioned a boy. He said he lost him in the blizzard."

She looked at the old man as though she hoped he'd confirm this, but he was still staring at his own blue fingers. The officer turned and looked out across the ditch, as though the boy might be standing in the field, watching them. Then he turned back. "Follow me," he blurted, and he ran back to his car.

Luke was staring at her. "What did he say?"

"He said to follow him."

The police car pulled out and passed them, it's lights still flashing. No siren. Luke looked back at her as though he wasn't sure he'd heard correctly.

"Follow him!"

Luke put the car in gear. "We're fucked," he said.

The old man had started to shake.

"Don't worry," said Irene. "Everything'll be all right. The police are taking us to the hospital. Did you lose the boy somewhere around that farm where we found you?"

But the old cowboy's teeth were chattering so hard he couldn't have answered if he'd wanted.

"We're fucked," Luke said.

"I WANT an immediate separation," Gwen said. "And then I want a divorce."

She shifted her eyes from the highway to Sam, as if to judge by his face the exact twist of her words. "I've already talked to a lawyer."

Sam had no idea how to reply. His mouth opened, but nothing emerged, not even a breath. He looked at his hands in his lap, resting on his seatbelt, and there was the ring they had picked out together that rainy day in Vancouver over fourteen years ago. A simple gold band. He darted his eyes her way and saw her naked finger on the steering wheel. She was waiting for his response. Any response seemed inadequate. The sound of his own breathing seemed inadequate. The way he twined his fingers and pressed his palms together seemed inadequate.

Perhaps this was just another of Gwen's threats. Except that there was something different in her look and in her voice: a calmness that was not a part of the Gwen he had known. They hadn't been fighting the way they usually were when she announced the end of their marriage. And the lawyer. She'd never actually mentioned a lawyer before, except to challenge him to call one. Plenty of consideration had gone into her little speech, and he had heard that consideration in her controlled delivery, but still Sam could not help but feel that she had looked at him and known his indiscretion and decided right there and then that she would not put up with him for another second. He was too late to save his life.

In the field next to the highway a million sunflowers swayed in the wind. They had not yet begun to flower. When the sunflowers were behind them, there was wheat. Then, on the other side of a hedge of caragana, more durum wheat. It was still green, but in a month or more, if it was the same durum his father grew, it would be brilliant orange, shimmering black. Black whiskers sprouting around the orange heads—whiskers too small to make out from a car speeding by at seventy-five miles per hour—would give the orange a shading like a five o'clock shadow. If it rained.

The railway tracks ran parallel with the highway, hidden here and there by stands of chokecherries. Or were they buffalo berries? A sign with a curved arrow, a grey wooden grain bin in the middle of a field. Next to a deserted farmhouse, a topless windmill, the remains of its workings hanging limply. Natural gas markers and microwave towers. Miles and miles and miles of barbed wire.

An hour had passed and they were almost to Rosetown when Gwen spoke again. "Say something, for Christ's sake."

Sam sighed, shook his head, opened his mouth and managed to make a few sounds. "I don't . . . I don't know what to say."

"We need to discuss this."

There was obviously a script he wasn't following: she had already had this discussion inside her head, playing through what she would tell him and how she would respond to his possible responses. Silence was not a possibility she had considered, but silence was exactly what the situation called for. Words were primitive, grotesque. Any sentence he considered forming was simply a pitiful attempt to drown out the voice inside his head that was telling him he was lost.

He was in Saskatchewan. The evidence was all around him. He was the passenger in a car heading for a home that had

long ago slipped away, even if he'd been avoiding the acknowl-
edgment of its absence for just as long.

No, that wasn't true. Until two days ago he might have
saved their lives together, but now he had no footing to support any argument for their existence. He was an adulterer.
Play with fire, his mother and father had warned him.
"Remember that time we burned down the barn?"

Gwen looked at him as if he were crazy. It had been Vern
and he who had burned down the barn. He hadn't even
known Gwen yet. He was talking about something that had
happened years before he'd ever imagined winning or losing
Gwen. Vern and he liked to pretend they were cowboys. They
built a campfire out of straw, just an imaginary campfire, but
imaginary hadn't been enough for Vern, so they'd gone to the
house and stolen a pack of Old Sam's matches. Vern was
already stealing his tobacco.

"It was Vern," he said, so Gwen would know he hadn't lost
his mind. The expression she gave in response, however, did
not suggest that the attempt to convince her of his sanity had
been entirely successful.

The fire had spread like a river finding an opening in a
dam. Sam ran down the hill for a pail of frog pond, but by the
time he got back the balestack was spewing flames and greasy
black smoke into the pretty blue of the sky, and the intensity
of the heat made it impossible for him to get close enough to
toss his gallon of green water onto the inferno. This, he now
knew, was what always happened when you tried to make the
imaginary become real.

Vern argued that it would be better if Sam took the blame,
because he was young enough—only six—that his behaviour
could be excused. Vern, at ten, was old enough to know better. So Sam agreed and confessed to the crime, saying Vern had

not known he had the matches, and he had lit the fire when Vern wasn't looking. In the end, it didn't matter much. Their parents were overwhelmed by the scale of their mischief. Old Sam said they both ought to have their hides tanned, but their father didn't seem to think that would be an adequate punishment for burning down a barn.

"True enough. They hang barn burners," Old Sam told them, with a weary shake of his head.

A few months later, when Vern stole Sam's favourite toy car and blew it to pieces with a .22, Sam told his mother what had really happened that day at the balestack. For this revelation, Sam was given a sound spanking and ordered never to tell lies. And so it was that at six Sam learned that, once surrendered, truth was not so easily recovered.

"I love him," Gwen said.

"Pardon?"

He turned to her. She gripped the wheel with grim fortitude, staring straight ahead. "I love Vern. And he loves me. And I can't live without love any longer. You don't love me, Sam. Don't lie to yourself about that. All you care about is your career. And there's nothing wrong with that—you really are good at what you do. Not just good. You could be a . . . anything you want. I really believe that. I don't think I should stand in your way any longer. Vern and I want to be very open about what's happening. We want to do the right thing. The children are the most important thing the three of us have to consider in all of this."

"Vern?"

She gave him a look that suggested he'd said something particularly offensive. "Well, what the hell did you expect?"

It was perhaps the most ridiculous rhetorical question Sam had ever been asked. "Not this," he blurted.

She kept staring straight ahead. "Well, then you're even more blind than I'd given you credit for."

He too looked ahead at the road to see what it was she saw up there that he couldn't quite make out. Nothing. Just an endless broken yellow line shut in by two unbroken white borders and a white Corvette they were fast overtaking.

"I guess that's right. I guess I must be the blindest man in the whole wide world."

"It doesn't matter anymore," she said. "It's out in the open now. Vern and I couldn't stand to live this lie any longer."

They whizzed past the Corvette, its driver glancing at them with revulsion.

"You and Vern wanted to do the right thing."

She turned to him and scowled. "What do you mean by that?"

"That's what you said: you and Vern wanted to do the right thing."

She held him in her gaze long enough to transform her face into the most profound look of hatred he had ever seen directed his way, and he had seen many profound looks of hatred from clients whose loan requests he had refused.

"Fuck you," she said.

Finally, she turned back to the road.

"Stop the car," he said.

Apparently she didn't hear him.

"Stop the fucking car!"

She braked gradually, signalling so that the Corvette was able to avoid rear-ending them, and they rolled along the shoulder for a hundred yards before they were finally stationary, her shoulders heaving with a heavy sigh, relieved of a burden that had at long last been lifted. She didn't look at him. He opened the door and stepped out into the wide world. The wind hit him immediately, clearing his head. He did not shout one last damnation at her, and he didn't slam the door, just shut it firmly so that it clicked into place. Superb German engineering. There were hints of beauty in the most unlikely places. As matter-of-factly as she'd stopped, Gwen proceeded again. Standing in the crested wheat just off the shoulder of the road, the hot wind whipping past him, he watched her disappear.

He stood there waiting for her to return.

Twenty minutes later he had begun to understand that she wasn't going to appear over the horizon any time soon.

He thought about death. For the first time in his life, he really wished he were dead. He had the feeling that if he were to lie down and fall asleep he might never wake up. Was that possible? Or would he have to make some greater effort? He didn't have the energy. He was just too tired.

For many minutes he stared at the surface of the highway, shocked to realize that there were bits of glass sparkling in the concoction of tar and sand that made up the asphalt. The highway was made of glass, stars of blue light, fragments of broken windshields. All those rubber tires supported by glass. Gradually, the fascination passed. For another while he threw rocks at an Elrose 15 sign and considered throwing them at the few cars that straggled by, the drivers swivelling their heads, curious about the man in the Italian suit glaring at them from the side of the road.

She was fucking his brother. For how long? Had it possibly been years? Was that why she had stopped making love to him? There had been so many excuses. After Benjamin was born, she told him she no longer felt like a woman, only like a mother, and he'd have to be patient. And then, when that phase passed, she'd simply told him she was tired. When he reached across the bed to touch her, she would kiss him and say, "Good night. Go to sleep." And, after all, Ben was still waking them at night. She was still feeling like a mother, though she did not make that excuse. She was just tired or didn't feel like it. And then after another year, when Sam had begun to feel like a toy that had been wound too tightly too many times, she had told him that she no longer felt that way about him. He had changed. He was too distant. He wasn't romantic enough. He was too uncommunicative. Too dark and brooding. (Weren't *dark* and *brooding* once considered romantic?) All he cared about was the bank. It was his fault she didn't want to make love with him.

The broken toy had changed.

The worst of it was that he'd believed all of these excuses. He'd blamed himself entirely. He'd scolded himself for making sex so important to his happiness. If he could get over the wanting of it, the fixation on it, he could start to do things that had once made her love him and their lives would be better again, and maybe she would even want to make love to him again.

Should he start hitchhiking? She'd expect him to catch a ride and roll into town in a couple of hours. But what then? He couldn't go home and he couldn't face his parents, and he couldn't stand the thought of the pleasure any of his clients and acquaintances would be deriving from his predicament. He imagined the entire town of Broken Head seething with stories, exchanging details of his cuckoldry over beer and peanuts, tea and sugar cookies.

How could they?

How dare they humiliate him?

The only possibility of salvaging any dignity was to kill them both.

It wasn't that he believed he could actually accomplish the deed, but it was the only thing he could think about that gave him any relief from his anguish. What would he use? One of his father's rifles? The little .22 Vern had once used to obliterate his toy Camaro? He visualized the barrel against Vern's forehead, the expression on Vern's face, the recoil, the bloody emulsion of bone and brain spattering the wall behind Vern's head, the impact of the body hitting the floor and settling with a slight bounce.

He'd noticed in movies how bodies bounced when they struck pavement or floor.

Was it dangerous to hitchhike in an Italian suit?

Saskatchewan. There was a tumbleweed stuck in the barbed wire fence across the ditch. He walked over, pulled it free, and threw it into the pasture, but it caught again in a clump of wild mustard. He climbed through the fence and gave it a kick to set it free and it bounced off across the field, stirring up small puffs of dust with its progress. If he'd done this to gain some sense of satisfaction or accomplishment, he found that he had not succeeded. He climbed back through the fence, careful not to snag his suit on the barbs.

Back on the shoulder of the highway, he took a deep breath and, for no definite reason, started walking south, in the direction of Broken Head, in the direction of home, but he was not going home, he was watching the broken line at the centre of the highway, thinking—yes, actually thinking that there was no sense in looking at life as a linear series of events building in some general progression towards death. No sense believing a life could be neatly encompassed by something definitively unified by a self named Sam McMahon. He was walking beside a highway in the middle of nowhere. What business did Sam McMahon have here? There was a farmhouse in the distance he'd never ever noticed before on the million trips he'd driven on this road, and now he might walk to that farmhouse and ask for a meal, and there might be a woman there who might take him in and feed him and make love to him and ask him to run her farm and marry him. Or she might shoot him before he ever reached the door. Or she might make love to him and tell him that she was just leaving for Paris, where she ran an advertising agency when she wasn't slumming on her parent's farm, and would he like to come along? Or she might pretend she wasn't home, watching him through the window, peering from behind the pink curtains as he knocked on the door, shouted hello, tried to peer through the pink curtains and finally skulked away. Or she might make love to him. Anything might happen, and he might be anywhere at any time and there was no more meaning to Sam McMahon then there was to a scribble in the margin of a Broken Head phone book found on the bank of a river in Islamabad.

He became so engrossed in these matters that he was not even fully aware he had stopped walking and was staring into the ditch, looking at a beer bottle that some happy or desperate teenager had tossed there, either frivolously littering or in some truly significant act of rebellion against his parents and the world.

"Are you all right? Do you need a ride?" a woman's voice asked.

Sam turned slowly, expecting to find that he was alone, and saw that a sports car had pulled to a stop on the opposite shoulder. German, he thought. No, a Toyota. A tiny Native woman was speaking to him through the open window of the car. No, perhaps she was Asian. As he stepped closer, he could see a video camera lying on the back seat of her car, and a briefcase in the front, but otherwise he saw with otherworldly clarity that the vehicle had never been occupied by anyone before. The exterior was perfect, and so was what he could see of the interior. Not a mark or a scratch or a discarded Kleenex floating on the upholstery. No hint of an accent in her voice. He felt dizzy—a little unsure that any of this was really happening. He actually wondered if he might be dreaming. Yes, maybe this was a bad dream. No, that hot breath was the real wind gusting against him. There were no winds like this in his dreams. Perhaps Gwen had sent the woman to rescue him.

"Are you . . . ?" he started to ask, before he realized just in time that the question was absurd. He thought of another, more appropriate: "Where are you heading?"

"That way," the woman shrugged, looking south, then north, avoiding his eyes. "Where are you . . . heading?"

For a moment he didn't know how to answer, but he found himself blurting out, "Broken Head."

"Oh?" She met his eyes. Hers were brown. Her nose was slightly too large for her face, he thought. She was smiling slightly, like Mona Lisa, as if she already knew too much about him and she was about to ask him something to which there could be no answer but "yes." There was nothing in her voice to suggest any origin but here. Not here. She sounded as though she might have been from the television. This could be a commercial for the car or maybe some soft drink. Or it might be one of the bank's expensive new spots. "I noticed Broken Head on the map," she said. "That's quite a distance, isn't it? Maybe I could take you to the next town. Is it . . . Elrose?"

She pointed at the road sign two hundred yards north of them. He had walked two hundred yards south.

"Yes, sure. That'd be fine."

He waited for a response before he realized she was waiting for him to get into the car. As he was about to round the car to do just that, she suddenly did respond: "Listen, this might sound strange, but would you mind if I took your photograph?"

He stopped. "Pardon?"

"Do you mind if I take your picture? I've never been here before, and it's such an incredible landscape, and when I saw you standing there in that beautiful suit . . ."

Sam squinted down at his suit, out across the vista and back into her eyes. Her eyes were a warm brown and angled like some predatory bird: falcon or eagle or owl, he wasn't sure which. "Oh, thank you . . ."

"Do you mind?"

He looked around again, searching for cameras in the ditch, or an audience watching from the other side of the fence. "You're a tourist?"

She had taken two cameras from her briefcase and was already getting out of the car. "Well, not really, to be honest. I'm kind of a photographer, but the photograph wouldn't be used in any . . . public kind of way."

"Not in any . . . public kind of way?"

"No. Not without your permission."

He approached her tentatively. She was standing in the centre of the highway. "Why do you want to take my picture?"

"Oh! It's just that the way you looked out here struck me as a good photograph. If you don't want me to, that's fine."

He looked around once more to see if he could see what she saw. A row of cedar fence posts so rotted the page wire was holding them up. Gwen was right. He was blind. He was the blindest man alive.

"Okay. Right here?"

She looked both ways to see if any traffic was coming. None. "That wind feels like a blow-dryer, doesn't it? I'd like one right in the middle of the road, if you don't mind?"

"No. That's fine." He smiled weakly. "I'm a middle-of-the-road kind of guy."

She chuckled, and he stepped onto the dotted line, and she took his picture. Twelve times. From slightly different perspectives.

"Should I look at the camera, or away from it?"

"Whatever's comfortable. I feel like we should have some kind of permit to be doing this."

"What do you mean?"

"Well, it's just so weird that there's so little traffic that you can do this. It's the kind of thing that takes so much planning in the city."

"Where are you from?"

"Toronto."

"Toronto," he agreed. "I like Toronto."

She kept taking pictures.

"What if I stand on the side of the road with my thumb out?"

She smiled and shrugged. "Sure. Whatever feels natural."

"Natural? Well, maybe that would be a little contrived."

She snapped a few more. "Maybe you could just look into the ditch the way you were when I first saw you."

"Was I?"

"Yeah. You were looking at something in the ditch."

"Oh? All right."

He took five steps to the edge of the road and stared into the ditch. The beer bottle was still there. He glanced over and she was studying him critically, obviously not happy with the way he was looking at the beer bottle.

"Did your car break down?"

"Pardon?"

"I don't see your car. How did you get here?"

He was silent for a moment, staring at that beer bottle, the peculiar brown of it, the label washed away by weather, the efficient hand-length of the neck. Perhaps that's why the stubby had died: the neck was so short you were forced to hold the body of the bottle, and that allowed your blood to warm your beer. Perhaps it wasn't just marketing that made the long neck win. He glanced her way, and she had started taking photos with the second camera. "How *did* I get here? Well, my wife stopped the car and left me here. She told me she wanted a divorce. She told me she's having an affair."

The woman lowered her camera until it was at her waist. "Oh. I'm sorry."

He shrugged. "It's not your fault."

And then Sam began to cry, his entire body heaving with sobs so huge he could not get control of his breathing and began to feel panicked that he might suffocate on his own terrible grief. The woman looked a little alarmed, and for a moment she raised her camera as though she had decided to take another picture, but then she let it drop against the strap around her neck, rushed to him and encircled him in her thin arms.

"Oh, my goodness. Let's get you into the car."

Surrendering, he grasped her tightly and allowed the tiny woman to escort him to the passenger door and put him inside the car. Her blouse was silk. She smelled of some secret scent, the origin of which he could not pinpoint. By the time she came around and got in the driver's seat, he'd let every particle of his sorrow spill out and, wiping the tears from his eyes with his shirt sleeve, was already beginning to feel ridiculous for exposing himself in such a childish way.

"Sorry about that."

"Are you okay?"

"Yeah, I'm fine. I'm all right. Sorry about that."

She smiled slightly. "It's not your fault."

"It just hit me."

"You're all right?"

"Yes. Thank you."

There was an awkwardness in her posture, in the way she avoided his eyes, that he noticed even though he was so busy avoiding her eyes. The embrace out on the road was not really between them. Here, in the car, they were two different people. They were strangers. He didn't even know her name.

"Thanks. For the ride. My name's Sam."

She offered her hand. "Hi, Sam. I'm Ai."

Despite her tiny hand, her handshake was surprisingly strong. "Pardon?"

"Ai. A-I."

He was confused—artificial intelligence?—completely unanchored—artificial insemination?—and his confusion was reflected in the expression on her face.

"Ai. It's . . . Asian."

"Oh? I've never met anyone named that . . . named Ai before. Sorry, I'm still a little dazed. Pleased to meet you."

A laugh escaped him, a bit hysterically.

"What's so funny."

"Oh, sorry. I was just thinking that if Gwen—my wife— asks who gave me a ride, I'll say Ai did."

She smiled weakly. "I've heard that one a few times."

He looked away. "Sorry."

She put the car in gear. "So, Elrose," she said.

"Yes, thanks. That'd be great."

She punched in the lighter and, with the same right hand, the nails painted bright red to match her lips, she took a cigarette from a package on the dashboard. "Oh. Do you mind if I smoke?"

Perhaps five feet. Perhaps ninety pounds. Her name was Ai. What the hell was he doing here? Was he here? He noticed now the faint smell of tobacco that could not quite mask the new-car smell. "It's your car."

"Not really. It's a rental. You're sure you don't mind?"

"No, that's fine. Maybe I'll have one myself."

"Go ahead."

"No, thanks. I don't smoke."

She glanced at him, her eyebrows raised speculatively.

"It's just that yesterday a colleague told me I should take it up. He said that's how you meet the movers and shakers. They're all smoking at the foot of the skyscrapers."

"Oh? Interesting strategy. Killing yourself for connections. Commendable." Suddenly she looked very serious, as though regretting her dark humour, and he tried to smile to reassure her that it was okay. "What do you do?" she asked.

"Banking. I'm a banker."

He could not decide whether it was her eyes or her lips that were familiar. She was dressed completely in black— looked as if she were on her way to the club where Erika'd taken him less than two days before, at the end of that other lifetime. Something popped, and they both looked: the lighter. She lit her cigarette, rolled down the window and exhaled out of the left side of her mouth into the wind. He shifted back to the right and looked out his window at the scenery. Yes, indeed, what was he doing here, and where was he going? What the hell would he do in Elrose? Make a phone call, but there was no one in Broken Head he wanted to talk to. Maybe it would be more sensible for him to head in the other direction, back to Saskatoon, and catch a flight to Toronto. He could book himself into a nice hotel, spend a few days getting his head together and formulating some kind of plan. If he talked to the right people about a position in Head Office, they'd no doubt be more than accommodating. He needed to keep in mind that there were always options. Any manager of Sam's abilities had to see this as an opportunity.

He could aim a gun and put a bullet hole through his brother's forehead.

"I didn't know bankers wore suits like that one."

He jerked his head to look at her. She was staring calmly ahead at the road. "Pardon?"

"It's nice. I thought you were supposed to be a little more conservative than that."

He sighed and shrugged.

"I like the cut."

Sam watched her release a long tendril of smoke from between her red lips. She glanced at him, and he could feel the weight of her eyes in his joints.

"Me too."

For a few miles he watched the fence posts march by, on their long trek to happiness. She turned on the radio and started searching for a station, finally settling on country and western over golden oldies. She was not particularly attractive. That nose, too large. But there was something about her eyes. Intelligence. She was obviously very bright. Whatever it was about her, for some reason he kept imagining kissing the spot where her collarbone showed through her skin. He could feel the hairs standing up on the back of his neck. All of this seemed too strange to be true—she couldn't have just stopped there by chance, at that moment. It had to mean something. If anything meant anything. They were supposed to meet. Someone or something had arranged it.

On the radio, Steve Earle started pounding his guitar. She

tapped her left black suede leather boot on the floor mat and lit another cigarette.

"So, what do you do, Ai?"

"I work in the film industry. I'm a locations manager."

"A . . . what?"

"I handle the locations for shooting. Right now, I'm working on a James Aspen film."

"James Aspen?"

"Yeah. He's filming in Saskatchewan. A western."

"Really? You're kidding. Here?"

"Yeah. Here in Saskatchewan."

"Really? James Aspen in Saskatchewan. I hadn't heard anything about that. And you know him?"

"I met him for the first time this morning."

"You met James Aspen this morning? In Saskatchewan! What's he like?"

She shrugged. "Well . . . he's very old."

"I guess he would be. I loved *Frozen World*. Bogart was really good in that. That's one of my favourite films of all time."

"It's pretty amazing."

"And *The Shoe Dropped*. When I saw that the first time, I couldn't talk about anything else for a week. Gwen finally told me . . ."

He couldn't finish the sentence.

"Have you seen *That Golden Sky*?" Ai asked him.

"No. Never. I'm not a big fan of westerns. Is it good?"

She tapped the ash off her cigarette. "It's one of my father's favourite films."

Sam nodded. She took another drag. The smoke spiked out her nostrils. He studied the world out the window through a brilliant new filter: they were driving into a James Aspen film. Those were James Aspen fence posts.

"What sort of locations are you looking for?"

His beautiful home, he was thinking, though as soon as he'd thought it he couldn't avoid the possibility it was no longer his, even though that's exactly what he was trying to avoid in his raw-nerved excitement at the fact that James Aspen, the great director, had suddenly touched a finger to his broken life. His house wouldn't likely work in a western anyway. He was fairly sure she'd said it was a western. The woman had a strange, uncomfortable look on her face.

"Well, who knows, maybe you can help me," she said. "Do you know any old barns? Really old?"

"How old?"

"Nineteenth century."

He shook his head. "I don't think so."

She shook her head. "I didn't think so." She glanced at him regretfully. "And I'm looking for one other very specific location right now. A prairie road—just a trail really—that you can see running forever. You know, right to the horizon." She pointed at the highway ahead of them as an example. "But then, all of a sudden, it's intersected by a big hole . . . or something. So that someone who was driving down it would just drive in without seeing it."

Sam nodded. "Oh, yeah. I know where you mean."

"You do?"

"Yeah. I know the place."

She turned and stared at him, her mouth slightly open, her brown eyes blinking. "You're kidding."

"No, it's . . . well, it's a long story, but I remember, when I was a kid, seeing the place you're talking about. Somebody was driving down this trail, going pretty fast and—my brother took me there once—you could see the trail running all the way to the horizon, and then he drove right off a cliff."

An image formed in his mind of Vern in the truck, driving so fast that Sam had to clutch the door handle on the corners. *Look out world, 'cause I've got a license to fly!* The cliff was one of Vern's favourite places. He loved the idea of that guy driving off into the sky. Vern was his hero that year, for a while, when he'd first got his licence, and he liked to show off to Sam by taking him for drives and exploring the countryside. Maybe Vern had always been his hero. Sam glanced at the woman and saw that she was waiting for him to continue.

"It's weird because—well, have you noticed that all the roads here are on a grid? Every two miles there's a road allowance." He pointed out the window at the crossroad up ahead and she nodded, though she looked more than a little confused. "And if you're driving down the trail I'm talking about, it looks like it runs all the way to the horizon, but all of a sudden, at the creek, before you'd see it coming if you were going very fast, the trail runs out. The valley's very narrow right there, and it's a sheer hundred-foot drop. But as you approach the cliff, you can still see the trail continuing on the grid on the other side of the valley. So this guy was going so fast he never saw the valley. And he drove right off the cliff. The car's still there."

Her eyes were open very wide, and she was looking at him. Sam checked the road.

The elevators of Elrose had poked into view a couple of miles ahead.

"Can you take me there?" she asked.

She wanted him to take her there.

"Well, sure, I guess." He felt himself sweating, despite the air conditioning, and brushed his forehead with his fingertips. "Actually, to tell you the truth, I don't know exactly where it is. But I'm sure we can find it."

"You said you were there?"

"When I was a kid. My brother took me there. He was older. He already had his driver's licence. He knows where it is."

"Your brother?"

"Yes."

"Does your brother still live here?"

"Yeah. He does. He lives . . . just up the road from where I live."

"Could we go and talk to him?"

He drew his handkerchief out of his breast pocket and dabbed his forehead. "Ummm . . ."

He imagined Gwen's face twisted in some kind of agony or ecstasy. "It's for this movie? For the James Aspen film?"

"That's right."

Sam nodded. They were reaching Elrose, and she slowed, and a moment later Elrose was gone and they were continuing south. He saw Humphrey Bogart in one of Aspen's films from way back in the fifties, and he saw Humphrey Bogart driving a stagecoach off a cliff, and he imagined driving into his brother's yard with this woman.

"Well, the thing is, I'm not so sure I want to talk to my brother right now." He could see by her look that the woman did not know what to make of this, but she waited. "My brother's been sleeping with my wife. That's why she left me out here."

The woman abruptly laughed, then looked horribly embarrassed. "I'm sorry."

Sam smiled, and shrugged to show her it was okay. "Well, for the sake of art, I'll just have to take you there, won't I?"

NOVEMBER 30th, 1970: NEAR BROKEN HEAD

I'M AT THE WINDOW of my cage, staring into the sad reflected eyes of my dark twin, because it's blacker than Toby's ass outside and the teenager with the pretty uniform left the light on when they gave up on the interrogation and I can't be bothered to pull myself out of this bloody chair and switch it off. I may never get up again. Though it would be more pleasant to sit in the dark and watch the shapes of things moving out there in the night. The snow's still blowing.

I told him to arrest John. I explained to him how he had murdered a horse. I was patient. Listened to his dumb questions and did my best to answer them. Tried my best to make him understand. Looked him in the eye. Tried my best not to make him feel like the young fool in the silly uniform that he and I both know he is. But this murdering of horses, of course, is not a crime in a civilized world. Beating a horse is a crime, but killing one is a job. No experience necessary.

I can hear the pretty uniform in the next room now, turning on his terrifying authority, interrogating the boys. The genuine third degree. "And your grandpa was pointing the gun at Mr. Chong?"

Silence. The clock on the old stove clicks like a mad thing. Three clicks per second, I'd imagine. It's always done that. I once tried putting cork pads under the corners to dampen the vibration, but it didn't work worth a damn. I imagine that when the world ends it will be set off by the eventual explosion of that stove.

It's the longest I've ever heard either of them boys go without wagging their tongues.

"We need to know what you saw, boys. You're not going to get into any trouble for telling the truth. Nobody's blaming you for what happened. I think your parents want you to tell us the whole story."

"That's right, Vern. Tell them what happened."

My son, the horse killer, back from his Russian movie, helping them shine the light in his own boys' eyes.

"Was your grandpa pointing the gun at Mr. Chong?"

"I don't think so." It's the older one. "I think he was just worried about the dog bitin' him." Vern. Named after her old man. Vern of the wispy moustachio, whose new cowboy boots cost him more than I used to make on a dozen cows. He knew exactly what happened to Nitro right from the start, but he strung me along, watching me make a fool of myself. "I think he was . . . just excited. He thought his horse was there. He wasn't actually pointin' his gun, but he shot to scare the dog, and Mr. Chong thought he was pointin' the gun at him, so he jumped on the ground."

Makes sense to me.

"And he left right away when you explained to him that the horse wasn't there?"

It's the other cop speaking: the older one, Officer Johnson, who was a private when I used to go for drinks in Chief Bailey's office.

"Yeah. Right away. He just wanted to know where Nitro was."

Bailey used to call him "John's Son." Tease him when he came into his office by offering him whiskey in the middle of the afternoon. John's Son would just shake his head and say he had too much to do.

"Why didn't you tell your grandfather that his horse wasn't there?"

Damned fine question.

"We did."

"Why didn't you tell him right away? Before he got to the barn?"

"Dad told me not to."

Damned fine answer.

"I just . . . It was just . . ." My son John begins his confession with the usual heeings and hawings. "He's right. Vern's tellin' the truth. It's my fault. I shoulda told Dad, but I knew he was goin' to overreact, and I guess I didn't want to face that yet. I'm responsible."

That's it. You've got your man. Lock him up.

"Grandpa was just excited," Vern says. "He didn't mean to . . ."

"I understand that, Vern. But do you understand that that doesn't make it right to point a gun at anybody?"

"He didn't. He just shot it to scare the dog 'cause it was gonna bite him."

"But he shouldn't even have been carrying a gun."

The boy doesn't answer, or not so I can hear anyway.

They want to take away my gun. Won't be long before they do that to everybody, so that they're the only ones who have them. Them and the crooks. The boy ought to ask Officer John's Son if he's ever pointed his gun at anybody, and what was the right and the wrong of that particular calamity. The way I heard it was he once shot a man in the back of the head while the man was leaving the scene of an attempted robbery. One strange thing, though, was that it was the officer's own bedroom the man was leaving, by way of the window, and the only thing missing from the bedroom was every stitch of the officer's wife's clothing. Leastways, her clothes were there, but his wife wasn't wearing them at the particular time of the shooting. I guess Officer John's Son must've prevented the man from stealing them.

"Why don't you stop pesterin' those poor boys and arrest me," I call out. That quiets things down in the kitchen.

I do feel ready to go, just so long as I don't have to walk. Let them haul me out of here and throw me in a cell and keep me there for the rest of my life. Couldn't be any worse than sitting staring out this window. Better still, let's get the whole disappointment over with. I'd be glad to have them march me out in the yard and give me a final smoke and tie me to a stake and put a blindfold on me so that the row of men with long rifles wouldn't have to look me in the eye when they shot me through the heart. I'd even be glad to sit down in one of them electrified chairs and *be* the final smoke. I imagine it would feel quite pleasant. My ass is still a little chilly at the moment.

Just don't put any itchy rope around my neck. That seems to me to be an altogether undignified way to make your final turn. Hanging there with your toes pointing at hell like a bloody ballerina.

Thinking about that firing squad has given me a craving for a puff or two, so I roll one and light it up.

Ahhh, life's little pleasures. All I need now's a cattle prod to the testicles.

They lowered their voices when I called out to them, but I can hear something again, so they must want me to listen.

"Are you takin' him in?" the son's asking, and you can make out the hope in his voice. Think of what he'd save on groceries.

"No, we don't need to do that. Mr. Chong's pretty upset, obviously, but we managed to convince him not to deal with this as . . . an official matter."

Is that so? We're not gonna make it official. No, let's keep
it unofficial, like the death of your wife's friend. But that *was*
official, wasn't it? That was an interrupted robbery attempt.
What we have here is an altogether different matter. This
evening's little charade never happened at all. Makes you
wonder whether there's any point getting up in the morning
when you go to all the trouble of pointing a gun at somebody
and then find out that it didn't even happen. It's the sort of
world where a horse could just disappear without anybody
giving a good goddamn.

I suppose Officer John's Son will expect my thanks for
keeping me out of the hoosegow. He can kiss my withered ass.

I take a drag on the cigarette and hear my own name,
"Sam!" before I realize it's me calling. Calling myself back
from somewhere I've gone missing, I suppose. I sit there waiting a long time before the young one finally comes.

"Turn off that light, will ya?"

He does, and my reflection disappears, and then it seems
like he's about to leave again—like he figures that's all I wanted from him and now he can escape the old lunatic before he
starts waving his gun around again.

"Come here," I say.

I know they're listening in the next room, so I wait till he's
really close before I say it, because they have no right to hear.

"He was a good horse," I tell him.

And, of course, the small one doesn't know what to say. He
just stands there blinking at me the way he did in the barn.

But that's all right. What could anyone say that would
make the slightest difference?

JUNE 29th, 2000: NORTH OF BROKEN HEAD

THE INTENSITY of his expression as he stared off into the ditch made me stop the car for him. Or perhaps "intensity" is wrong. The void. Whatever he was seeing had hollowed him out emptier than I have ever seen anyone before. Except my father. He had the same expression my father wears as he watches the television or that squirrel in the tree in our yard. That profile was the reason I stopped. And the beauty of his suit. The way it fit him as though the man or woman who had taken his measurements and sewed the darts had loved his body. And the landscape. The combination—the juxtaposition of that expression, that suit and that landscape that he was looking right through were too much to allow me to drive on by, even though I have never stopped for a hitchhiker in my life—even though I was filled with a fear so palpable that my hands were shaking and I kept the car in gear until I heard his voice and saw his blue eyes focus on me and I came to the tentative conclusion that he wasn't a psychopath.

By now I am fairly certain he will not kill me. Unfortunately, I doubt if I managed to steal even a half-decent photograph, as I was only beginning to get him to relax when he broke down, and I missed the best one of him weeping there on the side of the road. I let it go. James Aspen might scold me for being so sentimental, but maybe it's good that there are limits to my mercenary nature. My mother would think so. Or would she? I shoot my father's disintegration every Wednesday, but I could not stand there and flash the shutter while a stranger wept.

My mother may never forgive me for being here to miss that photograph. I'm looking for a location for a scene that hasn't even been written yet, while my father is dying. But my father's been dying for months. For more than a year. I can't stop my life to wait for the end of his.

That photograph probably would have been too melodramatic at any rate.

Now, in contrast to the stark emptiness I saw in him at first, the banker is filled with some sort of frantic energy, as though the shock of his grief has moved into his limbs and made him drunk. The mention of James Aspen has made him a little silly. Or maybe he's just lovesick. He's like a teenager on his first date. I get the feeling I'm about to be hit by his rebound. He can't keep his large hands still, moving them from the dashboard to his lap and running them through his thinning hair. His nails are manicured. He has long fingers, beautiful hands. He keeps pointing down the road ahead of us, as if he knows where we're going.

How could I have laughed when he told me about his brother?

But perhaps the location is found. All and all, I was not surprised when he told me he had seen the place in my dreams. Of course he had. Why else would James Aspen have sent me to find him? The only problem is that Sam the banker can't remember exactly where the location is hidden, and the only person who knows is the brother who cuckolded him.

"I know it's north of Broken Head, but I don't know how far. Or maybe it is south."

"You're not sure?"

"No . . . not really . . . but . . ."

He doesn't speak for far too long, probably twenty seconds, and I wait, expectant, dying for him to break the silence, unable to do it myself. I wonder if I should tell him that my father may be dying and I need to find this cliff as fast as I can and get back to Saskatoon so that I can catch a flight to Toronto. Meanwhile, we're going in the opposite direction. We've passed Elrose and are heading for who knows where.

"I'm sure I can find the place. I've got a fairly good idea of where it is."

I'm not sure what to say. This is my job, I could remind him. I'm a professional. Bankers understand professionalism. It would not be responsible to settle for a guide who doesn't know where he's going. However, under the circumstances, perhaps it's only appropriate.

"So it's north of Broken Head?"

"I think so." He shrugs and chuckles. "We'll find it. I don't have anything better to do. At least I'll feel . . . useful."

"If you're sure you can find it?"

"Yes. We'll find it."

He nods his head emphatically and squirms his large body, crossing his arms on his chest to massage his own shoulders through that beautiful suit. "Incredible. James Aspen. It's really exciting to be part of something like this, isn't it? I can hardly believe any of this is happening. It's like some weird dream. James Aspen's looking for a place that I know."

"I know what you mean," I say. "It always seems like our own world is so average and famous people exist in some other alternate universe."

"No. He's not just famous, he's an . . . icon." He drops his hands to his thighs, shaking his head as emphatically as he was nodding it only a moment before, leaning towards me, his face too close to mine. "And anyway, I don't feel we Saskatchewanites are average."

"No?"

"No. Average has no meaning here."

I can't help responding with another unfortunate laugh, and this time he does look a bit offended. "What do you mean by that?" I ask.

He raises himself off the seat, stretches his legs, then collapses so that he's actually sitting on his hands. You'd think he was stoned on amphetamines or something. "Well, for example, I woke up one morning last winter, and it was forty below. It hadn't been above twenty below in over three weeks, and now it had sunk to forty. Car wouldn't start, even though it was in the garage and plugged in. The block heater was burnt out. The bus didn't come, so Michael had to stay home from school. I called a cab to come out and get me because I had to get to work. The place would fall to pieces without me. You know? I've only been away three days, and it's probably in pieces by now. Anyway, when I walked out to the cab, there was this brutally cold wind blowing from the southwest. Nearly froze my ears off. By the time I got to work it was already ten degrees warmer. Two hours later it was melting. It'd been so cold for so long that people were positively giddy. They were walking into the bank in their shirt sleeves. One guy wasn't even wearing a shirt. Went from forty below to forty above in four hours. The average temperature in those four hours would be—what? Zero. But what does that mean? Zero has nothing to do with the oil in my car setting my pistons rigid in their cylinders or with that guy walking around without a shirt. If you watched closely, you would have been able to catch the exact moment the thermometer passed zero. But what would make that moment the average moment? It was just a zero moment."

All at once he stops talking, and I realize he is expecting some response.

"Minus eighteen?"

"Zero. Fahrenheit. We're in the West, now. You have to learn to speak Western."

"Zero," I nod. "So, you have a child?"

Like a pricked balloon, he deflates into his seat and stares out at the highway. I'm tempted to reach for my camera, but I know once again that I'll have to let it go.

"Yeah. Two. Boys."

He's quiet for a while, and he has the look of someone settling into the peace of resignation.

"I'm sorry," I say.

"It's okay. It's not your fault."

"Maybe . . . you and your wife can work things out."

"Maybe," he says.

I take a deep breath and change the subject. "So tell me the story about this trail again. Why was this guy going so fast?"

The question rouses him a little, and he pulls his hands from under him and studies one of them. The left one, with the ring. "He was joyriding. The car was stolen. God knows why he'd have picked that trail. Anyway, it was the wrong choice. It happened in the winter, but his body wasn't found until spring. The farmer who owned the land was fixing fence and he smelled something. That's the official story, at least. Vern—my brother—has this theory that the guy was being chased by the police."

"Really?"

"Yeah. Vern has a weakness for conspiracy theories involving the police."

He pauses, and the hand drops to the seat between us. I wonder if he wants to talk about his brother. My first instinct was to avoid the subject, but it's possible that he wants to get it out of his head by airing it.

"So what's your brother's theory?"

He doesn't flinch, but he's silent for a moment before he shrugs. "It's hard to explain. You see, my grandfather died the same month that this accident happened. Probably happened. Like I say, they didn't find the guy's body for months. Anyway, Vern figures there's got to be some connection."

"Some connection to your grandfather's death?"

"Yeah. My grandfather got lost in a blizzard, and by the time the police found him he was . . . pretty frozen. And before he died, he kept repeating this woman's name. So Vern thinks there must be some connection between the woman and the guy who went over the cliff. But there was no woman in the car. They only found the one body. It's not much of a theory, really. But it works for Vern."

I light a cigarette. "Does Vern live in a trailer?"

"Yes, actually." He turns to me. "How did you know?"

I shrug, embarrassed once again. "I was just joking."

He doesn't seem to see the humour.

"Yes, he lives in a trailer," he says tersely. "And he's sleeping with my wife."

I nod. So much for jokes. "And who was the woman your grandfather was talking about?"

He looks annoyed. "There wasn't any woman. He was frozen, delirious. He just kept repeating this name—*Irene*. I was only nine. They took me to his hospital room because he kept telling them he'd killed me, because he thought he'd lost me in the blizzard, and they wanted to show him I was alive. And I remember standing by his bed and him rolling his head to look at me and he said to me, 'She saved you too. Irene saved you. She's an angel. She's our angel, Irene.' I'll never forget the look on his face. Two hours later he was dead."

"Irene?" I say.

"Yes, Irene. Dad thinks he must have been so far gone he mistook one of the policeman who found him for a woman named Irene."

"That's my name," I say.

He looks at me funny. "Pardon?"

"Yeah. I mean, that was my name when I was a kid. I never liked it, so I took the name Ai."

He keeps staring at me, so I keep talking. "I was searching for my roots. My father's Chinese. Ai is Chinese. Or Japanese. The pronunciation is Japanese. It means love."

Sam nods slowly, swallowing. "Isn't that funny? Irene."

"Well, it was. But I never liked it. That's why I changed it."

He nods again. "Irene."

I nod, and we drive on in silence until we pass the next intersection. Grids, he calls them. Every two miles.

"Maybe Irene was his sleigh," I suggest.

"Pardon?"

"Like in *Citizen Kane*? Rosebud was his sleigh."

He nods and smiles a little nervously.

"I don't think so. Maybe a horse. He was a cowboy."

"Really?"

"Yes," he says.

I nod, "My father loves cowboys," I say.

He touches a finger to his forehead and traces a line down to the tip of his nose. "Is that so? My brother's a cowboy."

JANUARY 2nd, 1971: NEAR BROKEN HEAD

"Is THE BOY near that farm?" she asked him, but the old cowboy only murmured "Irene" between the chattering of his
teeth, before he closed his eyes, rolled his head back and let
out the most painful moan she'd ever heard. His extremities
were coming to life—his ears, his fingers, his toes recovering
their circulation—the blood finding its way back through the
blue and yellow flesh: Irene could see he was a smoker by the
nicotine patches on his fingers. He arched his back and held
his hands up before him, opening his eyes to look at the splin-
ters of flesh, writhing so that she could almost imagine a flame
like a torch on the tip of each finger. With each horrible
moan, Luke hunched harder into the wheel, staring at the tail
lights and the flashing dome light of the police car leading
them through the drifting snow and down the black strip of
highway towards Broken Head. It was over the next hill,
perhaps?

"Can you shut him up?"

"He's in pain."

"Me too, but do you hear me carrying on like that?"

She did not respond.

"What the hell are we doing? This is nuts. This is insane,
Irene. We're following a cop car."

The old man moaned even louder and, for some reason,
that made her think about the boy wandering lost in this cold.

"Did the boy have his jacket on?"

All the answer she got was another moan.

"Irene, we're following a police car."

"I don't see what else to do."

"Turn around and go the other direction."

"Oh, yes, that would be smart. Make them mad, when I've got them thinking we're heroes."

"You think they think we're heroes?"

"I do. They do. The old man does."

"He thinks you're an angel. Angels ain't heroes."

Was that true? She wasn't sure of the nature of either angels or heroes. It was something she'd have to think on, and she didn't have the time at the moment. There was a bad smell. With the heat, the old man was becoming all too ripe, his pores oozing the scent of stale tobacco and old flesh. He seemed to have peed his pants. That made her think of the boy again, and she looked out the window for him.

"We're saving his life, Luke."

The sound of his moan was so intense it made her close her eyes and watch the shadows of points of light inside her skull, waiting for the pain to recede.

"He seems to appreciate it," Luke said.

"They'd catch us if we went in the other direction," Irene said. "And what would we do with him even if we did get away?"

"Dump him out on the highway and let somebody else save him. Just 'cause he's dying doesn't mean he has to kill us too."

The old cowboy moaned again, this moan—each moan— more excruciating than the last.

"He's not dying. We're not dying. Nobody's dying. You go trying to take off, and maybe that's a way to end up dying."

"Nobody's dying," Luke scoffed.

The old cowboy shrieked that he wished this were not true.

"That's right, old man. She looks like an angel, but she's a demon. I was as numb as you when I met her, and she did the same thing to me. She brought me back to my suffering."

The old man agreed. The truth is, he told her without speaking, that the only way to be good was to be dead. Good and dead, so they said, and they knew what they were talking about. He had come too far and bled too much to have to be born again. Why hadn't she left him in a snowbank? Why hadn't she left him out there with the dead boy? Who was she to drag him back through the door and thaw his blood so that it could feed flesh already too damaged to be worth trading for another breath? The torture he endured was all her fault. Who was she trying to fool with her tiny charities? Her miniscule morality could not understand the real shade of his grandson's eyes, that blue so pale it felt like an iceberg slicing its razor edges across your eyeballs.

"Stop the car," she said to Luke.

"What?"

"Stop the car."

He slowed and pulled over onto the shoulder, and Irene jumped out of the car and scooped an armful of snow from the ditch. The police car had whirled around and was coming back towards them. She waved that they would follow, and got back into the car. The cop who was driving studied them before pulling another U-turn and slowly heading west.

"Okay, go. Follow them."

"What are you doing?" Luke said.

She took some of the snow and applied it to the old man's fingertips, and in a moment he stopped moaning and opened his eyes.

"Does that feel better?"

He nodded wearily and closed his eyes. "You're an angel," he said.

They reached the top of a rise, and the lights of a town appeared, winking at them through the storm, a swath of low buildings huddled across the bottom of a frozen valley. Despite the wind and snow, Irene imagined a pale wreath of smoke unfurling from each tiny dwelling. This, she supposed, must be Broken Head. She reached over the seat and put a hand on Luke's shoulder. He looked up into the reflection of her eyes.

"I'm sorry," she said. "But it'll be okay. I love you, Luke."

The old man moaned, and she applied more snow.

The police car pulled off onto the service road, passed motels, gas stations, then turned and drove beneath the highway at an underpass and into the town. Here the officer switched on his siren, and they followed him right through a stoplight. The drivers in the few cars waiting at the intersection swivelled their heads to watch the Studebaker pass, wondering at the Indians being escorted off to jail and going so obediently. The wonder was repeated by two or three pedestrians, heavily bundled and hunched against the cold, but mostly the streets were empty, the houses stiff on their foundations. Snowmen watched from yards, their carrot noses dripping icicles.

The hospital, the biggest building in town, was across the street from a row of large, regal homes where the doctors lived, just to be close by. The police car led them into the concourse marked Emergency, and Luke stopped the car a yard behind the police car's bumper, pushing the transmission into park and sighing heavily. The passenger officer—the older one with the beer and doughnut belly and the receding hair—ambled back towards them and opened Irene's door, while the young tough went inside.

"Why don't you get in the front, dear, and we'll help him out. Sam? It's Officer Johnson, Sam. Are you okay?"

"Irene," the old cowboy moaned in response, and sat straight up.

Irene was obeying the officer, moving from the back to the front.

"Good. Good. Why don't you get out of the car by yourself, Sam? Can you do that?"

The cowboy lay back down, groaning his displeasure at the request.

"You don't think so, hey? It would be better. We don't want to hurt you. How did you get lost out there in this cold anyway?"

The young officer returned with a nurse and a wheelchair, and in the end they had to drag the cowboy out of the car and roll him inside in the wheelchair. He was still moaning "Irene." Luke stared into the dash through all of it, never even glancing back to see what was happening behind him. Irene put her hand on his arm, and he glared at her as though her touch might be the only clue the cops would need to put them away forever.

When the old man was gone, and both officers had disappeared, Luke put the car in gear. "I'll back out and we'll go," he said.

"Okay," she said.

"They won't mind us going."

"Okay."

He put it back in park. "They'd catch us," he said. "We might as well wait for our medals."

The old officer returned, and Luke rolled down his window.

"You should go to that farm where we found him and have a look for the boy," Irene told him.

He leaned down and looked her in the eye. "What boy?"

She looked away. He had dull, terrible eyes. "He said he was out there with a boy. There's still a boy lost out there somewhere."

"You saw a boy out there?"

"No. But he said there was a boy. It's cold. He'll be in trouble."

"Oh, I see. Don't you worry about it, dear. I'm sure the boy's fine. We'll have to see how the old man does. Meanwhile, would you mind if I took a look at your licence and registration?"

THE TOYOTA coasted downhill towards the bridge that crossed the South Saskatchewan River, the second bridge to have been built here. Apparently, it was the same spot where General Middleton and his army had crossed the river in 1885, on their way to quell the Riel Rebellion. But in 1885 there were nothing but crude, flat-deck ferryboats that were no better than rafts. The original bridge was finished in 1951. The runoff in April of 1952 was so severe that the ice started backing up against the new bridge, and when they closed it down people drove out from Broken Head to stand looking down at the ice jam and feel all that metal and concrete shivering beneath their feet. The next day the pylons gave way under the pressure, and the bridge was swept away. By some miracle, no one was standing on it when it went. The black strip of highway crossing the river before them was built as a replacement.

"What a beautiful valley," Ai said.

"The South Saskatchewan River."

"I'm gonna stop and get a few shots."

"Sure."

She pulled onto the shoulder and stepped out to snap her pictures. Sam considered getting a breath of fresh air, but he was suddenly nervous about standing on the side of the highway with her. What if a client drove by? He sat waiting, watching her work the camera. Judging by the way she was pointing it, she was not interested in the river, but in the brown-skinned draws of the valley hills as they rippled up towards the headlands of the Plains. They looked a little like those photographs of skin taken through a microscope.

"Lovely," she said, when she got back into the car, and then, "So stark."

There was something in her voice that reminded him of when she'd asked if Vern lived in a trailer—something in the tone of her enthusiasm that suggested they were in the middle of Antarctica and she was the first person ever to frame its image. He could tell her about the significant history of the place—General Middleton, the bridge, the metal straining and collapsing under the force of all that ice. He could point out that there was a park and a campground a few hundred yards away where kids might be building sandcastles at this moment. But he didn't. It would only make the place sound exotic in a different way.

"Yes," he said. "Austere."

They drove on, crossing the bridge and climbing the hills she'd just captured on her camera.

"You know what it means: Irene?" he asked her, avoiding her eyes when she glanced nervously at him.

"Pardon?"

"The name, Irene. Do you know what it means?"

"I . . . I don't remember. Peace?"

"That's right. Peace. It's Greek."

"I never liked it," she said. "The name."

The automatic transmission geared down, and the engine revved to pace them up the steep incline. Peace must mean something too. Michael had once asked him what it meant, and the only way he could think to define it was in the context of war. Peace was an absence of war. And Michael had asked, "Peace is when there are no more bad guys?"

"Are we getting close?" Ai asked him, when they had crested the valley and the prairie stretched out before them.

"Yeah. We are."

They drove in silence, and he began a careful study of each successive grid, dismissing them as they passed, wondering what exactly it was that she was seeing. It was obvious she thought Vern was some kind of hillbilly redneck, and if she thought that of his brother she probably thought Sam was some quaintly ambitious stubble-jumping buffoon. On the other hand, she'd said she liked his suit.

Her name was Irene.

She lit another cigarette. He craned his neck around, noticing, again, the video camera lying in the back seat. "Do you make your own movies too?"

"No," she said. "James Aspen told me to buy it. He said he wanted me to get some video of the cliff."

A few hours before, she had been talking to James Aspen, and now she was talking to him. She took a deep drag.

"Do you like Toronto?" he asked.

She gave him another nervous glance. "Yeah. It's my hometown. I've lived there all my life. I guess it's not that popular out here."

"No. Gwen doesn't like Toronto. Vern doesn't either. He's never been there, but he doesn't like it." She didn't respond. "I like Toronto."

"It's an interesting city."

"Yeah. Maybe I should go to Toronto."

"Pardon?"

"Should I fight for them in court? Chances are I'd lose anyway. I mean, maybe I could win, but not without dragging them through hell. And they love their mother. They'd hate me for trying to take them away from their mother."

He watched some cows chewing their cuds as they watched the Toyota drift by.

"Maybe you can still work it out with your wife."

He glanced at her. She gripped the wheel, not looking at him. There was a tiny scar on the back of her right hand.

"They're so close to her, and with my job I'm always too busy. They'll probably hate me no matter what I do. They'll probably blame me for the divorce and . . . I could try to get a place in Broken Head and split custody, I guess. But . . . that would be like living in hell. I don't . . . Oh, I think this is it."

"Pardon?"

"The grid coming up is Aspen's trail. Make a left."

She slowed and turned, stopping on the approach to study the trail. The parallel paths ran between a barbed wire fence and a green field of wheat. It looked a bit rough.

"You sure?"

"I think so. I won't guarantee it."

And it was lucky he didn't, though all he'd have forfeited was her faith in his navigating skills, and when—after three miles of hard going, during which she smacked the bottom of the Toyota against two large rocks—they came to a stop in front of a slough and he said to her, "No. This isn't it," her expression didn't suggest she had much invested. She sighed and looked off across the slough.

"So. Where do we go from here? Do you think it's farther south?"

Sam made an awkward attempt at a kiss, which landed on her right ear when she turned her head to block him. Before he knew it, she'd opened the door and stepped out of the car.

He stepped out and faced her, the car between them. "I'm sorry . . ."

"What the hell do you think you're doing?"

"I'm really sorry. I guess I'm a bit confused."

"I guess you are."

"I'm sorry."

"Was this your plan? Get me out here and . . . ?"

"No, no, no, please. I'm sorry. It just happened. I won't do it again. I promise."

She shook her head, her hands on her hips, her feet slightly spread in a way that made her slight body look wonderfully powerful, looking away from him as though she were weighing his promise in relation to something in the sky.

She got back into the car, and he got back in on the passenger side. "You promise you won't do anything like that again?"

"Yeah. I promise."

She pushed in the lighter, and took out a cigarette.

"I don't usually . . ." Sam said. "I guess it was just . . . I feel so disconnected, and talking to you I felt I was making some sort of connection."

"Forget it," she said.

"You can just let me off in Broken Head. I can make arrangements from there."

"No. We need to find that cliff."

He nodded. "All right. It's farther south. I think I'll know the grid when I see it."

He stared between his feet. In all of the immaculate perfection of the car, he now noticed a quarter lying on the floor. Still shiny. Not much silver there. He picked it up and checked the date. 2000. A boy and a girl stood on a maple leaf, holding upstretched hands, while a huge sun rose in the background. The lighter popped, and she lit her cigarette. The two children on the quarter were posed like figure skaters, but they did not seem to be wearing skates. She took a drag so deep and luxurious that Sam began to feel a craving for one. The longing had been there all the time, but it was so unfamiliar he hadn't quite identified it. He wanted a cigarette. He wanted to put it between his lips and suck. He wanted to share a smoke with her, if nothing else. He hadn't had one since university.

He sighed, flipped the quarter in the air and let it fall to the floor where he'd found it. "I'm sorry," he said. "I've had a bad day."

"Forget it," she said, and she turned the car around and headed back the way they'd come. When they reached the highway, she flicked the left signal and touched the accelerator.

Her briefcase began ringing. Not the first bars of Beethoven's Fifth, or "The Dance of the Sugarplum Fairy" or "Goodnight, Irene," just a plain electronic ring. With her right hand, she opened the briefcase and then opened the phone, keeping one eye on the road. She glanced at the number, frowned and answered. "Philip. How are you?"

She listened and frowned again. "Is he worse?"

She glanced at Sam, and he turned to the window, trying to look uninterested. Wheat.

"Are you sure? What does the doctor say?"

They passed a grid cutting a boundary between a field of hard wheat and a field of barley. That could be the one.

"No, you *don't* understand. It *is* very important to me. Well, *he* understands. Why don't you talk to him about it?"

That might be the trail she was looking for.

"Well, I'm sorry, Philip. No, but I'll get there as fast as I can. No, I don't think there's any way I can be there before tomorrow afternoon." She glanced at Sam, and he heard the angry buzz of a voice from Toronto. "Listen, there's someone here right now. Can I call you back in a few minutes? All right. Talk to you soon."

She snapped the phone closed and threw it back in the briefcase.

"They're dangerous," Sam said.

"What?"

"Cellphones."

She laughed a bitter laugh. "Out here, you could read the newspaper while you drive."

"That's what the fellow who found our cliff thought."

This observation brought a moment's silence.

"Uh-huh," she said.

"Who's Philip?"

She paused, glanced at him with a look that said it was none of his business, and answered anyway. "My brother."

"Brothers," Sam said. "What were you arguing about?"

She didn't answer.

"I just wondered. You seem upset."

"My father's dying," she said. "My brother called to tell me that my father is dying and I have to fly home." She began to slow down, as though she were realizing only as she spoke to him what needed to be done. "I need to call the airlines and find out what's the next flight I can catch."

Sam massaged his forehead, trying to unknot the ache that was beginning to form. "I'm sorry," he said. "Was it . . . sudden?"

"No. Cancer. He's been battling it for years." The car stopped rolling and she stared out at something just beyond the horizon. "But Philip insists he might die this afternoon."

While Sam stared out the window, she made her call and booked her flight. He considered getting out of the car and walking away. It was only fifteen miles to Broken Head. He could cut across the fields, skip town and walk straight to the farm. It was probably only twenty-five miles as the crow flies. He could be home before midnight, and the walk might do him good. Gwen would not be glad to see him, but Ai would be thankful to be rid of him. At least he could make one woman happy. She could head back to Saskatoon and jump on a flight and be back in Toronto by midnight. Her father was dying, and she needed to be there to watch.

She hung up her phone, put her hands on the wheel and sighed. "I've got a flight tomorrow morning. Listen, I'm starving, so I need to get something to eat, and then I really need to find this cliff as quickly as possible. Are you sure you know where it is?"

"I'll take you to my brother," Sam said. "He can show you."

She turned to him, her eyes full of worried hope. Her nose was too big.

"Are you sure?"

"I love my brother," Sam said. "My brother's my best friend in the entire world."

She studied him. "That's nice," she said. "My family's not particularly close."

"Oh, we are. We're too close. Farms are like that. It's like growing up on an island."

She started the car and pulled back out onto the road. "Okay. Let's get something to eat and go and see your brother."

"You'll probably like my brother. Women usually seem to like him. See, that's what I don't understand about women. You complain about what assholes men are, but nine times out of ten you'd pick an asshole out of a roomful of saints. Why is that?"

Holding the wheel with her right hand, she scratched her right arm nervously, looking down at what she was doing as though she might not be able to accomplish it if she couldn't see the itch. "Maybe this isn't a good idea."

"Oh, sure it is. Don't worry about it. I should probably talk to him myself at any rate." She didn't respond. "I'm sorry about your father."

She nodded without looking at him. "It's not your fault."

—

When they reached Broken Head, she stopped at the mall to call her brother, and Sam said he'd stay in the car. She took a camera with her. He watched her cross the parking lot, and eye the motion detector with suspicion when the door opened for her.

He had to duck down below the dash when Mrs. Tarkington, the alderman's wife, wandered by with a new rake in her hand. He had recently helped the Tarkingtons prepare for their retirement. The Tarkingtons were well prepared. With the new rake, the Tarkingtons would be prepared for the fall. It was June. Perhaps they needed it for grass clippings.

"How's the restaurant in here?" Ai asked when she came back.

"Compared to what?"

"I haven't had anything since breakfast."

"Do we really have to? What about the drive-through at McDonald's?"

"I was thinking of something . . . else," she said.

One thing was certain; he was not walking into the mall with her. It wasn't just her. He didn't want to be seen by anyone. Not right now. But he couldn't suggest that they get something at home. Gwen was unlikely to be in the mood for cooking, and there wouldn't be any food in Vern's trailer, and he was not taking her home to Mother.

"Do you like Chinese?"

She gave him a long, suspicious look.

"Food. Do you like Chinese food?"

"Sure. Chinese would be fine."

They started across town, Ai following Sam's directions, but three times she insisted on stopping to photograph something—a row of identical bungalows on a residential street, a dog tied to a stop sign outside a video store and a pickup truck with silhouettes of naked women on the mud flaps. After they'd crossed the overpass and were closing in on the edge of town, he directed her to park in front of the Peking Palace.

"Why here?" she asked.

Sam scratched his head. "He's a client. From the bank. He needs the business."

"Oh, I see. You own the restaurant."

"No. I don't want to own the restaurant."

Bill Chan. Vietnamese boat person. Thirty-seven thousand dollars principal still remaining. Late with his last three payments after word went around that someone got food poisoning from the deep-fried chicken balls and those rumours ballooned into other rumours that the chicken balls were not really chicken. Just over a block away, Susan Evans, Michael's former grade two teacher and a client at the bank, was walking her dog in their direction. There was still time to get across the street and into the restaurant before she was within nodding distance. Sam jumped out of the car and rushed around to close Ai's door for her. She had already stepped out, looking shocked by his sudden enthusiasm.

"May I buy you lunch?"

"You don't have to do that."

"I insist."

And, with a flourish of his right hand, he directed her across the street.

JUNE 29th, 2000: BROKEN HEAD

SAM THE BANKER marches me across the street and holds open the door. Anyone would think we were entering the Ritz. Considering his recent attempt at a kiss, the behaviour makes me nervous. Suddenly I feel like I'm on a date, but I'm hungry enough that I've decided to take it all as an offering of apology for scaring me, and a chivalrous show of support for the daughter of a dying father. I have to wrap this up as quickly as possible, and get back to Saskatoon. Then again, my flight isn't until tomorrow, so there's no point in panicking. He is lying there waiting for me. Wait just a little longer, Dad. One more day.

I step inside to see a payphone set into a niche modelled to look like a seashell, and I think of that line from "The Love Song of J. Alfred Prufrock." What is it? *And sawdust restaurants with oyster shells.* The sky like a patient on an operating table. And Banker Sam's thinning hair. He should not wear his trouser rolled.

The phone also makes me think I should call my mother. And it makes me think of Philip, whom I just called to argue with from the relative privacy of the Broken Head Mall, keeping my voice low enough so the people trooping by, to and from the washrooms, wouldn't hear the bombs landing in our pitched battle.

He told me I'm selfish. He told me I'd always been selfish. I told him that someone who had always been given everything he wanted had no right to call anyone else selfish. I told him that Dad understands, and I'll be home by tomorrow afternoon. He told me that Dad no longer understands anything and tomorrow afternoon will probably be too late.

As we round the corner, we are greeted by metal tables and orange Naugahyde and chrome chairs on a worn orange carpet in a dim underwater room. There are no windows. A middle-aged woman sits on a stool, smoking a cigarette and watching a soap opera on an ancient twelve-inch colour television set. A few Oriental figures, a little like kitchen witches, decorate the dark red walls. The woman is certainly not from China. Not Peking—perhaps Peoria. There is no one else visible.

"Would you mind if I took a photograph?"

Slowly, the woman turns her head to us, releasing the smoke from her lungs as she does. The sight of the camera makes her narrow her sad eyes and tilt her head slightly, as though looking for another perspective. She does not, however, appear overly surprised. I imagine it has been a long time since she appeared surprised.

"Are you from the newspaper or something?"

"No, no."

"Suit yourself. Sit where you like."

I flash a few shots of the room while she fetches the menus, and Sam chooses a table against the wall.

"Sam," she says, when she reaches the table, and he nods, a bit embarrassed by her familiarity. "I see you've brought us the lost princess of the Peking Palace. Your loyal servant awaits your order."

I consider laughing politely, but I'm afraid that would encourage her. She seems to believe the comment is innocent enough, and that's fine with me. I'm hungry.

"Sheila, this is Ai," Sam mutters, not quite at a loss for words. "Ai, Sheila."

"Hello," I nod.

"Did you say 'I'?"

I nod, but don't offer any explanation. She turns to Sam, and he nods too. "Ai. That's her name."

"Don't get many I's in here," she says, handing over the menus. "Lots of IOUs, though. Any relation?"

I smile and shake my head. She rests her pencil on her pad. "New York steak's the special. Or a chow mein combo. That comes with . . ."

"I'll have the steak," I interrupt her.

She looks at Sam, perhaps wishing an explanation for this rudeness, but he offers none. Instead, he nods in agreement.

"I'll have the steak too."

"Yeah? How would you like it?"

"Medium rare."

"Same."

"Baked, stuffed, fries or rice?"

She meets my eyes.

"Baked, please."

"Same for me," Sam nods.

Sheila scribbles on her pad. "Anything to drink?"

"Would you like some wine?" Sam asks me, and I shrug willingly. I could use a drink.

"Okay."

"The French red."

Sheila scribbles and retreats, glancing over her shoulder once. When she disappears into the kitchen, I look around at all the empty tables.

"The French red?"

"They only have one French red. It's a Bordeaux. Pretty good, actually. I think the Chews, the people that used to own this place, must have bought a few cases a decade ago, and no one but me ever orders it, so it's well aged. And great value. Cheaper than the liquor store."

I examine the orange, cigarette-scarred utility carpet. "So, I'm the lost princess of the Peking Palace. That's why you brought me here?"

He actually blushes. "Sorry. I didn't think about Sheila when I suggested the place. She means no harm. She's been here forever. Since the Chews owned it. I think this is the only job she's ever had. I went to school with her."

"You and the Peking Palace have a long history?"

"Actually, yes. I had my first drink here." He looks around at the ghosts of his past slouched in the empty chairs. "It was Keith Hawkins' birthday, and his mother brought us here for a special supper. She and her husband were separated, which was unusual in those days. She was very pretty, as I recall. Young. I was only ten, so I didn't really register how young, but I noticed she was different from other mothers. She ordered a screwdriver, and Keith asked if he could have a sip. It was his birthday, after all. So, when she gave him a sip, she had to give his guest one." He looks around. "I thought this place was pretty exotic back then."

"Exotic?"

"Yeah." His look is all too serious. "Exotic. Like Keith Hawkins' mother."

A ghost bends and whispers in his ear.

Our meal comes without much delay, and the wine is okay, and, thankfully, Sheila has no more colourful comments. When I look up from my plate, I catch the banker watching me. I imagine he is thinking about introducing me to his brother. Considering what might be coming, I will need my strength. I should just ditched him—literally—and headed back to Saskatoon. But, a bird in the hand. With any luck, his brother will be able to draw me a map, and I'll be on my way in a few minutes.

Suddenly, a thin, middle-aged Asian man rushes out from behind the curtain, charges our table and vigorously shakes the banker's hand, using both of his own. It's a full-body handshake. Sam seems to have braced himself for the assault.

"Mister Sam! Mister Sam! Why you not tell me you coming? I make special something for you."

"I would have, Bill, but it was all a bit spontaneous. Ai was hungry."

Sam motions at me, and the man looks across the table. At first, his expression reveals shock, but then he smiles. "Oh. I know you?"

"No. You must be thinking of someone else."

"I'm sorry," Sam says. "Ai, this is Bill Chan. Bill, this is Ai."

Bill Chan nods, confused. He turns back to Sam. "You doing well?"

"I'm fine. How are you?"

"Very well. Very well. Very busy." He looks nervously around at all the empty chairs in the empty room. The two men stand in awkward silence.

"Things'll pick up," Sam says.

Looking grateful for this optimism, Bill begins to tell Sam how things are picking up at his other restaurants. Apparently he owns more.

"Do you mind if I take your photograph?" I ask.

He smiles a doubtful, pinched smile.

"You don't mind, do you, Bill?" Sam decides to help me out. "Ai likes to take photographs."

"Oh? Okay. You picture all you want."

He poses, smiling brightly.

"That's all right. Just relax. Talk to Sam like you were doing."

Again, he smiles doubtfully, but he obeys, and eventually he seems to forget about my camera.

Listening to this small-town restaurant owner's battle with English, I can't help but think of my grandfather. He was from Hong Kong, and my father hated him for his accent. My father has always been so proud of his English accent. Not that it made people in England or here think of him as an Englishman. Only the Chinese thought of him as an Englishman. Which meant he never had a place where he felt he really belonged. Not that he wanted to belong. He wanted to be a cowboy.

"Bill's a real star of local business," Sam tells me, trying to include me, though I would just as soon stay invisible. "He has another restaurant here in Broken Head, and another in Gull Lake. He's on the board of the Chamber of Commerce."

I nod that I'm impressed and click the shutter, catching, over Sam's right shoulder, Sheila watching with obvious amusement from her stool by the order window.

When my grandfather came to visit us, he loved to go down to Chinatown and walk along through the markets and chat with all the shop owners, and he'd feel more at home in Toronto than my father ever felt, even though my father had lived in Toronto for more than half his life. My father really hated his father for that. Or he seemed to. The way he talked about his father always made me think he hated him, and made me think I was supposed to hate him too.

"Ai works in the movie industry."

"Movies?" Bill Chan cranks the air with one hand.

"That's right."

"Actress? A movie star!"

"No, no. Much more mundane."

"She finds places to put in movies."

"Places?"

"Yes. The background. The settings."

"You find places?"

"Yes, I look for backgrounds."

He laughs and spreads his arms wide. "Like my place?"

"Yes, well . . . whatever they need for a scene."

I shrug and take another shot, and he nods and mentions to Sam some television movie that was supposed to be filmed here five years before, bringing big business to the area, that had never materialized.

Once, when I was a little girl and my grandfather was visiting, he took me to a playground in a park near where we lived. I was six years old, so I didn't need to be watched that closely, and while I was swinging and going down the slide he started picking the flowers in the park until he had this beautiful bouquet. But then a man who must have worked for the Parks—or maybe he didn't even work for the Parks, maybe he was just a concerned citizen, because I don't remember him having any kind of uniform—came over and started screaming at my grandfather, calling him this and that racist slur and threatening to have him arrested for picking the flowers. My grandfather smiled and nodded. And for a moment, I too hated my grandfather for being stupid enough to pick those flowers. And I hated his silly accent when he tried to answer. I really hated him.

"Canada is good. Broken Head is good. Business is good." For some reason Bill Chan is giving me his Chamber of Commerce speech, perhaps imagining that the photographs will grace the front page of the next Chamber newsletter. "I have everything I want. Nice clothes. I very happy. Canada is good."

"Where are you from?" I ask him.

"Yes?" Bill Chan asks Sam.

"Vietnam," Sam answers for him.

"Oh, no," the man says. "Cambodia."

Sam looks somewhat surprised and embarrassed.

"Cambodia?" I say. "When did you . . . leave?"

"Yes. I escape. Just me. No family. Very bad. Very bad men work us very hard making dam. Clothes only rags. Here I have good clothes." He indicates his green suit. It looks like he got it from the Salvation Army. "Canada very good. Thank you, Mister Sam." He throws his arm around Sam, who accepts the embrace with an embarrassed glance towards me.

They stand, awkwardly one, and I can see that there is a genuine kind of love for the banker from this proud client who escaped without his family from Pol Pot's Year One, and a genuine respect for the client from the suffering banker who is facing his own new beginning.

"There is one thing about Canada that Bill doesn't like," Sheila calls, as Sam extricates himself from the restaurateur's arms.

Mr. Chan thinks, grimacing slightly as if with the effort, and then looking apologetically at the banker as he speaks: "Very cold. You want more wine?"

IT'S BLOWING to beat heaven and hell and all the life insurance salesmen who won't ever die and go to either place. Could blow for quite a time. Wasn't that long ago—'51 it was, I do believe—we had one blow five days straight, and when it was over the driveway was under twelve feet of snow and John had to find a path through the pasture along the ridge of the hill and take the fence down to get the car out to the road so he could get to town. He was that age it was that important to get to town, and he wasn't likely to take the horse. But I recall the '51 blizzard was in February, and we only had to wait a month for it to start melting, and when it did there was so much water it practically took the dam out and it did take the bridge out at the river. Ice started jamming up against it, and next thing you know the whole thing come tumbling like the walls of Jericho. Only just built that bridge the year before. When the government's paying the bill, likely as not it'll fall down in a year or so.

Quite the winter, but this one could be far worse. By the time the ice goes out this year, there'll be a pile of dead animals and a bigger mountain of money spent on feed. Price of a bale of hay will be worth more than five pounds of beef. These young yahoos who're up to their armpits in debt to the banks will be lucky if they don't get buried completely. Oh, well. I'm sure they'll find some banker who'll be glad to read their eulogies.

Yep, quite a decent blow. Kind of weather that makes me want to go for a ride. Significant weather, you might say. The history of this country has nothing to do with kings and queens and princes and guillotines. Nothing to do with this here classy whore they call democracy either. This country is strictly a dictatorship of nature, and our history is a history of big harvests, big winds, big droughts and bad winters. The Indians used to keep track of how old they were by calculating how they were born in the year of the deep snow or the year of the skinny buffalo or that kind of thing, and nothing's really changed all that much. Other places have great wars; we have great winters.

I can hear them on the porch, pulling on their boots and snowmobile suits, getting ready to go out and feed the cows, and so as usual I send Young Sam to give them a hand, and he goes in his usual unwilling way because he wants to watch something important on the one-eyed monster. The Christmas tree's still blinking in the other corner 'cause nobody's got around to throwing it out yet.

"You stay here and look after Grandpa," I hear his mother say.

Now I've heard it all. The nine-year-old's looking after me, and meanwhile the blind, deaf and stupid walk out into the blizzard. Wait till the animals start dying and they come crawling for my help.

The son admits the count's off by one, but he insists that one less than he was expecting is just fine with him. Something about how a cow lost its tag and they put a new one in and then counted it as two different animals. Can you imagine? What's the point in having a count if you don't even know if it's right? What's the point in counting if you only try to find a way to pretend that your numbers work no matter what your numbers come out to? Must be the new math. A good hard winter will bury that kind of nonsense once and for all.

Meanwhile, the small one's back and, checking for holes in the top of his socks, reports his orders to the prisoner: "They say there's no room in the truck for me." Which shouldn't stop him from sitting in his proper place on his mother's knee. God knows how you do any work with a truck in a winter the likes of this one. It'll be stuck solid before they're halfway to the balestack. The old Clydes never got stuck. They'd just stride their way through anything you cared to put in front of them. If you did the math—the proper, old math—you'd find you were no far-ther ahead in time or money using these mechanical devices and modern conveniences. But that don't matter—everything's got to be done the new way. What difference if it takes longer and makes everything more of a pain in the pocketbook?

As usual, the small one's not in the room for fifteen seconds before he's got the television back on. What is it? That afternoon cooking show, *The Galloping Kookoo*, or whatever you call it. Some guy with a permanent grin who's a little light in his loafers, prancing about, telling you how to cook food you've never heard of, while he swills at a glass of wine every fifteen seconds. Only galloping that fella's ever done is in his boyfriend's lap. What's a fellow like that going to do to a nine-year-old's mind? Even more damage than watching boys get shot.

I can just barely see them out there by the garage unplug-ging the truck and getting inside, and they're not more than twenty feet away. It's so bad even young Vern, who likes to pretend cold and frozen flesh are a fantasy made up by us Good-as-Deads, has one of those ski masks over his face.

"I doubt that your brother believes in God, but I think he might be startin' to believe in the cold. Which do you spoze is the greater Master: love or wind chill?"

The boy looks up at me, but pretends he hasn't heard the question so that he won't have to ask me to repeat myself. That's a bad sign. Up until last month he wouldn't have let something like that go by—he'd have tried to understand the question so he could take a shot at answering it. But now I'm just some crazy old coot who goes around waving guns at

Chinamen and talking nonsense to himself. Pretty soon they'll lock me away in one of them homes where there's a nurse to hold your wee-wee and wipe your bum. Throw away the key.

So much for my hopes of passing on something to him. So much for my hopes of surviving in some little way in this stupid world.

"Are you gonna roll me a smoke?"

That question does manage to get his divided attention. He drags himself up off the floor and away from the Fruity Gourmet, as though he's worried he'll miss some of the recipe and won't be able to whip it up for us tonight. Ask your mother where she keeps the fresh basil and the cooking sherry. He's certainly not nearly as enthusiastic as he used to be, like he's worried there might be something besides a cigarette owing when I hand him over the fixings. These days everything's being weighed over again, and that damned Chinaman's always got his finger on the scale.

The small one doesn't say a word, but sets to work, forehead wrinkled like a freshly summer-fallowed field, fumbling the tobacco out of the package and sprinkling it onto the paper. His tongue's sticking out the corner of his mouth. When he gets to the actual rolling part, he screws his face up to such a point you'd think he was dismantling a bomb, but for the first time ever he does manage to twirl the paper around the tobacco, then to lick the stickum and get it closed before the whole shebang explodes. It looks like one of them marijuana cigarettes you see the hippies out in California smoking on television. But I'll be darned if the thing don't look halfway functional.

He hands it to me. I give it a once-over, then shove it in his mouth, take out a match and strike a flame off my thumbnail. The expression on his face would make a stone lion laugh. Believe it or not, when I hold the match to the tip, he draws in at the right instant and gets it going. I wait for him to cough, but he manages to avoid that embarrassment and eventually blows out a puny trail of smoke. His eyes are watering, and you can see the sweat beading out on his forehead, and his whole face turns a little blue, but for all that there's an undeniable look of pride in those watery lamps that makes me clamp a hand down on his shoulder and give him a good hard squeeze.

"Any boy who sits around watchin' that idiot box doesn't deserve the name Sam McMahon," I tell him. "Whaddaya say we go on an adventure?"

Well, next thing you know he's backpedalling faster than a rodeo clown with a Brahma bull's horn in his testicles.

"Mom and Dad said we weren't supposed to go anywhere."

"We're not goin' to the Chinaman's. We're just takin' a little ride out in the pasture to look for that lost cow."

"Mom and Dad said . . ."

"I don't give a damn what they said. You're with me now."

"But Mom and Dad said . . ."

"Are you sassin' your grandpa! I listened to your father talkin' back to me enough years, but I'm not ready to start puttin' up with it from the next generation quite yet."

"But Mom and Dad said . . ."

It only takes me thirty minutes of cajoling to get him into his winter duds. I think he's a bit dizzy from the smoke, and so he gives up on complaining, or maybe he just rightly detects that that cigarette marks the end of his simpering and mewling days, and the beginnings of the lifelong push up the everlasting hill—like he was moseying along in his diaper and crawled right into a rock with his name on it.

A rock with his name on it. I like that. You push it up the hill your entire life, and in the end they plant you under it.

Out in present weather, you have to keep your head down,

'cause the wind will freeze your eyelids shut if you go walking straight into it. The boy trudges along behind me so I can break a path—both on the ground and in the air. The leg's feeling a bit better. Only hurts most of the time. Better than all the time. When we get to the barn, there's already a three-foot snowbank against the door, but I push the bloody thing along the track— it weighs about a thousand pounds—and we traipse in through the snowbank, then switch on the light and pull the door closed again so as not to let out the cold. The horses turn in their stalls and give us a second look. Welcome to our humble adobe. They swish their tails as though they were keeping the flies away, and one drops a gift for the same. Do not open until spring.

It would be a good idea to take an extra mount, but there's only the two left now, and they're these willowy half of a quarter things they breed nowadays. Both boys' horses. The son doesn't even have one for himself. Never liked horses. Or horses never liked him. Now, there's a good judge of a man's character. Oh, well. If mine starts to get winded, I'll just have to trust that the small one's will be more rested due to the fact it's only carrying his skinny rack of soda-pop-fed bones.

More rested. Compared to Old Nitro, their entire lives have been one long picnic lunch.

The boy helps me saddle them up, but the questions have started spilling out of him again.

"Where are we going?"

"I told ya. We're goin' to find that cow."

"But Dad says the cows are all home. He says there's just one with two different numbers."

"Well, let's find her other number then."

"But what if there's no cow out there?"

"What if the sun don't come up tomorrow? What if it do, and the sky's black instead of blue? What if my name turns out to be Seymour and not Sam?" He's got nothing ready to come back at me with, so I go on. "We'll have to be careful, but it ain't that bad out there. Earl Withers died on a day worse'n this one. Went to the outhouse and got lost comin' back. Just drifted into the storm, and they found him two hundred yards from the house. I'm assumin' he made it to the shithouse, 'cause there was none in his pants."

The mare puffs out her stomach, so I knee her a good one and cinch her up tight. The agony of victory. It was her who got it in the gut, but she looks just fine and my leg feels like it's been skinned and flayed out on a piece of plywood.

"But the cows are all home," the small one whines.

"How do ya figure? The count weren't right, and I saw one wanderin' off. I recall she was bred early. Bull got out 'cause your Dad don't keep his fences properly mended. There'll be a new calf out there. How would you like to be born in this catastrophe? Not too pleasant. Wouldn't you hope there'd be somebody with enough gumption to come and haul you home? Wouldn't you?"

He nods his head, trying his pitiful best to look brave.

"I can tell you truly, I don't want to go out into this awful mess either, but if you and I don't, who will? The only other cowboys around are the ruined kind that ride around in pickup trucks. You think you could find that calf in a pickup truck?"

"It's really cold," the little pecker's whining again. "We won't be able to see where we're going. What if we get lost?"

"Weelll, if we can't find our way home, we'll just have to check in at the Ritz Broken Head and hire us a couple of girls. Whaddaya say? Goddammit, can you hold this bitch's head down for me?"

So he holds the rope, and I manage to get the bridle on her without any more extra pain in my leg than I likely deserve.

Ohhh God. To hell with deserve. What stupid beggar in the history of this sorry planet ever got what he deserved?

"Listen, I wanna tell you somethin'," I say to the boy, after I've got him up on his horse. Mine's ready to go, and I'm about to open the door so we can head out into that beautiful storm. "I wanna tell you somethin' about your Grandma."

He nods his head like one of those little doggies in the car windows.

"You know how everybody's always told ya that she died of a cancer of the breast? Well, there's no truth to that. She hung herself. In our bedroom. The same bedroom I still sleep in now. Left me alone to raise up your Dad on my own. I found her, and I cut her down myself. Your Dad was just a baby at the time. And I think your Daddy still blames me for that."

The small one's eyes are the size of silver dollars. "Grandma?" he says.

"Yeah. Mary. Your Dad's mom. Or didn't you realize your Dad had a mom?"

He nods the way he nods. With that click in his neck like there's a piece missing. "But . . . we went to Grandma's house for Thanksgiving. Grandma lives in Calgary."

"No, not that grandma. Your other grandma."

He looks away. "I don't have another grandma."

Which, come to think of it, is absolutely correct. There's no point talking to him about what's never existed in his way of thinking. Like this other grandma, his mother's mom, who has never existed in mine. And I'd just as soon not hear his mother jawing on at the breakfast table about her latest adventure to Timbuktoo or the shopping mall.

"Is that so?" I say. "Well, I coulda swore I remembered her body hittin' the floor when I cut that rope."

And I pull open the door and lead us out into that bitter wind.

INTERNAL EXAMINATION:

HEAD AND NECK:
The scalp reveals some hematoma, but the skull is unflawed and shows no sign of bone injury. Swollen meninges. Cerebrospinal fluid has vanished. The brain, badly decomposed, weighs 1300 g. There appears to be no substantial intracerebral hemorrhage. The neck is unremarkable, aside from decomposition. Excision of the mandible and maxilla is undertaken and same are retained for purposes of identification. There are no dental fillings.

THORAX AND ABDOMEN:
In general, the tissues and organs show decomposition, with a distinct malodour present. The blood is dark throughout and unclotted, and there is pinkish staining of the intima of the arteries.

The heart weighs 260 g and appears entirely normal in size and shape. The epicardium and endocardium are smooth, and the myocardium, valves and coronary arteries appear normal.

The left lung appears congested: 350 g. Extensive lacerations to the right lung: 380 g. A large hemothorax is displayed on the right side, and all of the ribs exhibit multiple fractures, with numerous jagged edges protruding into the pleural sac.

Liver, 950 g, is extensively lacerated, as is the right dome of the diaphragm. Examination of the gastrointestinal tract reveals the stomach to be empty, but otherwise appearances are normal aside from decomposition.

NOTES:
1. Blood and urine samples are forwarded to the provincial laboratory for alcohol testing.

2. The head injury, though significant, doesn't appear to be the primary cause of death. It is not possible to determine whether it resulted in immediate unconsciousness at the time of impact. Death was most probably due to the crushing of the chest and abdomen, with extensive hemorrhage.

FOLLOWING SAM'S DIRECTIONS, Ai headed the Toyota out of town on a dirt road that appeared where the pavement ran out at the end of Matterhorn Drive.

"Matterhorn Drive?" she asked.

"Developers. Mountains are beautiful. If you don't have mountains, you can always pretend."

She laughed heartily, and for a moment Sam actually felt defensive. He wasn't sure why. He wanted to tell her that until not very long ago this had been a pasture, and he could have explained to her how the spread of Broken Head across what was once open prairie didn't indicate that the population was actually growing, but only that the families in these houses in this new subdivision had not wished to buy the tiny houses downtown, and so those crumbling boxes now stood empty, or housed one or two elderly people who would soon leave them empty. He wanted to help her place Broken Head and the desperate pretensions of its developers into some sort of context, but he knew it would only make her laugh harder.

"Are you and your father close?" he asked her instead.

The levity the laugh had brought was instantly gone. "Not . . . really." She sat up straighter, flexed her fingers on the steering wheel. "You'd probably have found him charming, but he always seemed pretty distant to us. To his family. On the other hand, he's my father."

She pushed in the lighter and took another cigarette.

"Sheila's not so bad," Sam said. "She grew up in poverty."

"She's . . . delightful."

"Well, she's worked there her entire life. She can't be all that racist."

"I never said she was racist. Why don't you drop it, please."

"Sorry."

Sam was tempted to tell her about the terrible teasing Sheila had endured, how the boys had written Sheila-proof on their hands in a game of contagion tag they played at recess. A game he had taken part in. He might have told her, but again that would only implicate him. It was just something else to be ashamed of in a life that was filled with shame.

He was tempted to tell her how in grade seven he and three other kids had been caught smoking at recess in a culvert not far from here—the pasture the recently erected subdivision had erased had been across the road from his elementary school, which at that time had been right on the edge of Broken Head—tempted to tell her because he thought it was the kind of story that might make her see him in a new way (the young rebel in the schoolyard), but he was just as afraid she'd realize that was what he was trying to do, and she'd think he'd been only a twelve-year-old playing at being a tough.

He would like to tell her more about his grandfather, and how by all rights he should have been a smoker, considering the old man's influence; that his brother certainly hadn't escaped it, but Sam had managed and should be congratulated for not participating in her death wish. He thought about telling her.

The car began to fishtail.

"Wooooaah," Sam said, putting a hand to the dash as though to settle the Toyota, and she slowed, fighting the wheel, and got control.

"New gravel," Sam said.

She nodded and continued on at sixty klicks. "What if I get a rock through my windshield?"

"They never go right through," Sam assured her.

Her knuckles on the wheel revealed the white knobs of her bones beneath her skin. "What am I doing here?"

"Looking for a cliff," Sam said, lightly tapping his fingers on the dashboard.

She slowed even more, butted out her cigarette and pushed in the lighter again.

They descended into a wide valley with a small creek snaking along its lowest contour: the creek that had run through most of Sam's life. As they crested a ridge, they approached five Charolais cows sunning themselves in the middle of the road.

"Oh, my goodness," Ai said. She slowed as she approached them, and finally came to a complete stop. The lead cow lifted her head and sniffed the air, but didn't move. "Can we chase them off the road?"

"Honk your horn."

She honked. The cows jumped to their feet, and then stood their ground. She honked again. They studied the car, trying to interpret the language it was speaking.

"I'll chase them off," Sam said, and he opened the door and stepped out of the car. The cows eyed him curiously, chewing their cuds. He had not trusted Charolais since he had a bad experience with one when he was eight or nine. It was their neighbour's cow—the McMahons' were strictly purebred Hereford—which had got into their pasture, and when they tried to separate it into the corral it had turned to eye them, picked out Sam as the smallest and weakest link, and charged. Sam had jumped to the side and felt the cow brush by him.

Old Sam was furious and embarrassed that it had happened in front of the neighbour: "You showed it you were afraid! Did that old cow scare you?"

"Get on there, bosses," Sam said, imitating the way his father talked to his cows, but he couldn't help but feel that they were the bosses and it was he who was invading their world. He waved his arms without conviction and they walked a few yards farther along the grid before turning back to see what he was up to now.

Ai's door opened, and she got out, her camera raised. "They're not aggressive, are they?"

She had the door between her and them, so Sam didn't think her life was in too much danger, but he was not so sure about his own. He shook his head, trying to look nonchalant. She took a few shots of the blond cows standing on the gravel road, chewing their cuds, staring placidly at the man in the Italian suit. A meadowlark called. One of the cows seemed to be preparing to lie down.

"Okay," she said. "Chase them away."

Apparently she thought he had only been waiting for her to get her shots.

"Amen," Sam muttered to himself.

He charged, howling and flailing his arms like some fiery demon had taken over his soul. The herd scattered, wheeling off into the ditch, kicking their hind hooves into the air as though to fend him off from tackling them bare-handed and branding their warbled hides.

"Good work, Sam!" Ai called.

He turned and bowed for the camera.

"Nothin'," he said, and folded himself back into the car.

They rose out of the valley, skidded the benchland ten minutes

to the turn and proceeded east, pulling the dust like the train
of a wedding gown. Ai had not said one word in many miles,
and Sam only spoke to tell her to turn at the corner where the
fence posts were capped with old boots. A large knot was forming in his shoulders and stomach. He had done this drive a million times before, but never in this car, never with this driver,
never with his destination so unclear, and it all looked different—terrifyingly alien from this perspective. As they coasted
back down the grade into the valley where he had grown up, Ai
drove even more slowly, her arms tense as she fought the wheel
to keep the Toyota from spinning out of control.

"Like driving on ball bearings," Sam said, and she nodded
grimly, staring straight ahead, her tongue clenched between
her lips in a pose of concentration he recognized from his
mother.

"Do your parents call you Ai?"

Her tongue disappeared. "No. To them I'm still Irene."

She didn't look at him—seemed to be speaking to the gravel with the slight annoyance of one who has not been recognized, though introduced many times before.

"I just wondered. I once thought about changing my name."

"Really? Why?"

She did not sound interested.

"Because at the bank, down east, everybody calls me
Cowboy, and I thought maybe it was the name. Sam. It
sounds like a cowboy. I'm named after my grandfather, and he
was a bit of a cowboy. Well, a rancher, anyway."

"And you don't like being called Cowboy?"

"No. I'm not interested in living in the past."

"Why? The past is very hip at the moment."

"You think so? I don't think so. Maybe it's cool to make reference to the colourful idiocy of the past."

"What do you mean by that?"

"I mean, my sons will probably soon feel the aching longing of nostalgia for the nineties, a grander time they can only experience in images because they were too young to enjoy the real thing."

She nodded slowly, and he imagined he could see her perspective shifting, the world tilting in a slightly different direction, the engine humming at a somewhat shriller pitch, the light a little more golden than it had ever been before. As he looked down at the wild rosebushes in a draw at the edge of the road, it occurred to him for the tenth time in the last fifteen minutes that everything around them made reference to the colourful idiocy of the past. And he could no longer stop himself from telling her: "The Broken Head chief of police rolled his new car right here, down into that draw, but he was going in the other direction."

"Is that right?"

She did not sound interested.

"Yeah. The chief was a friend of my grandpa's. Chief Bailey. He stopped at our place to show Grandpa this lynx he'd shot while he was hunting moose down around Eastend. Southwest of here." They'd reached the bottom of the hill and were passing his house. Sam's car was parked in the driveway, and Michael was pumping away on the swing set. Ai's eyes were glued to the road, and she did not seem to notice the beautiful house or the perfect child on the swing. "Anyway, he stops, and he shows off this lynx, which Grandpa and Dad are pretty impressed by, because they've never seen a cat that big before, except in pictures. While he's showing off his kill, one of our barn cats climbs through his window and into the back seat of his car, but nobody notices it. So when they've finished their chat, the chief throws the lynx carcass into the back seat and drives off, and he

gets halfway up the hill when our cat leaps onto his shoulder."
She laughed. She had been listening. "He thought it was
the lynx and rolled the car?" she said.

"That's right. He panicked and let go of the wheel completely."

"Was he hurt?"

"The chief? Just a few scratches. From the cat, who wasn't
hurt either. The lynx didn't make it, though. You wanna turn
just up on the right here."

Vern's trailer hunched in the afternoon sun, streaks of yellowed rust leeching down like tears from each corroded rivet.
"Park over there in front of the shop." He pointed to the
gleaming steel Quonset, Gwen's Buick parked in the doorway
with the hood wide open, the yard scattered with the hulks
of abandoned technology: washing machines and driving
machines and agricultural implements. Between the trailer
and the Quonset rested a huge metal object that looked like
part of the wing of a Boeing 747.

"That's the shop? What's that over there, then?" She pointed
at the rusty trailer on the foundation of crisscrossed creosote
railroad ties that Vern had salvaged when they tore up the
branch line.

"That's where the dog lives. It's kind of ugly for a doghouse,
isn't it? I'm not sure why he doesn't live in the shop. I guess he
doesn't like to be too comfortable."

"Are you gonna be okay?" she asked him, studying him for
evidence of impending breakdown or violence. Her nose was
large, but there was even something beautiful about that nose.

"I'm fine. Don't worry about me. We'll find out where your
cliff is. Why don't you get some pictures?"

She nodded. "Thanks, Sam," she said, surveying the trailer,
her smile so wide, so full of irony, that he was sure he knew

what it must feel like to point out the man who had tried to erase you as he lined up against a white wall with black lines marked off in one-foot intervals. She picked up her camera.

Sam got out, stretched and leaned against her car, watching her snap an entire roll of film. He was imagining some hypothetical gathering of pierced and perfumed bodies near Queen Street poring over Vern's world framed on white walls. It was a few moments before Vern emerged, rubbing the sleep from his eyes and pulling on a grease-marked white undershirt as he trotted down the front steps he'd built himself from those old railroad ties.

Ai lowered her camera.

JANUARY 2nd, 1971: BROKEN HEAD

"What about the boy? What about that poor little boy freezing out there on his own in the cold?"

It did not matter how many times she asked them, the officers would not listen. Instead, they escorted them, one at a time, first Irene and then Luke, to the police car, and sat them in the back. They wouldn't even let Luke park the car in the lot beside the hospital. The young one did it himself, and pocketed the keys when he was done.

When Luke was seated beside her, Irene put her hand on his, but he would not look at her. "Everything'll be all right," she told him. Still, he would not turn to her. She squeezed his hand and said a prayer in her head, moving her lips so that He might read them if He could not hear her thoughts. It was not that she believed He was going deaf, as her mother had once told her, but she needed to be sure He heard her.

At the station they took Luke in the opposite direction, and even as they were leading him away he still did not so much as glance at her, and so she called to him. He turned as though she'd only managed to reach him through a deep sleep, and she could see in his empty eyes that he was lost somewhere inside himself.

"Indians," she heard someone say.

The young officer took her to a small room with no windows and asked her if she would like some coffee. "You should go look for that boy," she told him, and he nodded blankly and went away. There was a desk and two chairs in the room, and absolutely nothing on the walls, which were lined with that material with the holes in it that are designed to suck up sound. How did they do that, Irene wondered? How was the sound swallowed by those holes? Anyway, they could not block her prayers. He would hear her anywhere.

Where had they taken Luke? She imagined him in another room like this one, thinking of her. She imagined a boy stumbling through the snow, a smaller version of the old man, singing her name to the cold.

After twenty minutes the young officer came back and sat down across the desk from her. "How are you feeling?"

"Fine," she said, somehow grateful, despite herself, that he'd been kind enough to ask.

"So what's a pretty girl like you doing out on a day like today?"

He was looking at her chest. She crossed her arms and looked at the floor. "You should be looking for that boy. I hope you have somebody out there looking for him."

"What makes you think there's a boy?"

"The old man said so. You should be looking for him instead of wasting your time bothering us."

"Are we bothering you? We just want to talk to you about your car."

"It's not my car. It's not Luke's car either. He borrowed it from his cousin."

"From his cousin? What's his cousin's name?"

And so she told him Luke's cousin's name, and he wrote that down in his little book.

"The registration's in Calgary. We'll take it to the cop shop and show them when we get to Calgary. Won't that be good enough?"

"When was the first time you saw the car?"

"What difference does it make? You should be looking for that boy."

"When was the first time you saw the car?"

She recalled the thud of an engine beating its rhythm through the wall of her mother's new government home. Irene had walked to the window, and there was the car. Just a big old blue car. The door opened, and Luke stepped out, and her heart turned completely upside down. He had driven all the way from Calgary to the reserve without stopping except the once for gas. He must have come right through this place on the way. His heart was in his eyes when he knocked on their door. He was borne on the wings of love, her mother had told her. That car was his wings. A '52 Studebaker, the same age as her. She did not tell the officer these things. She told him only the day and the place and the shadow of the reason he had come: he was taking her back to Calgary to look for a job.

"And he told you it was his cousin's car?"

"Yes. It *is* his cousin's car."

"And did you wonder why his cousin would lend his car for so long? Wouldn't he need his car?"

"His cousin loaned it to him. Why would I wonder? Nobody ever loaned you nothing?"

"I'm asking the questions here," he said.

"That's right, you are. Why aren't you out looking for the boy before he freezes to death?"

"I am asking the questions here."

"You are, and they're stupid questions. There's a boy out in the cold you should be looking for."

"They're stupid questions, are they?"

"Do you need me to tell you again?"

He smacked her across the face. There was no time to react. She couldn't quite believe it. She sat there staring at him, feeling the imprint of his hand on her face. Slowly, pleased by her silence, a smile came over his face.

"Did you help him steal the car? Or is that a stupid question?"
She didn't answer.

"You did help him steal it, didn't you? Was it your idea to
rob the old man?"

"Rob who?" She started to cry. She did not want to show
him how afraid she was, but she couldn't help it. "We saved his
life. He was wandering out there in the cold. And that boy's
still out there. You should be out looking for him."

He sighed and shook his head. "What's this?" he said, and
set a brown leather wallet down on the desk. She had never
seen the wallet before.

"I don't know."

"You don't know?"

"No. I said I don't know."

"All right. I'll tell you then. It's the old man's wallet, and we
found it on the floor of your car."

How could that be? Was he telling the truth?

"It must have fallen out."

"It was on the floor of the front seat. The old man was in
the back seat. You never mentioned him being in the front."

She didn't respond. Luke. How could he? How could he
possibly have done such a stupid thing?

"Where did you pick up the old man?"

"I don't know. Out in the middle of nowhere somewhere. We
could show you. The boy must be somewhere around there."

"In the middle of nowhere? Can you be a little more specific?"

"I don't know. I told you we can show you."

"Tell me first."

"I don't know. I've never been there before. I could find it.
I think."

"The old man kept repeating your name. He seemed to
have a bit of a crush on you, like he'd been with you awhile.

I guess that's not so surprising with a pretty girl like you. You must be used to that. You didn't pick him up on the highway?"

"No."

"You were off the highway?"

"Yes."

"What direction? How far?

"South. Two, three, four miles. I don't know.

"In the middle of nowhere."

"In a farmyard. There was no one living there."

"How do you know there was no one living there?"

"It was an old house. The windows were broken. There was no one living in that house on a day like today."

"And what were you doing there?"

"Nothing. Driving around."

"Doing nothing in the middle of nowhere? In a blizzard?"

"The blizzard didn't start until after we got there."

"Oh. So you were there for a while? Were you breaking into the house to see if there was anything worth stealing?"

She wiped the tears from her eyes, trying to collect herself.

"We're not thieves! We didn't steal anything!"

He picked up the wallet. "What's this, then?"

"I don't know. Maybe Luke was looking for his identification. I've never stolen anything in my life. The old man came wandering through the blizzard without a jacket, and we saved his life."

"Then what were you doing there trespassing on somebody's land?"

"Nothing. Saving that old man's life."

"You must have had a reason for going there. If you were on the way to Calgary, then what were you doing a few miles south of the highway in the middle of nowhere?"

Irene stared at her hands, still feeling the blood in her cheek where he'd hit her face. It had not been so hard it would bruise her, but she could not help staring at the hand that did it, resting there on the desk.

"Do you understand why I don't believe you, Irene? Can I call you Irene?" He waited, but she would not give him permission. "You're riding around in a stolen car, with a stolen wallet on the floor, and here you were trespassing on somebody's land. There's a pattern here, Irene. We see a pattern. And we don't even know if that old man's gonna make it. We'd like to know how he got in that condition."

"It's thirty below. It's blizzarding. He was wandering around without a jacket. That's how he got in that condition. We saved his life."

"Did you save his life, or did you almost kill him? I'm weighing the evidence you've given me, and . . ."

Holding both his hands up before her, as though he were that woman, Justice, with her eyes blindfolded and her scales raised, he weighed Irene's fate in his hands, and he let the right hand sink, and she knew his left hand was her, rising into the air, unbearably light, like a feather, like truth, like the Holy Ghost.

"He'd be dead if we hadn't picked him up. That boy could be dead by now because you won't go and look for him."

"But there's this hole in your story, Irene. What were you doing in that farmyard if you were on your way to Calgary? You didn't go there to save him, did you?"

She stared at the wall, raising her chin a little to show him she was no longer scared and she no longer cared for his innuendo. "We went there to kiss."

"Pardon?"

"You heard what I said."

"Kiss. You said something about kissing."

She didn't respond.

"I bet you're a real good kisser, aren't you?" He got up and walked around the desk, smiling down at her a moment, then unzipped his fly.

"Would you like to show me what those lips of yours can do? Maybe you could show me? Maybe then we could be friends."

"I'll bite it off," she whispered.

"Pardon?"

"I said, if you try to make me, I'll bite it off."

He kicked her, and she crumpled into the corner.

JANUARY 2nd, 1971: NEAR BROKEN HEAD

SO, THIS MUST BE the end of time.

There's no sign on a post to tell ya, but even if I were to rein in this shivering pony and put one up nobody would be able to see the damn thing to read it. Ride right by and never know they were there. Here. Or maybe walk right by. Here is not a place you could drive to. Or I guess, being as it's the end of time, that would make this a when and not a here. When is not a place you could drive to. Or is that wrong? If time's over, then maybe it is only here, without the when of it entering into the question. It's always been here, and it's always been exactly like it is right now. Maybe here is the only place there ever was. I have always been here, and the boy has always been here, and we have both always been exactly this cold, and no one in the world has ever known where we were or are or if we even exist. We are looking for a calf, but there is no one looking for us.

The here of it is a little vague, if that's all there is to it. I know we're in that square mile I bought from Janson, and we're not far from the creek, approaching the old black willow where we used to picnic, but I know that through intuition more than sense. The wind's howling down the valley from the northwest, pushing us south, and I can barely make out the ground when I look down, and when I do catch a glimpse of it there's only the white of the fallen snow for the eyes to rest on a moment before it gets wiped away by the white of the blowing snow. There is nothing to here but these million shades of white. Isn't that what they say about the Eskimos, that they have a million names for white? Perhaps that's one of the things I have neglected in my sorry life, the learning of the possibilities of white.

We might be riding along in the clouds, the boy and I. He is still back there, isn't he? Yep, I can just make him out. Hunched over the horn, warming his hands under the saddle. Nothing like horse lather perfume. Should tell him to slick his hair down with a palmful of the stuff. Should warn him not to lose his mitts while he's trying to keep his fingers warm, but he couldn't hear me even if I yelled at him. There's no sound, nothing but light, but white, at this end of time. I've tied the horses together so his can't wander off with him, but I have to remember to check back over my shoulder every few minutes in case he falls asleep and makes that his last fall, or in case the rope should freeze right through and snap off like an icicle, or in case I do ride off into the sky and carry him and his horse dangling underneath me like a couple of frozen marionettes.

Check back every few minutes? How do you measure a minute at the end of time? With a shovel, I suppose.

It's a lovely day, this last one. A pure kind of day, and the sort of day made especially for those who need and accept purity. The dead, mostly, I would expect. It's the kind of day when the dead are on their best behaviour: even they go bad in the spring.

But from this time on there will be no more sprouting and spurting and rotting. It will stay like this for forty days—each one like the next, so that there will be no need to separate between them on this last day of all days. And when it's all over, the houses and churches and brothels will all be buried right over their roofs, and not even the cross on the steeple peeping through into the light, and the earth will be frozen right down to the hot, sticky marrow of its hot, sticky womb so that there's not a single seed left living even if the sun ever does manage to melt through.

And if it doesn't, so much the better.

Let it snow, let it snow, let it snow.

Oh, Sam, you old fool. Face it. It'll be cold for awhile, and then the sun will get the upper hand, just like always.

A man needs to dream, though.

By now they might be finished the chores and back in the warm house, wondering whatever became of us. If they even notice we're gone. Have to notice by the time the late night news comes on. Son won't miss that. Then they'll wonder why the small one ain't in front of the TV and start looking under the beds and in the closets and in the cupboard over the refrigerator and finally give up and watch the news to see if that tells them what's going on in the world. Maybe we'll even be on there. If they stay up real late, until after they play the national anthem and the blizzard comes on. There we'll be, riding by.

Goddamned bloody bastard who makes his old man go out in this hell because he's too lazy to look after the herd that was built up from a few scrawny animals by a better man's sweat and blood and handed to him on a silver platter just like everything else he's been given in life. Never had to work for a thing, and so he doesn't appreciate the value of the true suffering it takes to make a place for yourself in the world. At least his son will have had a taste of the kind of bitter medicine we used to have to gulp down by the shovelful every winter, day in and day out. There was sure no riding around in warm pickup trucks, the heater blowing like a bonfire so your fingers and toes are as warm as toast and you feel like nodding off. If you start to feel that way out here, you know your number is just about to be called. Bingo.

What the hell?

Oh, Christ, the boy's horse stumbled, and he's slid off, ass over tea kettle, right into a snowbank bigger than he is, thank the Lord for small favours. Horse is okay. Hope to hell the small one hasn't broken anything, or we'll have to turn back. Nope, he's bawling his head off, so there can't be anything too serious wrong. Horse must've stepped into a hole. Badger, likely. Saw that badger out here last summer and told the son he should be dealt with. Told him it'd dig a hundred holes to trip horses if we didn't put a hole between its eyes. But did he do anything about it? And now he's almost killed his own little boy. Should have dealt with it myself. Would have, if I were not so fond of badgers.

I get down to help the small one—grab him under the arms and pull him up to his feet, even though my goddamned leg feels like somebody's driving a nail into my hip.

"You're okay."

"I wanna go home," he's screaming.

"So does your horse, but I don't think she knows where it is anymore."

"I wanna go home!" he wails even louder, so I lean in close and say what needs to be said.

"Better not cry, or your eyes'll freeze shut. That's why your horse tripped. She was cryin' like a baby 'cause she wanted to be back there in her warm stall, and her eyes froze shut. Couldn't see the badger's hole. Now she's blind."

Which is true, if seeing nothing but white is blindness, and I guess it's as good a definition as any. The ice on her lashes has frozen over her eyes. Not that that should make a difference. Nitro would have smelled a badger hole through six feet of snow.

I throw my arm around his mare's neck to hold her head still and melt the ice with my hands. When I'm finished, she blinks at me with those stupid, docile lamps. Or am I once again mistaking pity for stupidity? They're sibling offspring, after all. It might just be that those eyes are saying to me, "You stupid old man. Why the hell would you want to die out here in the cold? What is wrong with your silly, frozen brain? Have you not understood all there is to understand about white? I pity you mightily."

But why should she pity me any more than she pities herself? Maybe that's all it is: she's asking herself what she's doing out here with a boy on her back and a crazy old man leading her away from the last best warmth.

Or maybe not. Maybe it's something else entirely. Maybe that's actual gratitude I see. Maybe there's even something in her that realizes that barn she calls home was built by me, and she owes me every comfort she's ever enjoyed, including that latest warmth of my hands that melted off her lashes. Maybe there's still such a thing as gratitude in dumb animals, even though it no longer exists in their masters.

I check my own horse. Not blind yet, but won't be long, so I melt away what's accumulated, and use the other side of my hand to wipe my own nose before I pull my mitt back on. Finally, I go back to the boy, who has sat down in the snow-bank like that's where he belongs, and I get him up on the flats of his feet.

"There. Now they can see there's nothin' to see."

He does not seem to find much comfort in these words.

"Are we lost, Grandpa? We're lost, aren't we, Grandpa?" he asks, hoping I'll deny that I don't know where we're at, and so I accommodate him.

"Not to worry there, small one. I know exactly where we are. I'll get ya home and into a warm bath just as soon as we find that cow and calf. I'm sorry you have to be out in this, but it's really the only thing we can do. Think how cold that poor little thing is about now."

And he nods, downcast, and maybe just a wee bit ashamed, and I get him back up on the back of his pitiful and pitying mare and get back up on my own equally sorry animal, and we ride off into the clouds, floating there, the last shepherds on the last cold ride, going nowhere, finding nothing, except, perhaps, a whole new appreciation for white.

THE COWBOY blinks down at me, his eyes puffy and unfocussed as though he's just risen from a long nap. He has one of those chiselled faces, a pair of those pale blue eyes that make you forget what you were about to say. His white T-shirt shows where he paused in his work to wipe his hands on himself. The job was not perfect: his hands are still dirty.

"I don't believe I've had the pleasure," he says, descending the blackened timber steps of his rusty trailer and extending one of those slightly blackened hands to me. The fingers are rough and scarred, and look twice as thick as his brother's. "I'm Sam's big brother, Vern." He is no taller than his brother, but his muscles are larger, his skin tanned and leathery. He also has more dirty-blond hair, a shade lighter than Sam's, and it's standing up as though he's just crawled out of bed. The scent of whiskey and cigarettes is on his breath. Smoky whiskey. Perhaps the reason for the bleary look and the messy hair is afternoon drinking and not an afternoon nap.

"I'm Ai."

I can feel the work on his hand.

"You're who?"

"Her name is Ai. A-I. It's Oriental. It means love."

Sam leans on my rented car, arms crossed on his chest, watching us as though he expects something unexpected to happen. The cowboy takes a long look at his brother, then looks back down at me with a smile that shows every one of his coffee and nicotine stained teeth.

"Is that so? Well, I'm damn sure I've never had that pleasure. Friend of Sam's, are ya?"

"Yeah." He's still holding my hand. I now understand that James Aspen is only a pale imitation of a cowboy. "I hope you don't mind me taking a few pictures?"

"No, no. Just so long as you promise to leave a bit of yourself when you go. To replace what you take. That's fair, isn't it?"

"I'll . . . do my best."

"I'm sure you will. I'm sure you will."

He releases my hand, and I let it drop to my side and float there, weightless.

"Were you planning on fixing this?"

We both turn to see that Sam has walked over to a relatively new car parked in the doorway of the large steel shed, and is peering under the hood. I say "relatively" new because it is the only machine in sight that could be described in such a way.

"Yeah. Sorry about that, Sam. I got cuttin' the hay and never did get around to it. It's just the fuel pump. Why don't I rectify the situation without any further delay? Shouldn't take me too long."

"That's okay," Sam says, taking off his beautiful jacket and tossing it beside a pan brimming with dirty oil. "You're busy with the hay. I'll do it myself." Sam's shirt is so white it's hard to look at in the afternoon sun—an entirely different white from his brother's T-shirt.

"Now, Sam! You wouldn't know a fuel pump from the business end of a . . . Greco-Roman."

"Whatever the hell that means," Sam says, picking up a wrench and leaning over the engine.

The cowboy stands, watching his brother adjusting the wrench. "Listen, Sam, I just wanted to say how sorry I was to hear about . . ."

"I don't want to talk about it."

"I told her she needs to think about this more. You know Gwen . . ."

Sam turns and glares. "I said, I don't want to talk about it."

The cowboy glances at me, an uncomfortable grin on his crooked face. "Well, all right. Maybe we can talk about it later."

"No. I don't want to talk about it at all."

The cowboy nods. "All right. If that's the way you want it. But remember there's another side to every story."

Despite the cowboy's charm and ruffled gentility, I have no doubt of his guilt. At the same time, I can see that he can't imagine himself as anything but innocent. He turns and speaks to me, even though I'm doing my best to pretend I'm not here. "Dad made a rule we couldn't drive a car until we could build one, but if Sam hadn't broken the rule he'd be walkin' to this day. Come to think of it, that's the only rule you ever did break, wasn't it, Sam?"

Instead of replying, Sam leans over the car with the wrench in his left hand, reaches down with his right hand and touches something, then brings the hand back up to look at the grease on his fingertips. He rubs his fingers together, testing the viscosity, then wipes them on his shirt. He might be a Zen artist capturing a gesture on his body. It is beautiful. I take a photograph.

"Jesus, Sam! What the hell're you doin'? Those are your good clothes. Let me do that."

Sam ignores him, extending the wrench towards an apparent target. "Ai's looking for the place where that guy drove off the cliff."

"Sam, that's not the fuel pump. Leave it alone."

The cowboy reaches down and confiscates the wrench with the ease and authority of a parent dealing with an unruly child. Sam stands up straight and looks directly into the eyes of the cowboy, and for a moment I think he's going to throw a punch. I wish I was not here. At the same time, it's fascinating. Despite the depth of the betrayal, I can feel and see that they are brothers and that what I'm watching is all part of some sibling power ritual that has been played out for forty years. They could be teenagers, both so different and yet strangely similar in their dirty white shirts. I take another shot and another. Neither of them even notices. Sam finally grabs hold of his banker self by the scruff of his neck, and takes a step back from the car.

"Where exactly is it? That cliff? Ai wants to put it in a movie."

The cowboy turns his eyes on me, as if he's only just remembering my presence. "You wanna what?"

"Yeah. I'm looking for a location that sounds much like the one Sam told me about."

"A location?"

"Yeah. For a film. I work in the film industry."

"Industry?" He scratches the corner of his mouth with his little finger. "You met Sam in Toronto?"

"No." I look to Sam, hoping he'll help me out.

"You ever heard of James Aspen?" he says.

"Sure. He's an actor."

"No," Sam says. "He's not an actor."

The cowboy shrugs and smiles at me. "Movies aren't my thing."

"He's a director," I explain, "and he's making a western, and we're looking for a location that sounds like the one where . . . that tragedy took place."

"I see," the cowboy says. He walks over to the car and picks up another wrench. "And you wanna put that actual place in your movie?"

"That's right."

He bends over the car and begins to work at a bolt with his wrench. "That's what you do for a livin'?" he asks without looking up from the engine. "They've got jobs like that? You find places to put in movies?"

"Yes. That's what I do."

"And somehow you managed to find Sam instead of a place?"

After he's spoken, his tongue appears in the corner of his mouth.

"I picked him up. He was stranded on the side of the road."

He glances at his brother, who has picked up a small cardboard box from the clutter on the ground and is examining its contents. "Oh, yeah?" the cowboy says.

"If you could just draw me a map . . ."

"You think it's a good idea?"

"Pardon me?"

For a long time he doesn't elucidate, as he is struggling with whatever he's doing under the hood, but at last he stands up straight with the bolt he's removed, holding it out towards me like a dentist showing off the culprit tooth.

"I'm just not sure it's a good idea to put that place in a movie."

I study the bolt, hoping it might explain his comment. "What do you mean?"

He shrugs. "Somebody died there. Maybe it deserves a little more respect than just puttin' it in some movie."

He leans down over the engine and goes back to work. Sam looks at me, but the empty look in his eyes has returned, and he is obviously too obsessed with what's going on inside him to have any interest in my response. Perhaps he hasn't even noticed that I have been broadsided, completely exposed as an exploiter of places and their ghosts.

"We're not putting his story in the movie. I didn't even know anything about his story until today. I just want to put the location in the movie because something happens to the characters that's something like what happened to that man. But that's just a coincidence. It isn't based on him."

"Coincidence?" The cowboy is still working away on the engine, grunting at the effort. "I see," he says. "But the place is still connected to him, isn't it? I mean, you can't get much more connected than that, can ya? And anyways, who really knows what happened to him. Maybe you *should* tell his story. I think the problem is that nobody wants to tell his story."

"Oh?"

"You've told it a million times," Sam points out, setting the box back down on the ground where he found it. He has been listening after all.

"Sam doesn't like stories."

"Sure I do," Sam says. "I eat them up. Any kind of stupid story. But I'm beginning to get over my gullibility."

"Is that so?"

"Yeah."

They stand glaring at each other, having some sort of violent conversation with their eyes.

"What do you think happened?" I ask the cowboy.

"I don't know. Why? Are you a story collector too?"

"No. Just curious." He smiles crookedly at me, and I look away, shrugging to dismiss my own guilty curiosity. "I would like to see the cliff, though. I mean, maybe we won't even use it. Maybe you're right. I'll have to think about what you're saying some more. But I would appreciate seeing it. I really feel I need to see it."

"Like I told ya, I'm not so sure it's a good idea."

Sam rolls his eyes at me. "I'm sure I can find it for you."

The cowboy keeps working. It's he who knows, and I realize I'm not going to reach him by telling him that this is all about some job or even some work of art.

"I had a dream about my father and me driving off this cliff. My father's dying, and I have to find this cliff in the next couple of hours so that I can get back to Toronto," I say.

The cowboy stops what he's doing. Sam's mouth begins to open, but no words come out.

"What do you mean?" the cowboy says.

"I dreamed about the cliff last night."

"Dreamed?" Sam asks.

"Yes, I was driving with my father across the prairie, and we drove off this cliff. I told the director my dream, and he told me he wanted the cliff for the movie. I happened to pick Sam up on the side of the highway, and I told him I was looking for the cliff, and he told me the story. Then I got a call that my father's dying. I have to get back to Toronto, but I really do want to see the cliff before I go. I'd like to get some film of it and show it to my father."

The cowboy and his brother stare at me.

"And her name is Irene," Sam says.

"Pardon?" the cowboy asks.

"Irene," Sam says.

"That's true. I don't call myself Irene anymore. But my father still does."

They're both still staring.

"Her name is Irene," the cowboy says.

"That's right. If you could draw me a map, that would be great."

The cowboy slowly sets down his wrench on the fender. "I guess I should take you there."

"You don't need to do that," I say. "A map'll do fine."

No one speaks. I glance at the car. I left my cigarettes in the car.

"Yeah," Sam says. "Just draw her a map, Vern. Let her get going."

Sam has lowered his eyes and is staring at the ground.

The cowboy looks from Sam to me and raises his eyebrows. "Sam, she's a guest. I wouldn't want her to get lost. I'll take her there."

Sam keeps staring at the ground. For an uncomfortably long time, no one speaks. I go over to the car and get a smoke and light it up. When I look back, I see that the cowboy is still watching me. Sam breaks the silence, speaking very softly, and for a moment I think he's talking to me: "Whatever happened to that rifle Dad used to have? You know the little one we used to hunt gophers with when we were kids?"

The cowboy raises his hand to his chin. "Why, you got a gopher problem?"

"Yeah. I was hoping it was here."

"No, no. It's over at Dad's with the others. The only gun here is that old handgun Grandpa pointed at Mr. Chong that time. The Colt .45."

"Pointed at who?"

"Mr. Chong. You remember that."

"No. What do you mean?"

"That time we went up there to look for Grandpa's horse. Nitro. You remember that."

"No. I don't know what you're talking about."

"You were there. It's an old Colt. You want it? I think I've even got a few shells. It'd obliterate a gopher."

"It would, would it?"

"Yeah. It would blow it to pieces. Do you want it?"

"Who's Mr. Chong?" I ask.

"A neighbour," the cowboy says. "Used to be a neighbour. He moved away, must be over twenty-five years ago."

"I don't even remember him," Sam says.

The cowboy looks at me. "Sam has one of those memories."

"I remember you shooting my favourite toy car with that little rifle," Sam says.

"What?" the cowboy says. "I never did. I don't remember that."

"There's another side to every story," Sam says.

The cowboy shrugs. "Do you want me to get you that gun?"

"That's all right," Sam says.

I see now, as he raises his head, that tears are tracing their way down his cheeks, and he shakes his head slowly from side to side as he stares into his brother's eyes with an expression that is either of the deepest love or deepest hatred I've ever seen. I look away.

When I look back, Sam has walked across the yard and is getting into an old pickup truck.

"What are you doing?" the cowboy asks.

"Since the car's not fixed yet, I thought I'd borrow your truck." His voice cracks.

"Feel free," the cowboy says.

For a moment the starter grinds, and then it catches.

"Thanks for the ride. Nice to meet you," he calls to me, his eyes suddenly softer, as though he's reached another plateau in his grief.

"You're welcome," I say.

The truck leaps forwards as he pops the clutch and drives away.

The cowboy watches the truck out of the yard and turns to me.

"Well, he's in a bit of a lather today, isn't he?"

JANUARY 2nd, 1971: NEAR BROKEN HEAD

IS IT POSSIBLE the geese are flying in this disaster? I could swear I heard geese honking for a second there. Course not. It's January. Or it was when we left the house and walked out into this bit of weather, however many centuries ago that was. Couldn't be geese. Probably only one of them Injun wind spirits that suck your blood out.

Much prefer geese.

Yep, the boy's still back there.

Is it really January already? After Christmas, at any rate, 'cause I remember the boys unwrapping their presents, and Christ's pagan tree's still in the corner of the living room. Ah, there's worse sins than tree worship. Geese might not agree, but they've got other reasons to dislike Christmas. Bit too late for honking off on their winter vacation, though I suppose better late than never is all that counts on a day like today. Even the few stragglers who were stuffing themselves a little heavy on what was left under the swaths when the harvester got through would be frozen solid by now. Deliberating a little too long over the last supper. A little body, a little blood. And what's that you say, Judas? You're buying the next round? Where'd you collect all that silver? Must have returned the empties. Thanks for the thought, but if you need to put your lips to me, I'd prefer you plant one on my other end. That's right. Just like the goose taught ya.

My ass is pretty near the only part of me left that's got any feeling. The boy's still back there, hunched close to his pony to break the wind from hitting him in the face. Wind's shifting a bit, so I'm not as sure as I should be which way we're going. Maybe we should turn back. But I'd like to check that clump of poplar near the cutbank. That's likely where they'd be. Though you never know with a cow. She'll drop a calf on the highest hill in the coldest wind, just to make sure she's truly alone. But she's an older cow, so should have enough sense to find some shelter. Better check the poplars while we're this close. Just so long as we've got enough warmth left in us to get back home.

Likely couldn't hear any geese even if they were up there in the blowing. But it is nice to imagine them gliding over the storm. Who knows, it may be okay once you're up above the snow. If only this horse were a little taller. A little smarter. A little blacker. A little softer in the saddle area. Too long in the barn, I've been. This wind's colder than the Statue of Liberty's pussy in January. It is January, isn't it? At least for the birds it's a tailwind, pushing them on south. Old, grey goose looking down on a shroud of winter and dreaming of Mexico as he sails over my fool head. Never did get to Mexico myself. Missed all that warm water and all those sweet señoritas. And getting my gringo throat slit.

Won't worry about falling shit. Be frozen by the time it got to me at any rate. Might smart when it hits, but won't make much mess.

Yeah, it's January. Christmas is definitely over. Forgot to get Him anything for His birthday this year. So this is what He got me. And it's not even my birthday. That picture Mary once gave me is hanging in the bedroom now. Used to hang in the living room, but the boy's wife wanted it moved so she could put up one of her pictures. Some stupid thing with mountains. Mary's is a good picture: a collie in a blizzard, standing over a calf and howling for help. The collie's Christ,

Mary told me, and I suppose she was right. Blind seekers, we are searching out the weakest of the flock to save its sorry soul. Wish to Christ I was Christ, 'cause in that case I'd most likely be in a whorehouse or a lady's chamber and could maybe get a piece on the side. Evening, ladies, are you prepared to service your Lord? I can see by your eyes you have need of a little bit of Jesus in ya. What's the going rate for the redemption of a soul? Ask Mary Magdalene. Don't tell me that our Lord didn't have her oiling more than his feet.

My mind seems to be in the gutter. Riding's always done that to me. Simple physics, I suppose. Objects in motion. Friction keeps the one essential organ warm. DeWho's third law of whatever. Where was DeWho when the butler was inventing gravity? Not much point making it a law if it can't be broken. Leastways, that's what the doctor told me, just before he burst into flames. Goodbye, Doctor. Goodbye, Dad. Write if you get work. Close the door behind you. Wouldn't want snow blowing into the foyer. All I ever lacked in life was a foyer.

I'm losing it here. Better watch I don't drift off in a drift.

Boy's still back there.

God, I wish there was something to look at besides this white on white on white on white. If I use my wrist to wipe the snotsicle off my nose again, maybe I'll be able to get enough air to wake up my brain and smell my way to that stupid cow. What the hell was she doing out on a day like today anyway? Giving birth. That's a poor sort of excuse. Certainly not one I'd ever use myself, at any rate.

You'd think he'd have realized by now, after having two boys himself, and after being woke up in the middle of the night by the fearful bawling, and after wiping the endless river of drool off their chins and the snot off their upper lips and the shit off

their bums—after all of that, you'd think he'd have come to
some kind of understanding of what I, his father for
Chrissakes, did for him, and of what he owes to me. The
grunting and sweating between his mother's legs was the fun
part, but after that there's not much to recommend the
process. I soon began to realize that the prize I thought I'd got
when I caught her, those luscious breasts and that lovely moist
purse to put one more deposit in whenever the mood came
over me, was a mirage that faded away as soon as the boy took
root inside her. All of a sudden, she was never in the mood.
And so, I was patient. Or not so patient really, but I had to
take solace in depositing in purses that weren't quite so handy
to come by. Once the baby was born, she kept right on rolling
away and telling me she didn't feel the need for me, until I
thought maybe she'd felt the last of my need. And then she
surprised me. With a rope.

That's what he hates me for. I never replaced her with anything warm and filling. Suckling happily away at her nipples
all day long, he was the only lover she ever needed or wanted.
I soon began to realize I hadn't caught her at all; it was she who
had caught me. And now that my usefulness in that respect
was over—now that she had the seed she wanted out of me—
I could be assigned to the far side of the bed, my rifle and
shovel at the ready should the wolf come to the door. Which
is all well and fine, so far as she and the boy were concerned,
but what's in the bargain for the wolf?

A cow.

A blob, really. Just a slightly greyer shade in a field of white
and greyish white. Not in the shelter of the poplars. Out here
in the middle of nowhere. Miracle we found her. I wave and
point to let the boy know, but he seems to be studying the
back of his horse. I pull the reins and prescribe that particular

direction, and only then realize that the horse has been leading me, which means we must already be heading home and all of my efforts to force the ball-less wonder out could very well have been what caused us to miss our mark in the first place. I thought he just wanted back in the barn, but maybe he was trying to lead me right to her. I don't know him well enough. I didn't trust him. You've got to trust your horse, or you end up trusting in your own simple plans, and there's not much percentage in that.

By the time the boy sees her, we're not ten feet away, which doesn't at all diminish the effects of her shape upon his dark, deprived eyes. He sits up straight for the first time since we left the barn, and I can see him squinting his eyes up as though he can't really believe what's there, or maybe thinks he's approaching the pearly gates and had better start checking for his passport and figuring out what he ought to declare.

"She's there," he yells so loud I can actually hear him. Maybe thinks he's the one who discovered her. A regular Columbus. He lifts his bum right up off the saddle trying to make sure he really sees her there in front of him, nosing down at a patch of snow at her feet. And she is there, all right. All cow. All mother.

That, surely, is what John hates me for. Killing his mother and not even bothering to find him another. Except old Molly, who was harder than flint, and twice as sharp. Mary would have been a good mother. Except that she left him behind, didn't she? I never left him behind. But do I get any credit for that?

I get down and reach into the lump of snow the old boss's nose is giving attention to, and that white mound shivers under my hands. It's alive. Praise the Lord, the whiteness lives! I grab a handful of white and pull it up into the too-light world, the second time this has happened to the poor thing in the last few hours. A boy, wouldn't you know. Steer material. Nothing born in this kind of weather has a scarecrow's chance in hell of keeping its balls. Too much hard living to overcome. But we'll keep you around for the sacrifice, little fellow. No sense dying on your birthday.

Sam the Younger's eyes are open so wide he's liable to go blind from letting in too much light. He jumps down from the horse to help me, so I let him pat the calf's hind end while its mother bawls, a bit concerned, and licks at its head. She seems to know that we're not planning on eating her baby, for the moment, at least, and lets me sling him over the horse, in front of my saddle. That'll warm his empty belly. Maybe even get a little friction going in his willy, like it's done for me. Got to look for pleasure wherever you can find it in this cold world. Let that be your first lesson in life.

"Let's get home," I say to the boy, and he gets back on his horse without even a hand up from me. That's the fastest he's ever obeyed an order in all his decade of soft living.

I climb back on, myself. No need to think about steering now. Just let the horses take us home. The sun must be getting pretty low: the world glows like a fair lady's bracelet on a sunny evening in June. Shot of whiskey would be good right at this moment. Even hot chocolate would do fine.

The boy's almost smiling, like he's thinking of hot chocolate too.

JUNE 29th, 2000: NEAR BROKEN HEAD

THE SPRINKLERS WHIRLED, arcing into a million droplets, making Sam's yard the only patch of green in a brown world. Gwen's roses along the driveway were beginning to bloom. Michael was still on the swing set, throwing his head back to make himself drunk with the motion. Sam parked Vern's truck and stepped out into the oppressively bright sunshine. Was the boy wearing his sunscreen? Would Vern ever remember about such things? Not bloody likely.

When Michael saw it was Sam, he pumped himself harder, sprang from the swing, landed on the run and threw his arms around his father, hugging with all his nine-year-old might. This was love, pure and simple: the flesh and the blood and bone of it. How could he have ever greeted his sons without knowing what love meant? How could he have ever doubted that he was loved?

"Bring me anything?"

Sam shook his head. "Sorry. Not this time."

"What happened to your shirt, Dad?"

"Nothing. I just got a little grease on it."

"Cool. Why do you have Uncle Vern's truck?"

Uncle Vern. He remembered that he'd left his jacket lying there in Uncle Vern's yard.

"Just borrowed it."

"The starter's going. He said I could help him change it. I got my report card."

"You did. And did you do okay?"

"Yeah." He looked at the ground.

"Are you sure?"

"I didn't do that good at math."

"That's okay. I'm sure you did your best. We'll work on it together."

Sam gave him a bear hug, squeezing him too hard in an attempt to prevent himself from losing all control.

"Daaad!"

He held Michael's head to his chest so that the boy could not look up and see the stupid tears in his father's eyes. "You know your mom and dad love you, don't you?"

"I sure hope so," Michael said.

"And you know . . . you know that whatever happens, you can always tell me anything?"

Michael didn't answer. Sam released him, and the boy stepped back and turned away, as if to look at the flowering plum growing beside the lilacs. Sam pushed him out to arm's length so he could study him, but the boy would not look at him. Instead, he stared down between his feet at the grass. He reached down and picked up a pebble.

"What's wrong?"

"Nuthin'."

"You can, you know? You can tell your dad anything."

Michael shook his head solemnly, his eyes fixed on the pebble in his hand. Sam looked hard too. It was a black stone shot through with a vein of quartz. It would go well in Michael's rock collection. Almost any stone went well in Michael's rock collection. His criterion was quite inclusive. A stone only had to be pretty, and, God knows, most stones were.

"Sure you can," Sam insisted. "What is it? Is there something you want to tell me?"

"Nope."

"Did you break something?" Sam glanced towards the wall of glass.

"Nope."

The venetian blinds were all lowered and drawn as a guard against the afternoon sun; the private world withheld from nature's prying eye. No hawk would get an eyeful of breast, spy the mute fumbling for buttons.

"What is it, Michael?"

"Nuthin'."

"Come over here, and let's sit down."

He drew his son over to the patio furniture, and the boy came on stiff legs, still staring at the pebble in his hand. Sam sat, and Michael collapsed heavily into a chair.

"I know I haven't always been . . . Daddy works too hard. I know that. That's going to change. I want to spend more time with you and your brother. And your mother."

The boy shrugged and kicked at a corner of a paving stone. "What do you mean? We don't mind if you work. You have to work. We know that. You got to buy things. For everybody."

"That's true, Michael, but I don't need to work so much, and I want to spend more time with you. I want you to know how much you mean to me. If there's something bothering you, I want you to know that you can talk to me about it."

The boy threw the pebble. It bounced into tall grass and was gone. They would not likely ever find it again.

"Okay. I know. Okay."

"So what is it you want to tell me?"

"Nuthin'."

"Michael!"

His son looked him in the eye now, and Sam could see tears beginning to form.

"I can't tell you."

"Yes, you can."

"No, I can't." Michael looked at the ground.

"You can tell me anything. Anything at all."

Michael sucked in a breath. "It would make you feel bad."

Sam took his own deep breath, trying to fight back tears. "What do you mean, Michael? What is it? You can tell me. You can tell me anything."

Michael shook his head more slowly, biting both his bottom and top lips so that his mouth was just a hard line of flesh. "It'll make you sad."

Sam knelt before the boy, his hands on his shoulders, wondering what had come to pass in a world where a nine-year-old boy could feel it necessary to protect his father from some terrible sorrow.

"It's okay. You can tell me."

Michael swallowed, his perfect Adam's apple bobbing beautifully. He took a deep breath and closed his eyes and began to shake. "Mom and Uncle Vern made love." He sobbed, gasping for breath. A few seconds later he opened his eyes to see why Sam had not responded. Seeing his father's face, he simply added, "I heard them."

The sprinkler hissed, turning and turning, whirling droplets into the sun, where they refracted into tiny rainbows for an instant before disappearing. *Made love*, Sam was thinking, Where did he get that phrase? Why did he put it that way? Michael stared at the ground.

Sam nodded. "Yeah. I know. It's okay. I know. Thanks for tellin' me."

He gave Michael's arm a tiny squeeze, not too hard, maybe a little too hopeless a squeeze to have bothered at all, and he struggled to his feet, feeling a bit dizzy. He closed his eyes and breathed. Breathed. Breathed.

"Where's your brother and your Mom?"

"It's nap time. Ben's sleeping. Mom's in the house some-where." Michael shrugged, still staring into that perfectly groomed lawn. "I think she's cleaning the bathroom."

Sam ruffled his hair absently and headed for the house. Michael got on the swing and began pumping himself furi-ously into the sky.

The house was quiet. As he walked through the empty liv-ing room, he saw everything for the first time—the skylights, the fireplace made of rocks collected from this very piece of land, the polished oak floor, the signature where the stuccoer had signed his work. There was the mark where the sander had chattered on the hardwood; they'd promised to come and fix it, but they never had. There was the spot on the carpet where the dog had thrown up. The mark would never come out. And there was the corner of the genuine Eames table that Michael had smashed into. It had taken seven stitches to close the gash above his left eye.

FOR A MOMENT Irene thought she was in her bedroom, and the burning in her eye and back and ribs and shins was where Erasmus Hard Sky had hit her for talking back to her mother, and then she opened the one eye she could open and saw the underside of the desk. A large glob of pink gum had been left by an earlier detainee. Or perhaps a cop. Did cops chew gum?

The door opened, and a cop she didn't recognize, an old man in a fancy-looking uniform, stepped into the room. He looked down at her over his considerable paunch, his hands on his hips. "Jesus," he said, then turned and closed the door behind him.

Yes, Jesus. She hoped the cop was on his way to fetch Him, but she doubted it, so she began to pray, murmuring the words out loud in hopes He might hear her despite all those tiny holes in the white walls.

"Our Father who art in Heaven, hallowed be Thy name. Our fathers trusted in Thee and You didst deliver them. But I am a worm, not a woman, despised by the people. You art He who took me from the womb, made me hope when I was on my mother's breast. You were near me in my mother's belly, and You art near me even now, even here, in the belly of the terrible beast. Be not far from me, for trouble is near, and there is no one here to help, and I am afraid. O Lord, O my beloved Jesus, I am poured out like water, and my bones are out of joint, my heart wax melted into my bowels, and, Lord, I am afraid. Be not far. Be not far. Be not far. O Lord, shelter me, thy shepherd, I shall not want, and I will walk and will not fear, and I will eat at the table of mine enemies, the oil running into my cup running over into the house of the Lord, and someday I will dwell there forever with You, Jesus, my beloved, I will dwell with Thee forever when You pull me out of the net they have laid for me. You will give me the strength to commit my spirit unto You. I will, I will, I will, I will, I do, I do, I do, I do, my Lord Jesus, for You are my one true Love. Amen."

And she kept praying even when the old man cop came back into the room and began calling to her, "Miss? Miss? Miss? Can you understand me, Miss?" This time he had with him the other cop from the car that had stopped them—the older one who called himself Officer Johnson, who she had thought was scary, but who, as it turned out, was not nearly as frightening as the younger one. So far.

"Miss? Are you all right? We'd like to talk to you."

She did not answer, simply blinked up at them with her one good eye, and tried to tell them with her prayer that she was protected by Jesus and they should stay back. "Be not far, be not far, be not far, my Lord, for the devil is near, with his flashing eyes and his horrible white teeth." Now the two of them knelt beside her, and she cringed back into the corner, trying to will herself away, hoping Jesus might come and take her before their fingers touched her. But He did not. They grasped her by the arms, pulled her up and sat her on a chair. She clasped herself to her legs, kissing her knees through her jeans, and kept right on praying.

"Hallowed be Thy name. Thy Kingdom come. Thy Will be done. On Earth as it is in Heaven."

"Are you okay, Miss?"

One of them, Officer Johnson, took out a tissue and dabbed it on her sore eye. "Hold that there," he said, but she did not obey, and finally he withdrew the tissue and stood so that she could see nothing but his black boots, the same as the black boots of his young partner. A moment later even the boots were gone, and she heard them both walk out of the room and close the door and leave her safely alone.

She would go now, she decided. She would let Jesus take her in His cool arms and dance her backwards, one step, two step, three, and dip back down into the barrel with his long dipper. She should sing. She should sing a song to fill all those tiny black holes on the white walls. Her voice wasn't bad, Father Belanger had told her. She used to be in the choir in the front row, and Father Belanger called her—"Irene Hunter will sing for us now"—and she sang "The Old Rugged Cross" on the northern lip of the valley where the missionaries would climb up that dirt path to the wooden cross on their knees the entire way, and she sang herself through all the history of song—breathing, pounding, beating, crying, birthing, laughing, dying—into the notes there in the dark, her mother and Erasmus Hard Sky making a fine rhythm on the rusty squeaking springs of her mother's bed until she told them, "Stop that because Jesus might hear," and that's when Erasmus Hard Sky stumbled over in the dark and hit her for talking back to her mother, and her mother kicked him out of the house and told him never ever to come back again and rocked Irene in her arms, stroking her hair, and told her that Jesus was going deaf these days anyway, but Irene did not believe her.

The two cops were back in the room, and the one who had stopped them spoke: "Can you get up, Miss? We're gonna let you go."

JANUARY 2nd, 1971: NEAR BROKEN HEAD

WIND'S GETTING WORSE, if anything. Horse's head is down, plowing into it, so I have to hunch right forward to get the benefit of its blocking any breeze.

Boy's still there, the cow trudging along beside us, trotting to catch up and sniff her boy where he's keeping my hands warm in front of my saddle. Assuring herself he's still there and still alive and even kicking so hard from time to time that I have to hold him from falling on his noggin.

The view ahead is not nearly so interesting. Only white and more white and more white and more white and more white and, just for the sake of excitement, more white. Maybe my eyeballs are frozen. Maybe the damned horse doesn't know where we're going after all. Maybe we found the newborn just to give it a new place to die. And company.

We should be close. Five minutes ago I was sure I knew exactly where we were. I did. We passed the old threshing machine, there where I parked it the last time twenty years ago, the fall before I bought the Massey-Harris combine. Parked the old McCormick-Deering there by where the trail curls. Didn't I see it? I did. I'm sure. Unless I was hoping to see it so badly I managed to imagine it. If I did see it, we should have crawled inside and at least been out of the wind. No. Never wanted to die in a threshing machine.

Cow's sniffing her boy again. My boy's still there.

We should be there by now. Maybe we're lost. Better find some kind of marker. Christ, I've lived here for fifty years, but my brain's getting so fuzzy and the ground's so white I'm not sure exactly where I am. The creek should be right over there, to the left, I think. If I can get him to head that way, I should recognize what part of the bank we're at. But he won't go. And I'm too cold and tired to make him. He must know where we're going. He must smell the barn. Must have taught him something at horse school.

The white drops away for an instant, and hallelujah!

I see the distant shape of the chicken house hanging there, not half a mile away, across the crick. Built that chicken house myself. The throne room of my kingdom. Cock of the rocks. Foundation's filled with stones from the field by the house. McAllister laughed at me for making such a fuss over the foundation of a chicken house, but why not make it to last? Not like there's any shortage of stone. Hauled enough rock from the cultivated bits to build a fair-sized castle. My little share of the earth. Once, old man, all this was yours. But you gave it away. It vanished as swiftly as it does before your eyes right now, quivering there for an instant, then erased by the blowing snow, the blindness coming so fast that the boy doesn't even notice he's not going to die after all. He mustn't, at least, as he stays slouched in his saddle. Unless he's frozen stiff and can no longer react, even to the sight of warmth. Doubt it. No, he glances up at me for a second with a worried, old man's face, the spots of frostbite showing on his cheeks. Those hollow, myopic eyes. Wondering if we'll make it, and the house not a quarter of a mile away. Have to teach him to pay attention before his delinquent account comes due.

The cow sure as hell knows. She bawls at the blizzard, and she's lifted her head like she's looking for something white to look at. Wonder if she's seen or smelled or heard one of her sisters bawling, or if she can tell by the way the horses are picking up the pace as they balance along the edge of the draw, avoiding the deep snow, sniffing out a gentle approach to the creek. Probably all of the above. Cows may be stupid, but compare her knowledge of her surroundings with the boy's at this particular moment, and she looks like the genius. The skills acquired from watching a stationary box don't come in too handy out here. I'm not sure where they would come in handy. Might be good if you were a laying hen, I suppose. Though I've never known a laying hen to watch television. They might like the coyote, considering he always ends up under the fifty-ton weight. Only good coyote is a dead coyote. Laying hen and I can agree on that, if nothing else. Come to think of it, only argument I've ever had with a laying hen was over her eggs. But that about sums up their interests, so I guess I'd have to say that me and laying hens don't tend to see eye to eye.

The sensible approach would be to backtrack up beyond the cutbank—which must be over there in the direction of that particular whiteness—and go all the way around by the road and over the bridge and bring our bounty home by the driveway, but damned if I'm feeling warm enough to be so conservative at the moment. That's the way a truck would have to go, and we're lucky enough not to be in a truck. Hasn't been the coldest winter in history, but the ice should be plenty thick. Just avoid the rapids. Cross below them at the swimming hole. Only problem will be forcing the horses out onto slippery footing. But considering the amount of snow we've had this winter, these green horses will probably never notice they're walking on water.

We go over the edge, down the few feet of bank, and follow out a drift onto the ice. I have to hold onto the calf so he doesn't slip forwards or jostle off the side. Every time the little fella feels himself going, he tries to stand up, making our circus routine balancing act all the more difficult. He's settled for the moment, at least. It takes more than the moment to urge the horses onto the creek after the cow, but once we're on the ice there's enough snow and it's packed hard enough that they can walk without their feet slipping from under them. Figured. Just need to follow the drift of snow cover. Can see where it's open there, over the rapids, so stay clear of that. Meanwhile, the boy's finally noticed where we are, now that we're right in the middle of his swimming hole. The banks cut the wind a bit, so you can see yourself think, or hear yourself arguing with the part of yourself that's stopped thinking and turned completely numb. The cow's coming along beside us just fine, though she looks more than a little nervous about walking on water. Oh, ye of little faith. Eat this fish and do what I tell ya. Won't have ya hiding behind blind eyes when there's all this white to look at. Don't bother dying, even if you need the rest. Drink this water till you're drunk with love and drown.

Holy shit, we're in the drink!

Dearest mother of shit-kicking Christ, that's cold! Splashes right up to my waist, and I'm holding up the reins in one hand, holding the calf with the other and standing in the stirrups so as to keep as much of me out of the wet as I can, and the horse is doing likewise, though with no stirrups for purchase, but hopefully bottom. He's sucking in air, his one eye open too wide and looking back to ask me if this is the end of the ride. Sucks the balls right up to your tonsils. That is cold. That is damn cold. Calf's got his head up, and I'm wrestling to keep him from flipping off like a mad fish. Where's the boy? Don't see him anywhere. Must not have stepped in. Watching me drown. Horse is lunging forward. Water's only up to the calf's nose, and we better damned well not fall off, or we're stiffer than Satan's three horns. Terrible chill flares the fire in my leg like gasoline on a camp stove. The horse is plowing forward, so he is touching bottom. Should be damned thick here where the boys swim in the summer, and here we are, spinning around in it like it's a day in June. Where's the bloody suntan lotion and the lusty señoritas? Horse bolts up on his hind legs to get his feet on the surface, but it breaks away in front of him. I'm trying to hold onto the calf and stay on myself. My whole lower body's burning with cold. Numbness is the only thing saving me. He's up again, breaks through again, but it's shallower as he drags us nearer the other bank. Now even my feet are out of the water, and we're only in up to the horse's knees. He manages to step out onto the ice, and it carries him, and he leaps up onto the bank, where that wind cuts straight through us and freezes solid the lunch in my stomach and the blood in my heart.

The calf's gone. I turn and see it's fallen on the bank, crying there, while its mother's already sniffing and bawling her disapproval over my chaperoning abilities. There's no need to get excited there, momma, your baby's gonna make it. I may lose both my legs, but your baby's gonna be just fine. May have a bit of a bloody nose to show for the long fall, but no other badges. Don't look at me. You just dropped him nearly as far out of your hind end, and I'm not trying to make you feel guilty, am I?

Oh, well. What's a ride without a bit of excitement? Now we're good as home.

A pale shadow, the boy's horse, sweeps past me, galloping for the barn with nothing on its back. An empty saddle is rarely a good sign.

WOOD PANELLING. The sink overflows with dishes. Pizza boxes piled beside rows of empty beer, and whiskey bottles on the lime-green linoleum counter. The smell—of the dishes and garbage that's been left too long—is only slightly disinfected by the smell of cigarette smoke and alcohol. Perhaps there is the smell of another disinfectant as well: a row of bleached animal skulls is arranged on a shelf like knickknacks. The cowboy explained to me how he'd stripped them down to the pure white with some sort of acid. They are a powerful white indeed. Badger, deer, eagle, sparrow, gopher, cow, horse, dog. Morbid but beautiful. Certainly sculptural. They dominate the room, presiding over it all with their empty eyes. I can't help thinking of Dad. I take photos, having been let loose to document the lair in any way I choose while the cowboy has gone to "do his ablutions."

I tried to get him to take me to the cliff immediately after Sam left, but he insisted that he would have to clean himself up if he was going to take me anywhere.

When I've got all the angles I need, I sit down on the worn brown couch and light a cigarette—there's an ashtray the size of a hubcap, filled with the twisted butts of roll-your-owns, on its own metal stand beside the couch—and I listen to the hiss of the shower coming through the cardboard walls and the cowboy singing, "I want to be happy, but I won't be happy, till I make you happy too,"—a somewhat mournful rendition, making the possibility of the happiness sound more than a little doubtful—and I wonder what it all could mean.

Mean? It's all meaningless. On the other hand, when we get to the cliff he'll almost certainly find what he's looking for, even if it's only in his eyes. I can't imagine Dad sitting in this room. And I can't imagine the cowboy sitting beside the deathbed. Even if I wanted him there, I doubt he'd come. I'll just let him take me to the place I saw in my dream. Next he'll tell me that we have to go on horseback.

I wonder what'll happen to Sam. I hope he works it out with his wife. I think he was hoping I'd take *him* back to my father's deathbed. What would my father want with a banker?

I should phone Mom. Later. After the cliff. Dad will be delighted by the cowboy and the trailer and the cliff, I'm sure, even if I bring him only the photos. The image is more than enough. I'll sit by the bed and hold his hand and show them to him. Mom will forgive me when she sees me showing him these photos. My brother will sit there, watching, without a word to say.

It's not so much that I need to see him one more time before he dies. I've seen enough. It's that I need him to see me sitting there beside his bed.

What if the cliff is perfect for James Aspen? What will I tell the cowboy?

Who am I trying to kid? Of course it'll be perfect. I should phone Lance Taves and tell him that I'm flying out tomorrow, but I might as well wait until I have the good news. Of course it will be perfect.

The sound of the shower and the singing have stopped. Shouldn't be too long. I pick up a *National Geographic*—the March 1975 issue—from the coffee table and start leafing through, only then noticing that, revealed beneath where the *National Geographic* was lying, is a more up-to-date *Penthouse* magazine, some busty blonde leering at me from the cover.

Footsteps.

I jerk my head up, feeling absurdly embarrassed that I might be caught looking into those lecherous eyes, in time to see my host enter the room stark naked.

He doesn't so much as glance at me, allowing me to take in his progress to the fridge before I recover myself enough to look at the floor.

"Beer?"

"No, thank you," I say, carefully studying the photos in the *National Geographic*.

Still humming his mournful song, he paces back past me and down the tunnelled hallway to his bedroom. I put down the magazine.

I should run. Away, I mean. Either direction, to the bedroom or down the road, has been laid down in offering, and I am inclined to make it away. Not that I can't be adventurous, but there is something lacking in the courtship and the timing that all at once makes me a little afraid. I get to my feet and actually take two steps towards the door before I realize there might be a third option. The skulls tell me with their toothy grins. Perhaps it was only a conceit, but there was something so absurdly natural in his pirouette down the runway of his trailer that I realize he may want me to picture him—will certainly allow me to see him—as an animal roaming innocently in its habitat, with no other intent but its beer.

Slowly, reassuring myself, I sit back down and pick up the *National Geographic*.

Sure enough, he returns fully dressed in more traditional cowboy garb—a shirt with a yoke and pearl buttons and a pair of clean denim jeans—carrying a large shoebox and making no reference to his earlier appearance. I feel as though I've passed some sort of test.

"Can we stop and take Sam's jacket to him on our way?" he asks, taking it off the hook by the door. Sam left the jacket lying in the yard, and I picked it up and brought it in the trailer.

"Sure. I guess."

"Good. Might as well take this over to him at the same time."

He opens the shoebox—actually a boot box: a picture of the cowboy boots it once contained is printed on the top—to reveal a large gun. "Grandpa's. Colt .45. It's a serious gun. Make a hole in you the size of a basketball."

"It's . . . big," I say.

"Yeah, they always look bigger in life than they do on television. Or in the movies. Beautiful, isn't it? Means a good deal to me, this gun. It's the only thing of Grandpa's I have. But I get the feelin' Sam wants it, so I figure we'd better take it over to him."

He puts the gun back in the box, lays it down on the kitchen counter, takes out his fixings from his breast pocket and starts to roll himself a cigarette.

"Do you think that's a good idea?" I finally ask.

"Smokin'? They say it'll kill ya."

"What does Sam want a gun for? He's a bit . . . unstable right now, don't you think?"

He licks the rolling paper. "You're not sayin' you think Sam might shoot somebody?"

"Why do you think he mentioned the gun?"

"Who would he shoot?"

"I don't know. Himself."

He puts the cigarette in his mouth, moistening it, and draws it out a little too slowly, his eyes on mine the entire time. "Are you serious? Sam? But he's got so much to live for. Nah. If he meant he was gonna shoot anybody, it was Gwen's man friend."

He smiles provocatively.

"Maybe."

"Well, that wouldn't be such a bad thing, would it? Maybe that's what he should do." He lights his cigarette, shakes out the match.

"Pardon?"

"Well, why not? If there's anyone the world wouldn't miss, it's that fellow." He's not smiling.

"I'm . . . not sure I understand."

"What's to understand? I know him. He'd be nobody's loss."

"Is that so?"

"Sam didn't tell you anything about him?"

"No. No. No."

He taps his cigarette ash onto his floor. Avoiding his eyes, I watch the ash flutter to the dirty linoleum.

"Just as well. It's a sordid story. That's what they call it, don't they? Sordid. Anyway, it's not mine to tell, so we should get going."

He picks up the box from the counter.

"I don't think we should take that to him."

"Oh, don't you worry about it. I'm only stringin' you along. I don't think shootin' anybody has ever entered Sam's head. He's more attracted to monetary solutions. It was Grandpa's gun, and your dream of the cliff reminded him of Grandpa, and it was supposed to be left to Sam and I ended up with it, and he's in a bit of a state right now so he's got a little sentimental about such things. He's got Grandpa's name, you see, so he's the rightful inheritor. We'll take it over to him."

And he opens the door and steps outside. There's nothing I can do but follow. Nothing else occurs to me, at any rate.

"My dream reminded him of your grandpa?"

"Yeah. I believe my grandpa killed a person or two with this gun," he says as we walk towards the car.

"Why do you say that?"

"I can't say for sure. He just . . . said things. About how maybe sometime in his life he'd done some things that maybe he shouldn't have done, but that he could never take 'em back and so there was no point goin' through life worryin' and regrettin', 'cause you just had to go on with livin' or go crazy. You want me to drive?"

"No. I don't think we should take that to Sam."

"Why not?" He slouches against the car, waiting for my excuses, and I feel like a child. I take his picture, and he doesn't object.

"We should leave them alone for a while. They'll be talking. I need to get to that cliff. I need to get back to Toronto."

The cowboy shrugs. "It'll only take a second. What's the big deal?"

I shrug and take another picture.

"Don't you worry," he says. "You'll be at your cliff inside the hour. You want me to drive?"

"I'll drive," I say.

"If you insist," he says, and gets into the car.

GWEN WAS in the kitchen, sitting at the table, wearing her sweatpants and the "World's Best Mom" yellow T-shirt that Michael had given her for Christmas two years before, a mug of steaming something in front of her. Maybe it was true. Maybe she really had come straight home and picked up the kids from Vern's and put Ben to bed and cleaned the bathroom. Sam stood in the doorway, and they glared at each other for a moment before she broke the silence.

"What do you want?"

He walked to the counter and lifted his perfect teapot, but it was empty. What was she drinking from her favourite mug? Coffee at this time of the day kept her awake. A hot toddy in the middle of the afternoon, in the middle of the summer? She did that sometimes lately, with the intention of calming her mind, apparently, though alcohol generally made her even more anxious. She didn't have the constitution of a drinker— of a Vern—though that's probably where she'd recently learned to trust in her hot toddies. Not that hot toddies were Vern's drink. He preferred whiskey. But, when in Rome, eat pizza, even if you insist on ordering it with bacon. Sam sat down across the oak table from her. He'd had it built especially for this room, big enough to sit the entire extended family at Christmas.

"What happened to you?" she said, gesturing at his shirt with a single accusing finger.

"Just had a chat with Vern."

The corner of her mouth curled slightly, and she sipped

from her mug, blowing at it first to cool it. "I'm sure he looks much worse."

"I think you're wrong. I don't think he's in love with you. I don't think he'd know what love was if it . . . ." He fished for some absurd embodiment of love, then gave it up and let the sentence die. Her eyes burned blue. She flicked her hair behind her ear.

"You mean he's not interested in replacing you? No. I'm not interested in having anyone replace you. Why would I want to go through this hell again?" She waved her hands in a melodramatic flourish, as though she meant this kitchen were hell. His perfect kitchen, with its stainless steel appliances, with its black ceramic floor that shone so gloriously you could see the future in the tiles.

"Who the hell are you trying to kid? You know what a fraud he is. I have sat here at this very table and listened to you ridicule him. You forget that I know you too well. I remember the first time you met him. Remember? That night at the party out at Paradise? Remember? Hate at first sight. You said he was so phony and manipulative it made you want to puke. Remember? You actually told me that my big brother Vern made you want to puke. That was the word you used. Puke. That's one of the reasons I fell in love with you. Did you know that?"

"He treats me like a queen."

"Oh. He does. And is that what you think you are? A queen?"

She did not respond.

Sam crossed his arms and continued, "I just talked to Michael too."

"My, isn't that a novelty."

"He had something he needed to tell me. Something that really upset him."

At first, he could see he had touched her, pierced her armour, scratched a fingernail down her soul, but she took another sip and raised her nose defiantly. It was a nose of almost perfect dimensions.

"He told me too. We had a long talk. I told him there was nothing to be upset about. It's all very natural. What did you say to him? I hope you didn't make it out to be something sordid."

"No," Sam said. "Love is a beautiful thing."

"What would you know about love?"

Sam reached out and picked up her mug and, with a casual flick of his wrist, tossed it on the floor. It bounced but, miraculously, didn't break.

"I said, love is a beautiful thing."

She rose from her chair, picked up the cup, put it in the dishwasher, fetched the dishcloth and began to wipe up the floor.

"I hate you," she said.

And she did. He could see that she did.

"You hate yourself," Sam said.

She stopped wiping to look him in the eye. "Maybe. Maybe that's it. You made me hate myself, and I want to learn to love myself again. He's teaching me."

"Well, I guess he'd know, 'cause he's never been in love with anyone but himself."

She wrung out the cloth in the sink and draped it over the faucet.

"Get out of my house."

She said it calmly, almost as though it were a request, but her hands, clutching one another, said it wasn't.

"Your house?"

"My house."

He looked at the ceramic tile, the stainless steel fridge. "What about the boys?"

"Oh? You are aware we have children? I wasn't sure. The way things are going, you can bet they'll grow up to hate you just like you hate your father, just like he hated his father."

"I don't hate my father," Sam said.

In the silence that followed this pronouncement, Sam became all too aware of the sound of the kitchen sink dripping in a rough half-beat to his heart. She'd asked him to change the washer about fifty times, and he'd told her that it worked fine if you applied a little muscle. She'd said that when he applied muscle she couldn't turn on the tap. He'd told her to call a plumber. She'd said she'd ask Vern.

Sam marched to the sink, brushing past her, and torqued the cold tap, closing off the drip.

"You're right. It's all my fault. Everything's my fault. The death of love. The dissolution of the family. The desecration of the planet. Your father's bankruptcy. It's all my fault. I'm just glad I can bear up to the responsibility."

Wearily, she walked to the table and sat down. "Please don't bring my father into this ugliness," she said. "It has nothing to do with my father."

She flicked that lock of hair behind her ear. He shook his head. "How can you say that? For eight years you've blamed me for his failure, and now you're sleeping with my brother, and you want a divorce, but it has nothing to do with your father?"

"No," she said, looking at her fingernails. "I don't blame you for . . . what happened to him. I mean, I do. You let them do it. It was his whole life, and you did nothing . . ."

"Don't!"

She stared at the table, silenced. "I'm sorry. I know there was nothing you could have done. I know it was beyond you. But you could have walked away."

Sam swallowed. "I could have walked away."

"You could have. But that's not what this is about. It's too easy for you to hang our hopeless marriage on my father. It's handy. But it's not his fault. It's not my father's fault."

"I never said it was his fault."

"Oh, but that's what you implied. That's what you're telling yourself."

"I am, am I? And whose fault is it?"

She sighed and shrugged. "I suppose it's mine. I've got the scarlet A on my forehead to prove it, don't I? But it's yours too, Sam. You just go blindly along, never paying any attention to the damage you're doing. You excuse yourself from any responsibility because you've gotta keep your eyes on the numbers. On the dollars and cents. That's all that's really important, isn't it?"

"Someone has to pay attention to the dollars and cents. It *is* important."

"No, it's not. It's not important at all. It's just a fantasy that the big bad world made up to make it okay for people like you not to pay attention to anything that's really important."

"Is that so?"

"Yes, it is so."

"Well, I guess it's not surprising that someone who's never had to worry about a dollar or a cent her entire life would think that way."

She stretched her arms out on the table so that she could study the freckles on the backs of her hands. "You're not a safe place to be, Sam. Please, leave me alone."

He turned from her and watched the tap as a drop slowly bloomed. "I'm not a safe—and he is? And being a single mother is? We need to talk about this."

"I tried to talk, and you didn't want to. Now I don't want

to talk anymore. I want a separation. I want a divorce. What else needs to be said?"

He strangled the drop to nothing. "You said you'd called a lawyer?"

The words had not even left his lips when the doorbell rang. For a moment Sam imagined him there at the door—the lawyer, with his black briefcase hanging by his side. Gwen listened too, and it rang again, and together they followed the higher note of the *ding* down the scale to the lower *dong*, her eyes meeting his, and there was a moment's connection as they both wondered who had come to interrupt their terrible ballet.

"Who's that?" Gwen said.

Sam shook his head. "I have no idea."

He pictured Irene.

Ai.

Whatever her name was.

"I'll get it," Gwen said, and off she went.

"Just leave it," Sam said. "The blinds are closed. They don't know we're home."

"Michael's in the yard."

Sam watched her going, her step firm on the hardwood. She was his wife. They had a visitor, and she was answering the door. He ran his fingers through his hair and took one last look around him.

How DID I miss this place when I passed it with Sam? It's dug into the side of the valley, so it's partly hidden when you're coming the other direction: down the hill and into the valley. The house is Palm Springs modern, and it looks perfect here, the flat roof matching the horizon, but for some reason the prairie wasn't good enough for the landscaping. It's English country garden. Perhaps the house is Sam's and the garden is his wife's? A swing slowly pendulums, some ghost dangling there, regretting some sorrow.

"I'll take . . . the things to the door," I tell the cowboy, and he lifts his bushy eyebrows.

"No. I'd better do it."

He strides along a path of paving stones, the jacket draped over his shoulder and the shoebox under his arm like a dozen roses. At first, I think I'll stay in the car, but I can't resist getting a few shots, so I step out into that incredibly bright sunlight. I take a photograph, and another, purposely overexposing this one, and another. The cowboy has paused on the doorstep, as if he's actually unsure about something. At last, he reaches for the handle, hesitates for an instant, lifts his hand to knock, thinks better of his fist and presses the bell.

"Avon calling," he says, glancing back at me.

No one comes. He taps his boot on the paving stone, presses the button again. At last, the door opens, revealing a woman in sweatpants and a dirty yellow T-shirt that declares her the best Mom in the world. I remember her from high school. I know her from work. She's a little younger than I am, and prettier. She's blonde and blue-eyed.

"Oh, hello, Gwen. Is Sam around?"

She ponders the cowboy's presence there before her, ponders the box under his arm, and eventually notices me standing here with my camera half-raised, as if in salute. "Who's she?" she says, and I am about to stammer something, when I realize I have forgotten the answer.

The cowboy grins a bit awkwardly. "Oh, I'm sorry. Gwen. This is Ai, a friend of Sam's."

She studies me, waiting for a confirmation or confession, and flicks a lock of her hair behind her ear. My mouth is open. I close it to speak. "I gave Sam a ride."

The stare continues, but she offers no notion of response, and so I feel forced to go on with my explanation. "I'm looking for a location for a film. I'm in the film industry. We're making a western."

The cowboy nods to verify this statement.

Sam appears behind the woman and looks out at his brother, then at me.

"Hi, Sam," the cowboy says. "Here's your jacket, and here's Grandpa's gun."

He distinguishes the offerings by lifting the appropriate hand as he names its holdings. Gwen turns and walks away, disappearing back into the house.

"I didn't—this has nothing to do with me," Sam turns and pleads his innocence to his retreating wife. He runs a hand through his thinning hair, looking accusingly from the cowboy to me, as though our appearance has just snapped the final thread of their marriage. "Where's Michael?" he says, craning his neck, trying to see around corners. The cowboy looks around.

"Didn't notice him."

He drapes the jacket over Sam's shoulder and holds the shoebox out to him. Sam bats the box out of his hand, and it falls to the ground, the gun spilling out and skittering across the doorstep.

"Jesus, Sam. That's no way to treat Grandpa's gun." The cowboy kneels and picks it up, examining it for damage before he looks up to where Sam stands looking down at him. "Do you want it or don't you?"

"Go away," Sam says, and he steps back and closes the door.

The cowboy eyes me, wondering what to do now. I should walk to the car and get in and be gone, but I stand there, taking it all in, the way someone might watch someone else's house burning slowly to the ground. There is a hypnotic beauty in fire that cannot be matched by any face; a beauty that is impossible to capture on film. Perhaps it is the heat and the smoke. I take a picture. The cowboy tries the door, but finds it locked. He turns and looks directly at me one more time, challenging me for my stupid opinion.

"I don't think he wants to shoot you," I say.

He turns his back to me. I see his body clench, and he kicks the door. It doesn't give.

"Vern?" I say.

He braces himself a little more deeply, lowering his centre of gravity, and kicks again. The door doesn't give.

"Vern, why don't we . . ."

He kicks a third time, but before he can try a fourth the door opens and Sam steps out to face him. "What the hell do you think you're doing?"

There is the sound of a young child crying.

The cowboy hands Sam the gun. "You asked for it. Here it is. Put it in a safe place where the kids can't reach it. You gotta be careful with guns."

Sam raises the gun and points it at Vern's face. "Get out of here!"

That reaches me. I'm about to dash for the car, when I see a young boy standing near the hedge, watching us from beside the old pickup truck. He isn't crying. He's just watching, in awe, as the world comes rushing for him. He looks into my eyes, and I cannot take a step.

"You said you wanted the gun," I hear the cowboy say, "and I brought it to you."

"I said get out of here."

"There's a boy here," I tell them. "Could somebody introduce me to him?"

Neither of them responds, but when I look back I see they have stopped their performance to look at us. The gun is still in Sam's hand, but is dangling at his side.

"What are you doing?" the boy asks.

Both men shake their heads.

"I was just givin' your dad an old gun," the cowboy says. "It was your great grandpa's. Great Grandpa Sam."

Sam raises the gun to show it to his son.

"You're not gonna shoot Uncle Vern, are you, Dad?" the boy asks.

"No . . . nobody's gonna shoot anybody, Michael. Why don't you come inside and . . . watch television or something."

"Who's she?" the boy points at me.

No one answers for me.

"I'm Ai. I'm looking for a cliff to put in a movie. I look for places for movies."

"You're who?"

"Ai. My name is Ai."

He makes a funny face. "A real movie?"

"A real movie."

"Sweet. I saw *Independence Day*. It was pretty good."

"Was it? I haven't seen it yet."

"It's not bad. I've seen better."

"Michael," Sam's wife appears in the doorway, an even younger child burrowing his face into the hollow of her shoulder, "come on inside." She looks at me accusingly.

"Are you making a movie about Uncle Vern and Dad?"

"No," I shake my head. "I'm not making a movie about anybody real."

"I'm trying to get him into the house," Sam explains to his wife. "And I've asked Vern and his friend to leave us alone."

"My friend? Sam just introduced us, didn't he, Ai?"

"Put that thing away," Gwen motions to the gun in Sam's hand. "Come here, Michael. Come inside."

"He's okay, Gwen," the cowboy says.

"Come inside, Michael."

The boy gives me one more look, still trying to verify whether I'm real, and he leaves without saying goodbye, walking past his mother and disappearing into the house. Sam stands at his doorway, shaking his head.

"Please go away," he says to his brother and to me.

"And you go away too," the woman says. The three-year-old clings to her shoulder, hiding his face. "Your suitcases are in the trunk. The keys are in the ignition. But don't take the car. I need it."

She closes the door firmly.

Sam glares at us. He looks down at the gun in his hand, then hurls it at the hedge. The cowboy cringes slightly as it flies. When it's landed and bounced and come to rest against the delphiniums, he turns to his brother, shaking his head. "You shouldn't have done that."

The cowboy walks over to retrieve the gun, while Sam

marches to the car and opens the trunk and pulls out the two suitcases.

"Do you want . . . a ride somewhere?" I ask him, as I walk to my car, but he only glares at me.

He picks up the suitcases and throws them in the back of the pickup truck, gets into the truck and tries to start it. The starter grinds. He tries again. The starter grinds. He tries again. The starter grinds.

"I gotta change that starter," the cowboy says.

Sam gets out of the truck and starts to push past the cowboy, but the cowboy stops him by placing both hands on his shoulders, one of the hands still holding the gun. "I'm sorry, Sam."

The banker shrugs off the cowboy without even looking at him. He takes the suitcases from the back of the truck, and starts walking down the driveway.

"I can give you a ride," I call.

He doesn't look back.

"I guess you're right. I guess nobody's gonna get shot today," the cowboy says. He looks down at the gun and spins the magazine playfully.

I get into the car.

I start the car, but before I can press the brake and get it in gear the cowboy has slipped in the passenger door. "Let's go see a cliff," he says.

I consider telling him to get out. "Do you really think we should take the gun?"

He looks at it as though he'd forgotten he was carrying it. "Better not leave it here. Wouldn't want Michael to find it," he says.

How can I argue? I put the car in gear.

I drive slowly past Sam, but he doesn't even glance our way.

JANUARY 2nd, 1971: NEAR BROKEN HEAD

NOTHING TO DO but leave the calf on the ground and wade back in the water and search for the boy—dive in after him and dive again and again and again and do my best to find him before I pass out and get swept away under the ice. Before that. Which should not take long. My teeth are chattering like a telegraph machine sending me an invitation to my own funeral, and I'm still standing at the edge, looking into the black water. Never would have believed it could happen. Water flowing down from the rapids kept enough energy to cut a secret channel there under the surface, I suppose. Kept it thin, when by all rights it should have been at least two feet thick. Snow insulated it from the cold air so it could keep bubbling through, even over deep water that generally runs so still. Never would have believed it.

No reflection. Looks like oil. Not that I have any desire to see myself in my present state. Alive. Or at least partly alive. I can't feel my fingers or ears or cheeks, and even my bad leg's going numb, so there's that to be said for the experience.

Just need to make myself take the one step, at least fumble around for him. But let's face the face, there's no saving him now. He's gone. It can happen that fast. There's no angels up above to announce such moments, but he's definitely gone, and I'm standing here staring into his grave without one good word to say for my own eulogy.

I ought to go in and be done with it. If I just step right in and hold my breath long enough to float away under the ice, it won't take a second and I'll be down there with him, looking him in the blue of the eyes, that young face spattered across the nose with freckles, his cowlick frozen on his forehead, and there won't be any turning back for either of us, nothing to come between us, no survival instinct to save me from a fate worse than worms, which would be having to face my son and my daughter-in-law.

All I have to do is take one step. One long step. Just move the muscles the same way I've moved them a million times before, and I'll never have to do anything again. The water would probably not seem cold for long. I'd likely be asleep before the end of the story. Just drift off.

There's not much to recommend the alternative. Only more miserable life. The blistering and burping and bumping and bleating. The incredibly excruciating pain when my blood starts bubbling through my frozen toes on its doomed journey to what passes for my heart. The shame of looking into my own damned eyes every morning and thinking about how I killed him.

He's nine and I'm seventy.

I couldn't save a penny from a jackrabbit. The calf lies over there, laughing at me. Never seen anything so funny in his entire life, but then he's only been alive four hours at the most. Maybe that's long enough to know a fool when you see one. Worse than a fool. The boy was the fool, 'cause he came along for the ride. I'm only the coward. I'm afraid of the cold. Can't face it anymore, though I'm still standing here in it, watching the water flow by, which is the nearest way out. Float right on down to Mexico. No. If only. We're the wrong side of the divide. I'd go north, out to the Saskatchewan, and on up to Hudson's Bay. I'd never be warm again.

The boy will never be warm again.

Playing lifeguard's pointless—the current will have dragged him all the way to the bridge by now—but I should at least make some effort. If I don't have the gumption to die with him, I should at least step in up to my knees and fumble around a bit to make sure he's not somewhere in these hundred square feet of water we opened up like a big present from the devil. But he couldn't still be there. I know full well he's long gone, or I'd have seen him struggling. He was gone the minute he went under, swept beneath the ice, bumping along down there like a cloud scudding across the sky, tapping out a message maybe, if he knew some sort of code. What would he say to me if he still had words? What could he teach me? He's only nine, and he's arrived before I have. He already knows more than me. What right do I have to call him a fool? I should go down there and ask him for the answers. They're probably on the exam.

I take a step, and then another, and then another, and then another, until I am standing over the calf, and the cow looks up to ask me what I have in mind. To answer, I pick up her calf and start walking up the hill. She follows.

It is the longest walk I've ever taken, but I finally arrive at the barn.

The boy's horse is waiting in its stall. I unsaddle it, peel off the blanket and do the same with my own, then give the tired beasts half a pail of chop to stoke their fires. Should wipe them down, I suppose, but I'm too cold myself. All the while, the cow's nuzzling the calf, licking him all over, lowing softly, some lullaby about angels taking babies away to a better place than this one. Some warm place, where no one's likely to dump you in the water and leave you there to die. I kneel down and pat the calf's hind quarter, and his mother looks up at me, suspicious. I suppose I could bed him in here, and maybe he'd be all right, momma, but it would be best if I took him in the house and warmed him right through until he's good and dry. Maybe we'd get a little blood flowing in those poor frozen ears of his.

I lift him up, his mother more than concerned about this repetition of history, and I walk back out into the storm, the old lady right behind, sniffing her baby in my arms, bawling at me to leave him alone. Guess she's seen enough of my babysitting abilities.

Wind hasn't lost any of its flavour.

If I'd just left him to watch his television show, he'd be there waiting for me in the house, and I'd growl at him something about the wonderful ride he'd missed and how he's not worthy of my name, and he'd help me out of my wet boots and socks, and I'd go up and get into a warm bath and wait for the pain, while he stayed down and watched the end of his program.

But he's gone.

Can't feel a thing in my feet. Might be floating along above the ground and wouldn't know it. Damn cow's bawling in my ear, giving me instructions on how to make milk from water. Sorry, lady, but I'll never track down the proper ingredients. Would hot chocolate be okay? Would have made the boy a cup if he'd wanted, even though he didn't come out with me. Calf's bloody heavy.

The truck drives into the yard, and the son jumps out, looking at me with wild eyes like he's never seen me before. She's there too, her mouth open in the middle of her pretty face, and the other boy's watching.

"Where were you? Where's Sam? We came back and saw you were gone and went lookin' for you."

"Went for a ride. Took the horses. Found this calf."

"Where's Sam?"

I just keep walking, 'cause if I stop now I likely won't get there, and it wouldn't make much sense to give up this close to the finish line. The legs are moving, and I don't think I could stop them now if I wanted anyway. The son gets to the door first and has it open for me, and I walk in and set the calf down on the floor by the stove. Go to fetch a rag from under the sink.

"Dad, where's Sam?" the boy asks again.

There, beside the soap dish, are his stupid glasses, a ball of dirty masking tape holding them together. Too vain to wear them unless he was reading or watching television, so he'd carry them in his pocket and fall and break them. I could take them down to the creek and throw them in and go in after them.

When I get back to the calf with the rag, the whole family's standing around in their winter armour, watching me, wondering why I was standing there staring at his glasses that way, the question they're too scared to ask already in their eyes.

"Is Sam still out in the barn?" the son's wife gets it out.

I kneel down and start to wipe down the calf. He bawls weakly.

"Sam's gone," I say.

That clock on the stove is doing its three beats a second, and I can feel the calf's heart doing about the same. The wailing starts, a small gasp at first, and then a terrified "No!" that tells me she knows exactly what I'm trying to say, but the son figures it might help to be a bit obtuse.

"What do you mean, gone? Where did you last see him?"

I shake my head, trying to find some words. "You can't see. Everythin's light out there, and you can't see a damn thing. It's the damnedest light. Won't show you anythin'."

"Did he . . . Is he still out there on the horse? Where did you find the calf?"

"Where it was born. Right there on the ground. He's not a bad size either, is he? Born out there in the middle of a blizzard, and not three chances in hell he'd survive, and here he is, in a warm kitchen. What must he be thinkin'?"

"Dad. Where's Sam?"

"He was a good kid. We fell through the ice at the swimmin' hole. It should have been thick enough there. The ice's always been good and thick there. He was a damned good kid. Could somebody help me get my boots off? I can't feel my feet, so I'd best get them dry."

She's screaming, and I can't even tell her to stop.

"Stay with your grandpa," the son says, and grabs his wife and pulls her out the door and I suppose down to the creek to look into the black hole that I should have stepped into if I had any sense at all. Then they'd have put up a rock for both of us and told the story about how we died there together in the cold, saving that calf they found on the ground at the edge of the water. That miracle calf. They'd have raised it up for a bull, let it keep its balls, even though it had the conformation of a sway-backed mule. He'd have been our tribute, the boy's and mine.

The other boy stares down at me, a look in his eye that's only slightly less painful than his mother's wailing. He kneels and begins to unlace my boots, while I keep drying the amniotic fluid and snow water off the calf, and it bleats dully like it's not too sure about all of this but has calculated a decision not to complain too awful much, considering that this strange place is so beautifully warm.

When the boy pulls off my second boot, I look at him and catch him looking at me that way again.

"Yes," I say. "I've killed your brother."

JUNE 29th, 2000: NEAR BROKEN HEAD

THERE IS A pretty farmhouse to my right, the eaves and window frames painted an emerald green, but the trees surrounding it are dying, either from lack of water or lack of attention. Here, the cowboy has told me, trees really can die from lack of attention.

"That's the Brock Place, but nobody lives there anymore," is his latest lesson. "Bankers took so much of the land, the Brocks gave up and sold everything they had left. If they had anything. Must be ten years ago."

"Was it Sam?" I ask.

The cowboy looks at me. "Mighta been." He turns back to the road. "Sam keeps busy."

He drives with one hand, while rolling himself a cigarette with the other. The gravel was too much for me—it was all too much, and I could no longer concentrate—and he suggested he drive, and I pulled over and let him. If I hadn't, I don't know if I'd have made it back to civilization alive. I still don't know if I will. I'm not sure where the gun is, but I think it's under my seat. My father is waiting for me. I'm out of cigarettes.

"Can I have one of those?" I ask.

He pauses and looks at his right hand rolling the cigarette as though he hadn't realized until now that that's what his right hand was doing, and then he offers it to me. I take it and punch the lighter.

"Do you regret it?" I ask.

He cocks an eye at me and curls his lip as if he were amused. "That depends what we're talkin' about."

Am I provoking him? It's really none of my business. I have enough of my own regrets without pestering him about his. I'll look at his cliff and say thank you and get him to drive me back to town and leave him there. That sounds like a reasonable plan.

"Do you love her?"

The lighter pops, and he pulls it out and offers the glowing rings to me. I suck on the roll-your-own too hard and almost cough.

"Gwen? Of course I do. And I love Sam too." He pats me on the leg. "I've only known you for an hour, and I think I'm already in love with you."

I exhale, waiting for him to remove his hand from my leg, and finally he does.

"Really? You fall in love rather fast, don't you?"

He raises his eyebrows. "Like a ton of shit fallin' from a leanin' tower."

He shrugs and sighs and turns his full attention back to the road. After a while he pulls his fixings out of his breast pocket and starts rolling himself a cigarette. "To tell you the terrible embarrassing truth, I feel like a bit of a victim in all of this mess." He twirls the paper between his fingers and then licks the stickum. "I feel like I was set up."

"You were what?"

He punches the lighter. "Set up. I was set up. I mean, Gwen was lonely. What'd he expect? He works late every night. She never saw him. And he was constantly gone on his business trips. So, she'd invite me over for supper, just for company. Just to spend some time with somebody besides the kids. He knew I was spendin' more time with her than he was." He pulls out the lighter and holds it to his cigarette, taking a deep drag once he's got it going, before replacing the lighter again. At last he turns very deliberately to me, the cigarette glowing there in the left side of his mouth, as he speaks out of the right side. "If you wanna know what I think, I think he wanted it to happen. Which is why he set me up."

He squints at me before resuming his squint at the road.

"You're saying he was just looking for a way out of his marriage?" I ask.

The cowboy shrugs. "Either that or he wanted to lord it over me. Be morally superior. He's always liked doin' that. Some people like to face their own problems by being morally superior. It makes them feel better about themselves." He glances at me as though he's accusing me of something. "I think maybe he oughta take responsibility for his own marriage," he continues. "He wants out, but he doesn't have the guts to get out himself, so he set me up to do it for him."

"And what about you?" I ask him, chuckling to indicate that I make no judgments on anyone. "What are you going to take responsibility for?"

His eyes kill the road. "Myself."

There is a ringing in my ears, and it takes me a second to identify where it's coming from. My cellphone.

My father is dead.

It rings again.

"It's not for me," the cowboy says.

I open my briefcase and fumble open the phone. "Hello?"

"Ai. Lance Taves here."

"Lance! I think I may have found that location. I'm just about to have a look at it."

"Oh. Well. Don't bother. I've got some bad news. They've called the whole thing off."

"Pardon?"

"Yeah. At least for the moment. Herzog went completely bonzo and pulled the plug. In the middle of a meeting with the minister responsible, Jerry asked him why anybody'd be crazy enough to live in this godforsaken place, apparently because he didn't approve of the dressing on his salad. He says he's taking the production back stateside. He walked out in the middle of dinner. Aspen never even showed up. It's all a smokescreen, if you ask me, to cover up the fact that Aspen doesn't know if he's Jesus or Dead Eye Dick. Creeping senility, I suspect. I have serious doubts this film'll ever be made. Anyway. It looks like you're unemployed. At least for the moment. We'll cover your expenses until tomorrow, of course. I've already got you booked on a flight tomorrow morning."

"Oh," I say.

"We should meet, though. We may still work together in the future. You never know. I'll buy you dinner. How long will it take you to get back to the hotel?"

"I'm . . . not sure," I say.

"Well, where are you?"

"Somewhere near Broken Head."

"What?! What the hell are you doing way down there?"

"That's where the location is."

"Jesus. You really get into your work, don't you? Well, should we make it a late dinner then?"

"I think I'll be too tired by the time I get there."

"Yeah. I guess. Well, sorry about the bad news."

"That's okay."

"I'll have them give you a wake-up call for your flight."

"That would be nice."

"Talk to you soon."

"Bye-bye." I snap the phone shut and put it back in the briefcase.

"Everythin' okay?" the cowboy wonders.

"I'm fired. They don't want the cliff for the movie anymore."

He searches my eyes to see if I'm kidding, and apparently sees that I don't know how. "Good," he says. "Then no worries about showin' it to ya."

I take a deep drag on my cigarette.

"Are ya sorry to lose the job?" he asks.

"No. I'm not sorry. To tell you the truth, I'm a little relieved. It could have been worse."

"That's good. Why would ya want a silly job like that one anyways? I see you got a movie camera back there. If you like makin' movies so much, why not make your own?"

I shrug. "I had a boyfriend who used to ask me that."

"And what did you answer?"

"That he made movies, and somebody had to have a real job to support him."

"Are ya still supportin' him?

"No."

"Well, then? Do you still want to see the cliff?"

I crush out my cigarette. "Are we almost there?"

"Almost," he says. "Are you Chinese, or Japanese, or Vietnamese or Korean?"

I don't respond.

"I was just wonderin'." He grins impishly. "You all look the same to me."

"I'm from a place called the Leaside Towers. It's a high-rise apartment wasteland. Right near Don Mills. Where your breakfast cereal comes from."

He's still smiling, the smoke curling lazily out of his mouth, and he points out the side window at the field in the background.

"That's where breakfast cereal comes from."

JANUARY 2nd, 1971: BROKEN HEAD

IRENE HURT. It was so bad she laid back down on the floor and closed her eye, hoping the pain might have nothing to cling to if she let her mind go completely free. Free as the wind. They said they were going to let her go free, but she refused to snap at their baiting. She wouldn't give them the satisfaction of laughing in her face. She would lie here with her eye closed and escape from them that way. But on the back of her eyelids she could see the young cop's ugly smile. To escape him she opened her eye and the gum was still there, stuck to the bottom of the desk.

She prayed. After another prayer or two or three, the door opened and two cops escorted someone into the room. She recognized the running shoes. Luke.

"Tell her we're letting you go," the oldest cop with the fancy uniform said.

"Irene. Are you okay? What did you do to her?"

"We didn't do anything. She attacked one of my men. We'll leave you here to talk to her. Tell her we're letting you go."

The two cops walked out and closed the door.

Luke's running shoes stepped closer, and she felt his hand on her cheek, smelled the scent of his cigarettes. "Irene! Are you okay? What did they do to you? Those bastards. Tell me what they did to you. I'll kill those bastards."

"No," she answered him, raising herself with his help. "They're listening, Luke. Just keep your mouth shut."

"I don't give a fuck if they are. We'll get them for this, Irene. We'll tell everything to this lawyer guy I know in Calgary, and we'll get them. I told them even before I knew what they done

263

to you." He clasped her face in his hands, studying the eye she couldn't open. "Oh, Irene, what did they do to you?"

"Did you take the old man's wallet?"

His eyes shifted away and he shook his head slowly. "I took a few dollars for gas. For helping him. He hardly had any. What's wrong with that?"

"And your cousin's car *is* stolen."

He talked to those black holes in the white tile. "Not that I know of. It doesn't matter anyway. They're letting us go. They're scared. They know they went too far, doing this to you. They're letting us go, Irene."

"No, Luke. They won't just let us go."

"They will. They told me they're letting us go."

But she did not believe him, and so she began to pray again, and he held her, murmuring that they would let them go, while she called on Jesus to save them, which is how the officers found them when they returned a few minutes later.

"Let's go," the older man said.

"You're letting us go?"

"We're letting you go. Come on."

Luke helped Irene to her feet.

Outside, it was now very dark and still very cold, though the wind was gone completely. The officers escorted them to a police car and told them to get in the back.

"I thought you were letting us go." Luke said.

"We are."

"Where's our car? Aren't you giving us our car?"

"It's not here. We'll have to take you to it."

Apparently they'd left it at the hospital. Luke helped her into the back seat of the police car, and they drove off into the night, stopping at all the stoplights, back out under the underpass and north, into the darkness, on a highway they'd never been on before. They were not going to the hospital. She buried her face in Luke's shoulder.

"Where are you taking us?" Luke asked.

"To your car."

She kept her face in his shoulder until the police car began to slow down and Luke shook her and said, "Irene. There it is," and when she opened her eye, sure enough, the car was sitting on an approach, pointing away from the road, off into the night.

"All right," the old cop said. "There's your car. Now you take off down that trail to make it look like you got away from us, and that's how we'll report it. You got away. We're letting you go because you saved the old man. That was a good thing you did. So that's what we're doing for you."

Luke nodded his head, staring off in the dark. "What if we get stuck?"

"Get stuck? Why would you get stuck?"

"In the snow."

"You won't get stuck. That trail'll lead you right back to the TransCanada."

The driver, the same driver who'd stopped them, got out of the car and opened Luke's door.

"Did you find that boy?" Irene finally spoke.

The officer shook his head. "There's no missing boy."

"The old man said he was missing. Young Sam. He called him Young Sam. He could still be out there."

"There's no boy missing."

"Come on, Irene," Luke said, "forget about the boy."

Irene let Luke help her out and walk her to the car. Every step she took was like a knife in her chest. The officer got back into his car, and the two officers sat there at the edge of the road, watching. Luke tried the ignition, and it started.

"Still warm," Luke said, wondering at this, and he put the

car in gear and started down the trail, which was two lines of white in the black. The trail was not too bad, though, so he went faster. As they picked up speed, he began to laugh. "They did let us go. I told you they'd let us go. We had them scared."

She watched the two dark lines of the trail leading into darkness, wincing each time they hit a bump. Inside her head, she tried to think of a prayer. But her head was empty. There was nothing inside her but two black lines on white.

"What was that song from the radio this morning?" she said. "Luke. Do you remember how it went?"

"What song?"

"The song on the radio."

The darkness rushed at them in ice crystals.

"The Beatles song?"

"No. The song about Irene."

"Good night, Irene," Luke began to sing, "Good night, Irene. I'll see you in my dreeeeeeams."

Two black lines leading to black.

"No. Not that song."

"What song?"

"The other song about Irene."

"The one the cowboy sang?"

"No. The one from the radio. The one they were playing on the radio. Don't you remember that song? They were playing it on the radio, and you turned it off."

"I don't remember. I'm not sure. I don't know which song you mean."

And only black.

And Irene felt Jesus reach down through the windshield and grab her by the waist and take her, clasped to his icy body. He spread his wide wings and lifted her up into the bottomless sky, where she would dwell forever in the arms of her Lord.

JANUARY 2nd, 1971: NEAR BROKEN HEAD

A TICKLE in my throat's telling me some bug has already invaded. With any luck it'll kill me in the next ten minutes. Annoying as all get out. A smoke might help, but I don't have any dry fixings on me. Maybe I'll ask the boy to fetch them. The other boy. Vern. Her father's name. It's a definite risk. He might say no. He is not used to doing my fetching, no matter what the situation, and he's not likely altogether sympathetic of my present position. He did help with my boots, but he's left me in my stockinged feet. My feet are frozen, but I can feel the cold wool on my ankles. I bend and pull off my sopping wet socks without even asking him for help, and he sits there without offering any and watches me rubbing my poor old feet. Trying to get the blood moving, but why am I bothering? My fingers are already tingling, and I'm remembering exactly how bad it'll hurt.

The boy's looking for his brother's blood dripping from my hands. His face has that kind of look. Not so much an accusation as a surrender from all possibility of connection. Like I've grown horns and am no longer of a familiar species. I'll have to get used to that kind of look, I suppose. Or I'll have to find other things to look at.

"Could you get me a dry pair of socks from my room?" I ask.

He nods and goes, happy to be away from me.

"And grab the bottle in my sock drawer when you're there."

That plaque on the wall wishes me to be held in the palm of God's hand. That would be warm. Likely He'd just close his fist and grind my bones into a little stale flatbread. Man can not live by Sam alone. The calf bleats, calling for its mother, but she can't answer, though she's not that far off, standing on the front walk, staring at the boot scraper the boy fashioned out of a horseshoe. She's waiting for her own boy to come back to her. The little thing's hungry, it's tongue hanging out the corner of its mouth. I hold out my hand to let it suck my fingers.

"It's all right. She's only a hop and a skip away. Just on the other side of that wooden thing over there with the knob."

Vern comes with my socks and the bottle, handing them to me without offering to help me on with the socks. I can see he'd like to help with the bottle, though.

"Your mama'd probably walk right in here if Vern went and opened the door for her, but that might not be too good an idea. We don't need any pie at the moment, do we Vern? Or are you hungry?"

He turns away. Not much of an audience for killers who tell jokes, it would seem. Maybe I should go out and tell it to the cow and see whether I can make her crack a smile. The calf's still sucking at my cold fingers, and I don't have the heart to take them away, so I vice the bottle between my knees and screw off the cap and take a mouthful and let it burn down into my centre.

Standing at the door, waiting. That's a mother. She'll wait right there until he comes back to her. No matter how cold and hungry she gets. Well, she might stray away for a few mouthfuls of straw. Won't begrudge her that. She's a good mother. What must she think? What must this place be, in her estimation? In the calf's? A place this warm in the middle of a blizzard, the hot air coming out of the little grill there in the floor, coming up from some fire down near the centre of the earth, or somewhere between here and there. Of course, he's got almost nothing at all to compare this particular experience to, except being born in a snowbank, and riding through thirty below on the back of a horse. Might very well think this is what every day will be like. Land in a snowbank, pulled out and plopped on the back of a monster, carried through whiteness, no idea where he's heading, fall in ice-cold water, pulled back into a wind that'd freeze the sulphurous fires of hell, but all for the final gift of that blessed place where the heat comes out of the floor. Quite a day, all right, but with nothing to compare it to, how would he know that they're not all exactly like this one? Doesn't realize he'll never see this side of the door again. And his mother will never see the other side, so all she'll have to go on and pass on to the other mothers is his stories of that strange warm place where the ground was perfectly flat and the light was an all-too-pale shade of yellow and a man wiped her beautiful boy down with a rag that smelled like nothing he'd ever smell again. And the wailing. That might be the music of the place. He might go through the rest of his life wanting to hear more of that lovely music. A mother's terrible keening. But then, what sound would a calf love more than that?

Make your hair turn white, that sound.

He'd suck my hand right down to his four stomachs if he could. I take the empty tit away, and use it to help pull on the socks and pick up a wet boot and try pulling that on. They'll likely be back soon, and there'll be no escaping their eyes, and the wailing will go on for days. I get the boots on, but my fingers can't manage with the laces.

"We'll just warm ya up and get ya back outside to her, and you can have a good big drink of warm milk. A good big drink. What do ya say about that?"

I look at the boy when I say this, and he kneels and ties up one boot and the other. He's watching me with his big eyes, not that different from his brother's eyes. Blue. Round. Those black spots in the centre. I hand him the bottle. He screws off the cap and takes a drink. He doesn't cough.

"A good warm drink. I'm just gonna step outside and let your mama know you're all right. Vern'll stay here with ya, so there's no need to be afraid. He knows the place. He'll get ya whatcha need."

I teeter back onto my feet and head for the door, imagining I can already hear his parents coming to tell me the terrible emptiness of that ragged hole in the ice, but when I open the door only the cow's there, waiting. I turn back a second and look Vern in the eye, and he looks back and says, "You forgot your parka." I nod and close the door.

The cow looks at me too, sniffing at the scent of her calf, and I place a hand on her nose. The wind's still blowing, but we're in the shelter of the house and the chill is a relief from the flare of the blood that's already begun to flow.

"There, mother," I say. "Your boy's waitin' inside. Don't wander off."

And then I do just that, heading out the driveway, in the opposite direction of the crick, so I don't run into the boy and his wife. Wouldn't want them to have to look at me again. Wouldn't want them to have to tell me they forgive me. I've been forgiven one too many times already. Just can't remember when. Maybe it was Mary. Maybe it was the boy himself. Or maybe it was his son.

Or maybe only the weather. It's cold, but the warm was beginning to hurt.

JUNE 29th, 2000: NEAR BROKEN HEAD

SAM HAD NO conception of how long he'd been walking along the grid road, lugging his suitcases, when his father's dented pickup truck stopped beside him. He looked around and saw he'd passed Vern's driveway and was halfway to the home place. After tossing his bags in the back, he opened the door and climbed inside. The dusty smell made his nose crinkle, and he held back a sneeze.

"What's goin' on?" his father asked. He had on his orange cap, and it had a stain of grease that roughly matched the one on Sam's white shirt.

"Nuthin'."

The old man held him in his hard gaze a long, long time, but didn't ask again—didn't want to be hurt as much as Sam had. They drove into the yard without saying another word, his father grinding through the gears in silent fury. Not for the first time, he reminded Sam a little of his grandfather. Something in the way he clenched his jaw or the undirected fury in his eyes. But she was wrong. He did not hate his father.

His mother already had the table set, but seeing Sam and his suitcases, she was adding another plate when Sam stepped into the kitchen.

"Well, howdy, stranger," she said.

He'd stopped in the doorway to look around him. Of course, he'd seen it many times, had been seeing it all his life, but he suddenly noticed both how much and how little it had changed in all these years. They had a new fridge and stove, new linoleum on the floor, and the walls were a fresher yellow, but the furniture was the same, the plants in the windows were pretty much the same. They were even the same green curtains.

"What's going on?" his mother asked, needing to know, no matter how much it would hurt her. And, when she asked him, he couldn't help thinking of the day she'd been told, right here in this very room, of Sam's terrible death, under the ice, floating away into darkness. Her youngest son. Vern had told him about it enough times. The way his mother had cried out for him. Sam remembered strangely little of that day he did not die. The whiteness of the blizzard had erased all his memories. He did recall the moment the ice cracked, and how he slipped from the horse's back and up to his neck in icy water. He had no recollection of how he got out of the creek, or of scampering the two hundred yards to the house. He must have run himself a hot bath, because Vern remembered him coming down from the bath and asking for hot chocolate. His parents and his grandfather were out in the blizzard searching for him. Everyone was afraid he was dead. His mother had never got over it. None of them had, least of all Sam. It would have been better if he had gone under and never come up.

He met her eyes. She could read it all in the look on his face.

"Can I stay with you guys for . . . a while?"

"I . . . guess."

And then, as though by way of explanation, he said, "I hope you weren't expecting Vern for supper." As if he'd just left him lying in a pool of blood. As if he were brave enough. His mother sighed that she wasn't and gave Sam a deep silent hug. She did not grieve the older boy the way she had the younger, and Sam thanked her for that. Pulled into those soft arms, he buried his nose in her hair, but he couldn't help looking over her shoulder to where his father had lifted his eyes to meet Sam's.

"You should never have let it happen," the old man said.
The way he held his jaw.

The family—mother and father and son—sat down to eat.

It could have been 1970. There were boiled potatoes and boiled peas, and meatloaf with tomato sauce and bacon on top. Pickled beans. Pickled beets. The best dills on earth. Spanish onions in a shallow dish of vinegar. Fresh baked buns. Date squares for dessert. More than enough for everyone, as though they'd been expecting him since that day he'd walked out to get the bus for university twenty years before. The same yellow plaster walls, though the cracks had been plastered and painted over. The same little plaques with their reassuring wishes: May the Road Rise to Meet You and May God Hold You in the Palm of His Hand.

The same Mom. The same Dad.

Sam was alive. He was three or four or five or six or seven or eight or nine or ten, and he was more loved than anyone else in the universe. He was warm, and he was filling his stomach with beautiful, solid food. He never needed to go anywhere, to be anything, to love anyone else but his mother and father, and they needed nothing else but him. All else was vanity. All else was pain. After lunch he would help his father with whatever he needed help with. They would do it together. In the middle of the afternoon, without a word, they would leave the job behind, complete or not, and walk back to the house for tea. Perhaps Mom would have done some baking.

They ate for a long while in silence, their forks scraping on their plates, his mother frowning about something she would never share with them, his father's jaw clicking when he chewed, the way it always had. Sam kept looking at the spot on the floor where the calf had been beside the stove. The one they'd saved,

the one long since dead. He'd come down from the bath, and
Vern was sitting petting it and drinking from their grandfather's
whiskey bottle, and he'd asked Vern if they could have hot
chocolate. Vern looked at him like he was a ghost. "Everybody's
lookin' for you," he said. "Grandpa just went lookin' for you."
His grandfather had got up and walked out the door and into
the cold. "Irene," he had said, and then he had died.

Sam rose to his feet.

"I never meant to hurt you," Sam said.

Both of their forks stopped in mid-air.

His mother touched his arm.

"I've got to go for a walk," he said.

Sam's father set down his fork. "Where do ya think you're
goin'?"

"Everything'll be all right," his mother interrupted him.

"Yes," Sam said. "Everything is going to be all right."

And he squeezed his mother's shoulder, and walked past
her, past the stove, and out the front door.

There was a warm breeze. He walked down to the creek and
stood on the bank where the swimming hole used to be. It had
long since silted in, and Vern had found a new spot, between
their place and his, where they sometimes took the boys. The
creek changed, just like everything else. It was just another
thing you learned if you lived close enough to a creek to learn
such things.

He kept walking, out across the big pasture Old Sam had
bought from Janson. The air was soft, and the light glowed a
brilliant orange. How easy the world could be. It would be
practically impossible to die on an evening like this one, when
all you had to do was breathe to be alive.

He didn't know where he was going, but he kept walking,
cutting off the trail and following a cow path he remembered

from when he was a child. It headed eventually to a clump of willow that the cattle used for shelter, and the willow were gnarled and worn and tufted with fur from the cattle's rubbing, but he left the path before he reached them. He headed away from the creek, climbing a steep hill. A cactus caught in his sock, and he had to stop and remove it. It stuck to his finger when he tried to throw it away, but he finally got rid of it.

At last he sat down on a small knoll about halfway up the valley, nowhere in particular, but with a view of his own house about half a mile away. A safe place. He had to be a safe place. How do you do that? The shades were drawn, and he saw the lights go on as the sunlight dimmed. Behind him, when he looked to the west, the sky was awash with the setting sun. Purples and oranges and pinks.

He waited silently, but Irene did not come. It was not a surprise. He knew she would not come.

It didn't matter that she did not come. What would he have said to her?

As it began to get dark, he saw the lights of his father's pickup meandering along the trail below. He was looking for Sam. Sam did not want to show himself, but that would have been cruel. They were worried about him. At any rate, it was nice to be looked for. He got up and walked down to where the truck sat waiting, the lights turned off.

His father saw him as he approached, but was turned the other direction looking out his open window when Sam climbed into the cab.

"Been watching her since noon," his father said, motioning towards a cow that Sam now saw lying in a patch of rosebushes beside the creek.

His father had not been looking for him.

"She's late," Sam said.

"Yeah. She's the last. Might have to take her home and pull it."

They watched a while. The hooves were already visible when she strained with her labour.

"Maybe I'll just slip down and see if I can help her," his father said, lifting the calving chains from the floor between them. He opened the door, got out and walked slowly towards her. She stopped to nervously look at him once, but was overtaken by another pain, and lay back on her side and strained, the white hooves and socks pushing out to where Sam could see them clearly in the moonlight. His father reached her and looped the chains around the hooves, and when she strained, he pulled.

His father motioned to Sam to come and help him. As a child he had watched his father do this many times, but his father had never called for his help. A white shirt and suit pants was not the proper thing to be wearing to pull a calf. But his father was getting old and no longer had the strength.

He waved again, motioning the route Sam should take to come from behind and not startle the cow. Sam got out of the truck and obeyed, approaching slowly, though the cow just lay there panting and never looked back. When he reached them, his father motioned for him to grab one hoof, and his father grasped the other, and they pulled.

The calf emerged easily, slippery and gasping, into the night. Sam stood back, then kneeled and wiped the amniotic fluid from his hand onto the grass. His father made sure the calf's airway was clear, patted it on the side and lifted its tail.

He could have pulled it without Sam.

"Big girl," he said.

Sam nodded. For a moment he wanted to tell his father they should call her Irene, but he thought better of it.

She had no need for a name.

EXT. PRAIRIE. DUSK.

A cowboy stands beside a Toyota. He points his finger the way the camera aims: down a prairie trail
that becomes a gravel road running into the horizon
in the hazy distance.

>   COWBOY
>   You see? Looks like you could drive
>   right to the horizon? Now, follow me.

He motions to the camera, then turns and walks along
the trail, and the camera follows, jiggling unsteadi-
ly. The cowboy talks as he walks, but his voice is
muffled or entirely impossible to make out.

>   AI (off shot)
>   I can't hear you.

The cowboy peers over his shoulder.

>   AI (cont'd)
>   You'll have to speak to the camera, or
>   I can't hear you.

He turns and walks backwards, continuing his story.

>   COWBOY
>   . . . and we actually lose the cops,
>   'cause they can't drive like us, but
>   we know they're bound to radio ahead,
>   so we figure we'll double back on a
>   back road and head for home, so we take
>   off down this trail we're on now, doin'
>   about ninety miles an hour, watchin'
>   for the cops on our tail, and keepin'
>   an eye on where we plan to disappear
>   over that horizon . . .

The cowboy motions to where the road meets the blue,
but by now a valley has revealed itself between where
the trail runs out and where the road continues on
the other side.

> COWBOY
> . . . and we just keep drivin', right
> into the sky.

He stops, and a moment later the camera is beside
him, looking straight down a hundred-foot cliff. His
finger points to a hunk of twisted metal rusting in
some rosebushes.

> AI (off shot)
> That's their car?

The cowboy nods.

> COWBOY
> Yeah. They never bothered to try and
> get a truck down there and tow it away.
> Course, they only ever found his body.
> Do you think she could've walked away?

He looks into the camera. The camera jerks away and
pans the valley from one horizon to the other, the
creek snaking along the bottom, the draws climbing up
steep clay banks to the flat prairie, until we arrive
back at the cowboy, looking down.

> COWBOY (cont'd)
> Just goes to show ya, even the flat old
> prairie's got a few surprises . . .
> under her skirt.

> AI (off shot)
> Up her sleeves?

He shrugs.

                    COWBOY
        Whatever ya say.

The camera sweeps across the vista again, pausing
momentarily at that rusted metal in the rosebushes.

                    AI (off shot)
        And her name was Irene.

The cowboy is rolling himself a smoke.

                    COWBOY
        Somebody's name was Irene. There's a
        lot of women in the world.

He offers the camera a cigarette.

                    AI (off shot)
        No thanks. You're right. It is
        beautiful.

The cowboy nods and lights the cigarette.

                    COWBOY
        Beautiful way to die.

He exhales.

                    AI (off shot)
        You think so?

                    COWBOY
        Drivin' off the horizon? Sure. No
        better way to go.

                    AI (off shot)
        Ever tried it?

The cowboy considers this for a second.

                    COWBOY
        I'm drivin'.

He strides back towards the car, the camera joggling
behind.

>   AI (off shot)
>   Vern. Vern!

He gets in and starts the engine. The camera closes
in on him as he smiles at us out the window. He revs
the engine.

>   COWBOY
>   Comin'?

>   AI (off shot)
>   No. I don't think so.

>   COWBOY
>   Somethin' wrong?

>   AI (off shot)
>   Well . . . I don't see it ending this
>   way. I think I'm looking for something
>   more . . . conventional.

>   COWBOY
>   Conventional? Why?

>   AI (off shot)
>   All I need you to do is to walk off in
>   that direction and not look back.

The cowboy looks the direction she's pointing, and
chuckles, and then the camera pans to show us why:
the western horizon is bruised with a spectacular
purple, orange and pink sunset.

>   COWBOY (off shot)
>   I guess that makes me the hero.

>   AI (off shot)
>   That's right.

The camera pans back to his face. The cowboy shuts off the engine, disappears for a moment and gets out of the car displaying a large handgun. He smiles and stuffs it into the front of his jeans.

> COWBOY
> Okay. So, give me the gist. Who am I supposed to be, exactly?

He takes a deep drag.

> AI (off shot)
> The last cowboy.

The cowboy releases the smoke, peering into the camera.

> COWBOY
> The last one? I guess that's why I'm walkin' and not ridin', is it?

> AI (off shot)
> Yeah. That's why.

> COWBOY
> Well, what's he like? What am I supposed to . . . act like?

> AI (off shot)
> You. He's exactly like you.

The cowboy looks doubtful.

> COWBOY
> Really?

> AI (off shot)
> Yeah. Exactly. Just be yourself.

The cowboy points to himself.

> COWBOY
>
> Me? Myself?

He nods and turns to look at the sunset.

> COWBOY (cont'd)
>
> All right. How far do you want me to go?

He looks back at the camera.

> AI (off shot)
>
> All the way. Right into the sky.

The cowboy nods knowingly, a smirk on his face.

> COWBOY
>
> Uh-huh. That's a long ways.

> AI (off shot)
>
> A long walk.

The cowboy keeps nodding, giving the camera a deep and serious stare, then drops his cigarette and grinds it out with his boot.

> COWBOY
>
> All right.

The cowboy laces his fingers and stretches his arms out as far as he can to crack his knuckles, then tips his hat.

> COWBOY (cont'd)
>
> Toodle-oo.

He begins to walk away. He walks five yards, ten yards, fifteen yards, never looking back.

> AI (off shot)
>
> Goodbye.

The cowboy ambles into the sunset for what seems like forever, getting smaller and smaller and smaller, the sky changing colours, changing textures, the clouds drifting and changing shape, the world growing darker, growing deeper, growing older, until the cowboy is only a dot, and then even the dot disappears.

ACKNOWLEDGMENTS

The author wishes to acknowledge the generous support of the Ontario Arts Council.

Thanks, also, to my editors, Diane Martin and Angelika Glover, and my agent, Hilary McMahon.

A special thanks to Elizabeth Mulley for her valuable advice, to Su Rynard for her reassurances, and to Ai Tsuzuki for her wonderful name.

The body of *The Last Cowboy* has been set in Adobe Garamond. Designed for the Adobe Corporation by Robert Slimbach, the fonts are based on types first cut by Claude Garamond (c.1480–1561). Garamond was a pupil of Geoffrey Tory and is believed to have followed classic Venetian type models, although he did introduce a number of important differences, and it is to him that we owe the letterforms we now know as "old style." Garamond gave his characters a sense of movement and elegance that ultimately won him an international reputation and the patronage of Frances I of France.

LEE GOWAN grew up on a farm near Swift Current, Saskatchewan. He is the author of *Going to Cuba*, a collection of short stories, and of *Make Believe Love*, a novel that was nominated for the Trillium Award. His first screenplay, *Paris or Somewhere*, won three screenwriting awards and was nominated for a Gemini. He currently directs the creative writing program at the Scool of Continuing Studies, University of Toronto. He lives in Toronto with his wife and their young son.